MURDER
at the
WEDDING

BOOKS BY HELENA DIXON

HELENA DIXON
MURDER
at the
WEDDING

Bookouture

Published by Bookouture in 2021

An imprint of Storyfire Ltd.
Carmelite House
50 Victoria Embankment
London EC4Y 0DZ

www.bookouture.com

ISBN: 978-1-80019-543-1
eBook ISBN: 978-1-80019-542-4

Murder at the Wedding is dedicated with much love to the Bay City Rollers, their families, friends and fans. Thank you for the music and keep on rolling.

Torbay Herald – *May 1934*

Net finally closing on wanted man!

Exeter police reported today that they were close to capturing Ezekiel Hammett, wanted for the murder of Denzil Hammett in the city before Christmas. The public are reminded not to approach Hammett but to report any sightings at the nearest police station.

The statement given by Inspector Pinch was in response to growing criticism and concern from the public that Hammett had evaded capture for so many months. A substantial reward is still on offer for information leading to the arrest of any person involved in the historic murder of Mrs Elowed Underhay in June 1916. This crime is also thought to be connected to the wanted man.

Nuptial Joy

The wedding is due to take place shortly between Miss Lucy Medford, only daughter of Lord and Lady Medford of Enderley Hall near Exeter, and Lord Rupert Woodcomb of Thurscomb Castle, Yorkshire. The bride is expected to be attended by the groom's sister, Mrs Daisy Watts, née Banks, and Miss Kitty Underhay, the bride's cousin.

Lord Medford is well known for his manufacturing inventions during the Great War. The groom inherited his title and the Thurscomb estate following the sad demise of his late uncle last year. The Right Honourable Alexander Galsworthy, MP for Fincham, a childhood friend of the groom, is to be best man

The wedding is to take place at Thurscomb Castle in the private chapel and it is believed that the happy couple will honeymoon afterwards in the South of France.

CHAPTER ONE

Early May 1934

''Tis a good thing we're nearly done, miss, the light is going a bit now.' Alice settled back on her haunches and gave the newly pinned hem of Kitty's frock a critical frown.

Kitty stepped down from her position on the footstool where she had been balanced while her friend had adjusted her new dress. 'Thank you, Alice. I don't know what I'd do without you.'

The sunshine from earlier in the day had now declined and the shadows on the walls of her grandmother's salon in the Dolphin Hotel had grown longer. The loss of the sunshine had also brought an increase in the chilly breeze blowing toward the hotel from the river, rattling the leaded panes in the large bay window. An elegant cream embossed wedding invitation was propped up on the mantelpiece beside the clock and a small fire crackled merrily in the hearth.

'Shall I ring down for tea, miss, while you go and change out of that frock?' Alice asked as she got to her feet and started to tidy away her sewing materials.

'Oh yes, please do, I'm starving. You will stay for tea, won't you?' Kitty asked. She knew her friend was very conscious of her status as her maid and wouldn't presume to stay unless Kitty gave her a formal invitation.

She went to the bathroom to change back into her day dress, returning the new pale-green satin evening gown to its hanger. This was the last of her new purchases that needed to be altered before she and Alice took the train to Thurscomb the next morning.

Her cousin's upcoming wedding was certainly taking a toll on her purse. Lucy had invited her to come for a few days before the actual ceremony to keep her company and to assist her with the final touches. With only four days to go there would be plenty to do. Her aunt and uncle had been detained on government business in London and were not expected to arrive at Thurscomb now until the day before the ceremony.

Instead, Lucy was currently chaperoned at the house by her father's cousin, Hattie, who Kitty had met over Christmas at Lucy's home, Enderley Hall. She could well understand Lucy's desire for more female company as Hattie – well meaning as she was – could be very wearing. Plus, Hattie's penchant for subtly acquiring anything shiny probably meant that Thurscomb would be running out of teaspoons any day now.

Kitty rejoined Alice just as the tea trolley arrived. Her friend took Kitty's dress from her and draped it carefully over the back of one of the carved rosewood dining chairs that stood in the bay.

'I'll have that hemmed in a trice.'

'Thank you, Alice. Do come and sit down and have a break. Are you all set for tomorrow?' Kitty asked, frowning at her friend when she went to claim the teapot.

'Oh yes, miss, all packed and ready. It will be quite an adventure going to Yorkshire. I haven't ever been any further than Plymouth before.' Alice ignored Kitty's attempt to serve her and took over dispensing the tea and scones.

Kitty subsided gracefully onto the chintz-covered armchair in front of the fire and accepted one of the delicate floral-painted china cups from Alice. Alice was only eighteen and the eldest of eight children. The family, although hard-working, were not well off and she wasn't surprised by her friend's lack of travel experience.

'I must admit I'm looking forward to seeing Thurscomb. Lucy said that even though it is only a fortified manor house, it looks more like a castle, with its battlements. So much so that Rupert and the locals always refer to it as Thurscomb Castle – and now everyone does. One wing is almost derelict as they had a bad fire there some twenty or so years ago but it's still a huge place.' Her cousin had telephoned her several times since her arrival at Thurscomb and Kitty had learned quite a lot about the house.

'It all sounds terribly grand, miss. I reckon as it must be a much bigger place even than Enderley from the sounds of it.' Alice took a seat opposite her.

'Oh much. It's such a shame really that Lucy isn't being married from Enderley, but the church there is still without a vicar and the repairs to the roof have finally begun. I suppose it does make more sense to marry at Thurscomb in the private chapel.' Kitty couldn't help shivering a little when she recalled the events of Christmas at Enderley, when the late Reverend Crabtree had met an unfortunate end in the belltower.

'I'm looking forward to it, miss. I suppose as there still isn't any news from Inspector Greville about catching Ezekiel Hammett?' the maid asked.

Kitty sighed. 'Nothing certain. I'm beginning to believe he will never be caught despite the offer of the reward, and I shall never have the opportunity to question him about my mother's death.'

The car crash she had suffered a few weeks earlier had been directly caused by Hammett and his sister. Even now she still found herself looking over her shoulder when she was out, half-fearing some other attempt on her life.

'They will get him, miss, I'm certain of it. At least going to Yorkshire will give you a break.'

'Yes, you're right, Alice. Fresh scenes, new county and new experiences.'

Alice's eyebrows lifted slightly as Kitty slathered her fruit scone generously with clotted cream, before adding strawberry jam from the small glass preserve dish.

'I do wish that Matt were able to travel with us tomorrow though. It's too bad that he has to stay behind and give evidence in one of his cases before he is able to get away,' Kitty said, before taking a bite from her scone. Captain Matthew Bryant's profession as a private investigator had been keeping him very busy of late. Although she had begun to wonder if his work was all that was causing Matt to avoid her. She pushed the nasty, niggling thought aside. Since her recovery from her motoring accident they had both been exceedingly busy.

'Did Miss Lucy say as there would be a car to meet us at the station when we arrive?' Alice asked.

Kitty nodded and licked a stray crumb from the corner of her mouth with the tip of her tongue. 'Yes, Rupert is arranging for us to be met so we won't have to worry about the luggage. I take it Robert will be our taxi driver when we leave in the morning?' Kitty shot a sly glance at her friend.

Alice's cheeks bloomed a delicate pink. 'I believe so,' she said primly.

Kitty hid her smile behind her teacup. Alice had been walking out for a few weeks now with Robert Potter, the son of their regular taxi driver.

'I must say I would have liked to have driven to Thurscomb myself, but Grams and Matt were both so appalled by the idea that I was persuaded to give way.' She gave a regretful sigh. Kitty had acquired her own motor car at Christmas. She was very attached to her small red Morris Tourer and considered herself a good driver. However, the attempt on her life back in March when her car had its brake cable cut causing her to crash, had unnerved those nearest and dearest to her.

It had taken some persuasion after the repairs to her car had been completed to convince her grandmother that she was safe to motor about the bay. Since then, with regular driving practice, Kitty's confidence had returned and she considered the drive to Yorkshire to be within her capabilities.

Lucy's desire to have her spend time with her before the wedding had also been a factor in the travel plans. It was quite a distance from Dartmouth to Thurscomb and the train would undoubtedly be considerably speedier. There was a limit to how long she could be spared from her duties running the hotel.

Kitty had begun to wonder lately if Lucy might be entertaining second thoughts about the wedding. There had been something underlying their last few conversations that had left her feeling slightly worried. It wasn't anything her cousin had said, rather it was in what she didn't say that made Kitty feel a little uneasy. Still, no doubt it would all become plain when she saw Lucy in person.

Robert Potter arrived early the following morning to take them to the station in Torquay. Alice scurried around the taxi giving directions for their bags. Kitty stood to the side with her grandmother not wishing to interfere with her friend's organisation. Matt had arranged to meet Kitty on the platform before she boarded to see her depart.

'Now, Kitty darling, do enjoy the wedding and please give my regards to your aunt and uncle. I shall expect a full report on what everyone wore, the flowers and the food.' Her grandmother drew her warm navy wool cardigan more closely around her narrow shoulders as protection against the chilly morning air. Daylight had just started to dawn with the promise of a fine, fresh day.

'I will. You are quite certain that I can be spared for a week?' Kitty asked. It was approaching the main season for the hotel and she was conscious that she was leaving quite a heavy workload for her grandmother to manage. Kitty's recent near squeak had made her realise her grandmother's age and increased frailty.

'Of course, darling. Young Dolly has been enormously helpful typing letters and taking on some of the administrative duties.' Her grandmother gave her a reassuring smile.

Alice's younger sister, Dolly, had been attending secretarial school part-time and assisting Kitty and her grandmother with the tasks of running the hotel. She had proved an able and willing worker, despite her young age.

'That's everything ready, miss.' Alice stood next to the open rear door of the taxi.

Kitty kissed her grandmother's soft cheek savouring the delicate scent of the lavender perfume she always wore. 'I'll telephone when we arrive,' she promised, before climbing into the back seat of the motor car.

Alice jumped in next to her and Robert closed the door before taking his place behind the wheel. Unaccountably a lump rose in Kitty's throat as she watched her grandmother's upright figure recede behind them. Usually, she enjoyed an opportunity to escape from the large, ancient half-timbered hotel and all her responsibilities. Since her accident, however, she had become increasingly aware that things were changing and her workload was inevitably growing.

*

Matt checked the time on his wristwatch as he waited at the front of the green and cream painted station building. He calculated there would be just enough time to see Kitty and Alice safely aboard their train before he had to speed across town to the magistrates' court. The familiar sight of Mr Potter's black taxi rolled into view and halted before the station entrance near the newspaper kiosk.

A uniformed porter rapidly came to assist with transporting the luggage to the train waiting to depart at the platform.

Alice and Robert accompanied the porter with the trolley to stow their luggage on board the waiting train. Kitty slipped her linen-gloved hand into the crook of his arm and smiled up at him from under the brim of her smart new pale-blue hat.

'I hope you'll be able to get away to join us soon.' She fell into step beside him as he adjusted his longer strides to match her shorter ones.

'I don't think this case will take much longer. I should be called today with my evidence which pretty much supports that of Inspector Greville.' The inspector was well known to Kitty as he had been involved with all of the cases she and Matt had been embroiled in.

'I'm sure you'll both be successful in securing a conviction.' Kitty halted as they reached the platform. He was conscious of a faint air of constraint between them. The station was quite busy despite the early hour and he knew she often felt self-conscious at such times.

He smiled back at her aware that she needed to board the train as it was due to leave in the next few minutes. 'I'll come to you as soon as I can,' he promised. 'Don't get into any mischief without me.' Her ready smile at his gentle teasing heartened him. This break to Yorkshire for Lucy's wedding was just what both of them needed.

Alice was already being assisted into the carriage by Robert Potter. Matt helped Kitty as she followed her friend inside the first-class carriage. Kitty popped her head back through the open window and he snatched a farewell kiss as the guard blew his whistle for the locomotive to depart.

He stepped back as the train began to chug its way out of the station in a cloud of smoke and steam. Robert Potter stood at his side as they watched the train set off.

'Well then, I expect I'd best get back to Dartmouth. Father will be wanting his motor back,' Robert said, tipping the edge of his cap.

'Yes, and I had better get across town to the court.' Matt had made his way into Torquay on his trusty Sunbeam motorcycle. He accompanied Robert back out of the station to their respective vehicles.

'Best hope as all this wedding stuff don't go to their heads,' Robert remarked with a wry grin as Matt prepared to say goodbye. 'Mind, I reckon as you'm more in danger than me, if you don't mind me saying so, Captain Bryant. One wedding often gives rise to expectation of another, or so I'm told.'

Matt smiled back and clapped the young taxi driver on his shoulder. 'Yes, you could be right there, my friend.'

He raised his hand in farewell as Robert hopped into his father's motor and drove away. Would Kitty feel that way after her cousin's wedding? He blew out a sigh and prepared to mount his trusty Sunbeam motorcycle. After the accident when he had been convinced for a moment that Kitty was dead his mind had been all over the show. After the loss of his wife and child during the war he had struggled to permit himself to become attached to anyone again.

Kitty's accident had thrown his feelings into confusion once more and he wondered if she sensed that sometimes when they were together. Matt frowned and turned the key to start his motorbike. Perhaps the stay in Yorkshire would help him to clarify his thoughts.

CHAPTER TWO

In spite of the comfort of the first-class carriages and the attentive services of the various porters during the changes of train along the route, Kitty still felt quite frazzled when they finally arrived at their destination.

'I do hope Rupert has remembered to send the car.' Kitty looked around the small empty platform for any sign of a waiting chauffeur, while Alice deputised a lethargic-looking uniformed youth to collect their bags.

'Brr, it's a bit nippy, miss.' Alice shivered inside her best navy wool coat as a sharp breeze stirred the air. No one else had departed from the train at their stop and apart from the youth, who stood idly by next to the laden trolley, the station seemed deserted.

It was already growing dark and the lighting at the station was poor. 'Perhaps the driver has been delayed,' Alice suggested. She had already ascertained from the boy that no one was waiting for them and there had been no telephone message relayed to the stationmaster so far as he knew.

'It's possible. Let's go inside the waiting room and I'll go and enquire if the stationmaster will telephone the castle for us.' Kitty led the way into a small, cream painted waiting room furnished with a few wooden chairs and a small, black pot-bellied stove that at least threw off some welcome heat.

She left Alice to warm her hands and watch the luggage while the youthful porter escorted her to the stationmaster's office.

The stationmaster, a large bluff-faced man, was enjoying his pipe and the crossword when Kitty knocked at his door. He shooed the youth away and straightened his cap.

'How can I help you, miss?'

'My maid and I were expecting to be met. Lord Woodcomb was to send a car for us, and I wondered if I might be able to telephone the castle to discover what has become of it?' Kitty asked.

The man goggled at her for a moment through the aromatic cloud of tobacco smoke. 'Lord Woodcomb?'

'Yes, we're here for the wedding at Thurscomb Castle.' Kitty wondered momentarily if they had mistakenly alighted at the wrong stop and that was why there was no car waiting for them.

The man's round, ruddy face cleared. 'Of course, young Lord Woodcomb. Begging your pardon, miss, for a moment I thought you were meaning old Lord Woodcomb, God rest his soul. By all means come and help yourself.' He stood to the side as Kitty entered the tiny office, disturbing the large ginger cat that had been slumbering peacefully under the desk.

Kitty found the number from her handbag and dialled. It took a moment to be connected via the operator and the connectivity seemed poor.

'Thurscomb Castle,' a male voice finally answered. Whoever it was sounded elderly and frail so she surmised it must be one of the servants.

'May I speak to Miss Medford or Lord Woodcomb, please. It's Miss Kitty Underhay.'

'One moment, please.' The owner of the voice seemed to disappear, and Kitty was left clutching the black Bakelite receiver waiting for someone to return.

'Kitty darling, where are you?' Lucy sounded puzzled.

'At the station with Alice. There doesn't seem to be a taxi and you said Rupert would arrange for the car to collect us.' Kitty tried not to sound sharp, but it was dark, dinner time, and they had had a long journey.

'Are you at Ripon?' Lucy asked.

'Yes, that was what we arranged.' Kitty was quite perturbed now. It wasn't at all like Lucy to sound so disorganised.

'Of course. Darling, I am so sorry. The car will be there soon I promise. We'll hold dinner back until you get here.' Lucy's voice sounded almost tearful at this point so Kitty assured her that she and Alice would be perfectly warm and comfortable in the waiting room until the car arrived, and finished the call.

'Thank you so much for the use of your telephone.' Kitty replaced the receiver, then fumbled in her purse for some change to pay for the call.

'Oh no, miss, that's quite all right. You go along to the waiting room and I'll send the lad to help with your bags when your car gets here.' The stationmaster beamed at her and Kitty guessed he was probably relieved that she was about to vacate his office so he could reapply himself to his crossword.

'Thank you.' She walked back along the platform to rejoin Alice in the waiting room. Her friend was seated on one of the wooden chairs beside the stove. She sprang to her feet as Kitty entered.

'Did you manage to telephone, miss?'

'Yes, the car is on its way. I think there must have been some sort of mix-up. Lucy sounded most odd on the telephone.' Kitty held out her hands towards the heat of the stove. She hoped that the car wouldn't take long, she was longing for a hot bath and a cup of tea. Her cousin's mention of dinner had already started her stomach rumbling.

''Tis probably pre-wedding nerves,' Alice said sagely.

The lad came into the waiting room some ten minutes or so later to say that the car had arrived. Kitty and Alice gathered their things and followed him out of the station towards a rather battered-looking black Rolls Royce. A chauffeur dressed in green livery nodded to them and opened the rear door of the car for them to get inside, before helping the boy load the luggage.

Kitty wound down the window to tip the boy before they pulled away, shivering a little as she pulled it back up. They had only driven a short distance when Kitty noticed a faint odour inside the car. Glancing across at Alice she could see her friend's nose was crinkled and she guessed that she had noticed the smell too.

The interior of the car was dark, and they had left the lit area of the town to venture along the narrow country lanes. The leather rear seats were covered with woollen travel rugs and Kitty wondered if they had somehow become damp. It was all very peculiar.

Eventually the car bumped its way along a narrow track lined with hedgerows. All around them darkness was falling rapidly with only the light from the car headlamps picking out the way.

'I think I see the house.' Kitty touched Alice's arm and they peered ahead through the gloom to see a large light-coloured stone building up ahead. The entrance took them over some kind of bridge, through the building and into a big square courtyard surrounded on three sides by buildings.

The chauffeur pulled the car to a halt outside the huge arch topped oak front door, which was set in the front of the tallest of the buildings. The door opened immediately spilling light out onto the gravel-covered yard and a tall, thin, elderly butler appeared.

Kitty and Alice scrambled out of the car as Kitty surmised that the butler must have been instructed to look out for their arrival.

'Good evening, Miss Underhay. Miss Medford is entertaining in the drawing room. If you would like to follow me.'

Somewhat reluctantly Kitty left Alice with the silent chauffeur to deal with their bags. She hoped Rupert's staff would be as kind to Alice as her aunt and uncle's staff always were when they visited Enderley.

The butler led the way into a large, square stone walled room with a vast inglenook fireplace set in the far wall. A suit of armour stood guard on each side of the empty fireplace. The Woodcomb family crest was engraved in a shield on the stone mantel. Around the walls were displayed various large and gloomy landscapes painted in muddy greens interspersed with the mounted heads of long dead animals. A maid in a black uniform took her outdoor wear and showed her to a sparse and chilly cloakroom to freshen up.

Kitty sighed when she saw the state of her short blonde hair and did her best to neaten her curls before reapplying her lipstick. The air inside the castle seemed as cold as the outside and she hoped that the drawing room at least would have a good fire. She made a quick telephone call to the Dolphin to reassure her grandmother of their safe arrival and prepared to follow the maid.

The girl led her through the hall and along a wood panelled corridor to a spacious drawing room. Kitty was relieved to see that although this room too had stone walls and a vast fireplace, at least this one had a fire in it. Lucy, in a dark green evening gown, was standing in front of the fire holding a glass and talking animatedly to Rupert. The large diamond on her engagement finger glinted under the light from the large electric candelabra.

Lucy's pretty face lit up when she spied her cousin and she hurried across to meet her. Muffy, her small and scruffy devoted dog, followed hard on her heels.

'Oh, Kitty darling, I am so sorry about the car. Do come over by the fire and warm up.' Muffy capered around her ankles as Lucy escorted her over to where Rupert was waiting.

'Kitty, it is lovely to see you again. I'm afraid it was my fault about the motor. I had asked my driver to collect you, but it seems he was detained on another errand.' Rupert's expression was apologetic as he bent his dark blond head to kiss her cheek.

'It's quite all right, it was only a few minutes. Alice and I were quite comfortable in the station waiting room.' Kitty smiled back at her host suddenly feeling slightly shy. She hadn't seen Rupert since the previous summer, and she was suddenly aware of the alteration in both his demeanour and his social status.

Back then he had been lively and flirtatious, his handsome good looks winning him easy popularity with the young women. He had also been something of a rebel, heavily involved in politics and keen to advance the cause of the working man. This, along with his aspirations to become an artist, had not endeared him to her aunt, Lady Medford.

'Lucy has been longing for you to get here. You both had quite a time of it again at Enderley over Christmas. Then that ghastly business in Torquay. Let's hope our wedding proves to be excitement of a different kind.' He smiled at Lucy, causing her cousin to blush.

'Well, I blame Matt. I never used to keep tripping over bodies until I met him.' Kitty laughed. She was relieved to see that whatever might be worrying her cousin it didn't seem to be her relationship with Rupert.

Lucy pressed a cocktail into her hand. 'Do come and meet everyone. Hattie, of course, you know already.' She led the way across to where Hattie was ensconced on a vast ancient brown leather-covered sofa where she was talking away to a rather bemused distinguished-looking older man with silver hair and an expensively tailored suit.

'Hattie, how lovely to see you again.' Kitty's words were almost drowned out when the plump older woman leapt up to embrace her, enveloping her in peach chiffon and some kind of exotic perfume.

'I'm so pleased to see you again too, Kitty. Do let me introduce you to Mr Ralston Barnes the third. Ralston, this is Miss Kitty Underhay, Lucy's cousin. She is to be bridesmaid at the wedding.'

The man had risen on their approach and now extended his hand for Kitty to shake. 'I'm delighted to make your acquaintance,

Miss Underhay. Miss Merriweather has been telling me all about you.' The man had a pleasant American accent.

'Ralston's daughter, Moira, is married to Alexander Galsworthy, but we call him Sandy. He's Rupert's oldest chum from school. Sandy is to be best man,' Lucy explained helpfully as she discreetly indicated a couple standing near one of the large, faded tapestries that covered the walls of the room. The woman was also expensively dressed in a pink satin evening gown, which did little for her bony frame and sallow complexion. Sandy was a beefy man who looked well pleased with himself. Kitty suspected that he might have been rather good-looking a few years earlier but now appeared to have gone to seed somewhat.

'The other couple are Sinclair Davies and his wife, Calliope. He is also an old friend of Rupert's,' Lucy continued, indicating a thin nervous-looking man with receding hair accompanied by an exotically beautiful woman with dark hair and eyes, dressed in a gorgeous red gown that Kitty immediately coveted.

'Goodness, you have quite a house party.' Kitty sipped her drink and tried not to shudder at the strength of the brandy it contained.

'Of course, you haven't yet met Mrs Adalia Watts, Aubrey's mother.' Lucy frowned momentarily.

Mr Barnes appeared to suppress a snort.

'Aubrey and Daisy are longing to see you again. They should be here in a moment to join us for dinner. They live in an apartment in the gatehouse.' Her cousin's easy smile returned, and Kitty hoped she would be able to remember who everyone was.

Daisy, Rupert's sister, and Aubrey, who had previously been her uncle's secretary, had been engaged when she had last seen them at Enderley the previous June. She recalled that Aubrey's mother had not approved of the engagement and in the end the couple had eloped to London in order to marry. Kitty was somewhat surprised that Adalia would be visiting them at all given her dislike of Daisy.

'I must confess I feel rather under-dressed.' Kitty wished they could have arrived with enough time for her to change. She was conscious that her tweed skirt, pale-blue silk blouse and cardigan must be quite crumpled from sitting in the train for so long.

'Nonsense, darling, everyone knows you've only just got here,' Lucy assured her. 'By the time dinner is over, Alice will have had time to unpack your things but really don't worry about changing this evening.'

'You are quite charming as you are, Miss Underhay.' Mr Barnes made a polite half bow in her direction.

Kitty barely had time to thank him for the compliment when the drawing room door opened. Daisy entered on Aubrey's arm accompanied by a pale, slender woman in a fussy dark-blue dress.

'Now for the fun. The queen has arrived,' Mr Barnes murmured out of the corner of his mouth and winked at Kitty.

CHAPTER THREE

The sonorous note of the dinner gong sounded from somewhere in the hallway so Kitty had little opportunity to do more than say a brief hello to Daisy and Aubrey before they exited the drawing room.

The dining room proved to be yet another vast stone walled room. This time surrounded by huge wooden dressers laden with blue-and-white painted china meat plates and serving dishes. It was quite chilly despite the fire burning in the hearth and Kitty was suddenly glad of her warm woollen cardigan as she took her place at the table beside Mr Barnes.

He made the formal introductions to his daughter and her husband. Hattie, seated on her other side, performed the same offices for the other couple. Aubrey was seated with Daisy on one side of the table further down and his mother on the other. His pleasant be-spectacled face bore a harassed expression as his mother began to quiz Lucy over the evening's menu.

The brandy cocktail she had consumed in the drawing room had left Kitty feeling a little light-headed and she was looking forward to her dinner. The table was certainly set nicely with silverware and an evergreen and floral centrepiece. She hoped Alice would be given dinner early too as she too must be feeling hungry after their journey. The tea and sandwiches they had been served on the train seemed a long time ago now.

Between Mr Barnes and Hattie she was kept quite busy in conversation as she ate her first course of mushroom soup, followed by roast pork with all the trimmings. She noticed that Mrs Watts made a great deal of fuss over each dish, declining any sauces and picking at whatever was placed in front of her, which appeared to embarrass Aubrey and caused Daisy to roll her eyes on more than one occasion.

Sandy meanwhile seemed to be consuming a great deal of the wine, which also appeared to be causing both Moira and his father-in-law some disquiet. Calliope was engaged in conversation with Daisy, while her husband talked to Rupert. There was a gentle buzz of conversation in the room, and, on the surface, everything seemed quite cordial. The way Kitty had expected with such a joyful occasion so close at hand.

Yet she couldn't shake off the faint sense of disquiet that had been bothering her ever since Lucy's last telephone conversation, before they had left the Dolphin. Perhaps Alice was right, and her cousin had been having some pre-wedding nerves. Kitty decided it must be that and that she was so tired from travelling that the surroundings of the castle were playing on her mind.

Dessert was a delicious lemon meringue pie with cream and Kitty felt much better by the time she placed her spoon and fork down on her empty plate.

'Miss Merriweather has been telling me that you are quite a detective, Miss Underhay?' Mr Barnes dabbed the corners of his mouth with his linen napkin.

'I'm afraid Hattie has misled you, Mr Barnes. I have been caught up in a few investigations but it's my friend, Captain Bryant, who is the private investigator. He will be joining us here as soon as he can get away. I am really just a hotelier.' Kitty smiled and took a small sip of her wine.

'Hmm, really. It must be fascinating—' Mr Barnes broke off abruptly when the conversation at the other end of the table suddenly grew louder.

'Rubbish, Sinclair, old chap. That's always been your problem, strong on the theory but weak on the practicalities.' Sandy

thumped his fist down on the table making the crockery jump as he emphasised his point. His face was flushed, and Kitty noticed he had little beads of perspiration forming at his hairline.

'Oh boy,' Mr Barnes muttered, his gaze fixed on his daughter's anguished face.

'Steady on, Sandy, my dear fellow. Come, everyone has finished dessert. Gentlemen, let us adjourn to the library. I've a rather fine port I should like your opinion on.' Rupert looked at Lucy and she indicated to the ladies that they might care to return to the drawing room for coffee.

Sandy rose somewhat unsteadily to his feet and Rupert guided him out of the dining room. Aubrey, Sinclair Davies and Ralston Barnes followed behind at a distance. Lucy and Mrs Watts led the way back towards the drawing room. Hattie had bustled her way to Moira's side and was chirping away in her ear as Kitty fell into step next to Calliope as they walked along the draughty corridor.

'I do love your gown,' Kitty remarked in an attempt to strike up conversation.

'Thank you, I acquired it in Italy last month.' Calliope gave a regal and somewhat dismissive nod of her sleek, dark head, clearly disinclined to continue the conversation.

'Kitty darling. I am so happy to see you. It seems ages since last summer. Do come and sit with me and tell me all the news. We are to have the fittings on our dresses for the wedding tomorrow.' Daisy caught her up and slipped her arm through hers, leaving her little time to dwell on the snub she had just undoubtedly received from Calliope.

Kitty was more than happy to join Daisy on the sofa while the maid served and dispensed the after-dinner coffee. Daisy's blonded hair was still dressed in the most fashionable style, although Kitty thought she looked a little pale.

'I think you have rather more news than me. Tell me all about your wedding. Lucy said you and Aubrey married in London?'

Kitty kept her voice low, not wishing Mrs Watts to overhear in case the subject of her son's marriage was still a source of annoyance.

Daisy glanced in Adalia's direction. 'Aubrey and I decided it would be for the best if we married quietly. Adalia enjoys poor health, and we didn't wish to cause her any stress by preparing for a large wedding. We married in a small church with just a couple of witnesses. It was rather nice, actually.'

Kitty smiled. 'It sounds very romantic. Lucy said Aubrey's mother is staying with you for a while?'

Daisy's perfectly pencilled brows rose. 'Yes, she arrived unannounced two weeks ago with rather a lot of luggage.' She shot her mother-in-law a glance. 'And she has given no indication of when she intends to depart.'

'Miss Medford, please, could I ask you to move your little dog? It's just that I am so terribly sensitive to animal hair.' Adalia had claimed the chair closest to the fire and coughed theatrically into her lace-trimmed handkerchief while glaring at Muffy.

'Oh dear, and she is so fond of you, too.' Lucy ushered her pet away from Adalia with the aid of a biscuit.

'Poor Muffy,' Kitty murmured.

'Poor me,' Daisy responded. 'I'm sure she would quite like me removed in much the same way.'

Hattie turned on the wireless to find a music programme, causing Adalia to wince and press her fingers dramatically to her temples. Kitty could see why Ralston Barnes had said that they would see some fun.

Moira Galsworthy was seated at a distance from Calliope Davies who appeared to be studiously ignoring all of them, focusing her attention on the pages of a fashion magazine.

'Please don't mind Calliope,' Daisy said. 'I overheard her speaking to you in the hallway. She dislikes all of us. I'm sure that she's only here because Sinclair made her come. Moira hates her like poison.'

'Oh?' Kitty was surprised. She wouldn't have thought that the elegant Calliope's path would have crossed much with Moira.

'Sandy was considered quite a catch a few years ago. You know he is the Right Honourable Member for Fincham and he has a junior cabinet position? Well, he and Calliope had a bit of a thing together back then. But, of course, Moira was an heiress and Calliope, although I believe is well connected, was not. Ralston Barnes, Moira's father, is a millionaire, something to do with cattle or wheat or something. Moira set her sights on Sandy and Sandy, well, he needed a little financial boost if he was to make his mark politically.' Daisy nodded sagely before taking a sip from her coffee cup.

Kitty could see now why she had thought there were tensions around the dinner table. 'How terribly complicated. So Sandy has history with Calliope but is now married to Moira. And Calliope married Sinclair. What a nightmare for the seating at the wedding. I take it Sinclair and Sandy are at odds too?'

Daisy shrugged. 'It's hard to say. Sinclair was Rupert's mentor a few years ago. You know my brother and his political leanings. Well, Sandy is a member of the Labour Party and Rupert has since rejoined. Sinclair regards Rupert and Sandy as having sold out, I think. Sinclair on the other hand has done a complete about-face. There is a rumour that he is heavily involved with Oswald Mosley's Blackshirts. You know, those ghastly rallies? As you can imagine, that's made things rather awkward. I think my brother wishes that he had not invited Sinclair, but he was unaware I think of his change of political beliefs until he arrived.'

'Is that what was going on earlier at dinner?' Kitty asked.

'Ever since they arrived it's been clear that Sandy is very fond of the bottle. That's usually when everything becomes rather heated. Sinclair starts to espouse his new beliefs. Poor Moira gets dreadfully upset and, of course, Calliope just sits there looking complacent.'

Lucy drew up a chair to sit near them. 'What's all the chatter? Do tell me all the news.'

Kitty bent down to fuss Muffy, who had come to lie at her mistress' feet. 'There's nothing to tell really, darling, we were just exchanging idle gossip.'

Lucy glanced over at Adalia who was now occupied with fanning her face and complaining to the maid who was collecting the cups. 'Hmm, I must admit I shall be glad when mother arrives. Hopefully she can occupy your mother-in-law, Daisy dear.'

'I rather fear that no one will ever succeed in that mission.' Daisy chuckled.

'I must go and try and entertain Moira until Rupert returns with the rest of the gentlemen. I always feel a little sorry for her and Calliope is so rude to everyone. Kitty darling, may I come and see you in your room later?'

Kitty's senses were immediately alerted. 'Of course.'

Lucy squeezed her hand. 'Thank you.' She rose and went to join Moira.

'Is something wrong with Lucy?' Kitty asked.

'I don't know. Something has seemed to be troubling her these last couple of days. I don't believe it's the wedding, although hosting a party such as this is quite something.' Daisy's expression was thoughtful. 'I'm sure it's nothing serious or to do with the marriage. She and Rupert seem to be terribly happy.' She glanced towards the fireplace where Aubrey was now attending to his mother's demands and sighed.

Kitty finished her coffee and set her delicate china cup and saucer down on the table next to her chair. She hoped Daisy was right and that Lucy was still happy to be marrying Rupert. It did cross her mind that if Lucy were having doubts, she would be unlikely to confide in the groom's sister.

When the men finally returned to the drawing room, Sandy was not amongst them. Mr Barnes went to his daughter and murmured something in her ear. Moira flushed and hurried from the room.

Hattie immediately claimed Mr Barnes' attention, drawing him into conversation, while Sinclair continued his debate with Rupert, ignoring Calliope. A wave of exhaustion passed over Kitty, so she made her farewells and set off to find her room, accompanied by one of the housemaids to show her the way.

CHAPTER FOUR

Kitty followed the young maid up a flight of ornately carved oak stairs into a long, poorly illuminated, stone walled corridor. They passed several closed wooden doors hung with elaborate iron hinges that Kitty suspected led into other bedrooms. The maid halted eventually in front of a similar door.

'Here you are, miss. If you want anything there is a bell in your room.' The girl bobbed a curtsey and turned to leave.

At that precise moment all the electric lights in the corridor flickered and went out, plunging them into inky darkness.

'What's happened?' Kitty asked. The corridor was pitch black and she could barely discern the white of the maid's cap.

'It's nothing, miss, please don't be alarmed, they'll come back in a moment when Mr Beck has been and seen to the fuse. They'm always going. There is a lantern and a flashlight in your room in case they go and they have to get someone in to mend them.' As the girl spoke there was a crackle, and much to Kitty's relief the corridor lights blinked back to life.

'Thank you.' Kitty entered her bedroom to see Alice, still dressed in her maid's uniform, attending to the fire.

'I were all of a fluster then, miss, when the lights went out. Thank heaven they come back on. This isn't a place you would want to be by yourself in the dark. Black as a bag it is without the electrics.' Alice shuddered and replaced the poker in its stand. 'I got the girl to bring up more coal for the fire. It might be May, but it soon drops down cold at night still.'

'It certainly feels warmer in here than it does downstairs,' Kitty agreed. 'Have they looked after you, Alice? Did you have a nice dinner?'

Alice nodded. 'Oh yes, miss. Everyone has been very good. I think they was glad to see me. There isn't many permanent staff and having so many people come to stay is leaving them a bit short-handed. You know, if the bells keep going. Miss Moira has her own maid they said, and her father has a manservant, but they keep themselves to themselves. Apparently, the old Lord Woodcomb didn't entertain.'

Kitty took a seat on one of the old-fashioned dark-green velvet-covered chairs beside the fire and eased off her shoes. She stretched out her feet and wriggled her stocking-clad toes in satisfaction in front of the heat while she took in her surroundings.

Lucy had allocated her a very pleasant room. The mahogany framed bed was set back in a stone archway. A tapestry in soft greens and golds depicting a hunting scene covered the wall above the bed. A huge mahogany chest of drawers and a matching dressing table were placed under the window, which was now covered with a thick dark-green velvet curtain that matched the fireside chairs. An old-fashioned floral-patterned porcelain jug and basin stood on a separate wooden stand.

Alice's bed was in a small room opening off from Kitty's and she guessed that her cousin had tried to match the arrangement she and Alice usually had when they stayed at Enderley. She had been keen to keep Alice with her as she enjoyed her friend's company. She also knew that Alice wouldn't be very happy if she were to be banished to the servants' quarters in the attics.

'I've put hot bottles in the beds, miss. The bathroom is down the corridor right at the end, but the hot water isn't very hot and it's proper cold in there.' The maid's nose wrinkled disapprovingly.

Kitty decided her idea of a nice, hot bath was unlikely to be forthcoming at this hour of the evening, especially as she didn't fancy risking the lights failing while she was up to her neck in soapsuds. She accepted her things from Alice and ventured off to find the bathroom.

She was back quite swiftly. 'Goodness, I see what you mean. It's not a place to dawdle.'

'I fetched us some cocoa and some biscuits from the kitchen while you was changing.' Alice grinned as she offered Kitty a very welcome hot drink.

'Whatever would I do without you?' Kitty smiled back and resumed her seat in front of the fire, tucking her feet up and wrapping her thick, red flannel dressing gown around her.

Alice placed the small plate of biscuits on the table next to Kitty. 'You'd probably go and get yourself killed, miss.'

A knock at the door interrupted their conversation. Alice went to open it while Kitty sat herself up in her seat.

Lucy greeted Alice and came to join Kitty by the fireside. Muffy trotted at her side and sank down on her mistress' patent leather evening shoes, before looking hopefully at the biscuits. 'Oh, Kitty, I'm so glad you're still up. I know how tired you must be after such a long day.'

Alice took herself off to her own quarters leaving them to talk privately, although Kitty was quite sure her friend would be listening in to the conversation.

'Lucy darling, whatever is the matter? I knew something was wrong the last few times you telephoned. Is it Rupert? Or the wedding?' Kitty watched as her cousin stared into the flames.

'Everything is fine with the wedding and our engagement.' Lucy absent-mindedly twisted her diamond engagement ring round on her finger. 'This is going to sound absolutely ridiculous, but I have to tell someone.'

Kitty eyed her cousin curiously. 'Whatever is wrong? You know you can tell me anything.'

Lucy sighed and looked squarely at Kitty. 'Do you believe in ghosts?'

Kitty blinked. 'Ghosts? No, I don't. Why?' She wondered if living in such an old building had started to affect her cousin's senses.

'Neither do I. Or rather, I didn't. At least not until the other night just before I telephoned you.'

Muffy whined and sat up for Lucy to scratch the top of her head.

'What has happened to make you doubt yourself?' Kitty was curious now to hear what Lucy might say. Her cousin had always been a very rational person.

'I'll give you the grand tour of the place tomorrow and I'm sure Rupert will regale you with all the stories about the castle. I think the house is the same sort of age as the Dolphin.' Lucy waved her hand dismissively. 'Anyway, as you might imagine with a house as old as this and with its history, there are stories.'

She paused and Muffy nudged the palm of her hand with her nose until Lucy took the last biscuit from the plate and offered it to her.

'And?' Kitty prompted. It was most unlike Lucy to believe in rumours and folk tales.

'Well, one of those stories involves the derelict wing. You probably couldn't see it very well when you arrived as it was getting dark, but that part of the house is quite damaged. There was a large fire some twenty years ago. In fact, it's become most unsafe. Rupert's uncle didn't make any repairs to the castle at all for the last forty years or so. We're having the unsafe walls taken down from the damaged wing and reusing the stone to make some repairs up on the roof in the main part of the house.'

Kitty wasn't sure where this story was going but nodded her head to encourage Lucy to continue.

'According to Rupert, the fire-damaged part of the house was built on the original foundations of a convent that used to stand there. The story goes that one of his ancestors wanted the ground for his own house – this house – and forced the nuns to leave. He built them another place; I think. One nun refused to leave, however, and they knocked the convent down around her. She was crushed accidentally under the masonry and when she was dying, she cursed the family. According to the story, whenever a death is about to occur in the house she appears.' Lucy halted and looked at Kitty. 'Some of the servants think the ghost was responsible for the fire.'

'I take it that you think that you've seen her, the nun?' Kitty asked. She could think of no other reason why Lucy would be so unnerved.

Her cousin nodded, the jewelled clips in her chestnut bob twinkling in the firelight. 'The other evening. Sandy, Moira, Ralston, Sinclair and Calliope had all arrived the day before. I'd changed for dinner and came downstairs to telephone you. There was a terrific draught in the hall, and I noticed the door hadn't been closed properly. I thought it might be Sandy. He had already made it a habit to go out of the front door into the courtyard to smoke. Moira disapproves of his smoking and, of course, he tends to avoid smoking in her presence. I went to close the door and looked outside. There was no sign of Sandy but there was a glimmer of light in the damaged wing, and that's when I saw the ghost.'

Muffy looked hopefully at Lucy in case another biscuit might be forthcoming, before collapsing back down with a disgruntled sigh.

'Tell me exactly what you saw.' A frisson of unease danced along Kitty's spine. 'It could have been one of the servants checking on something or keeping an assignation. What made you think it must be something supernatural?'

Lucy shook her head at the suggestion about the servants. 'I saw a flicker of light and stepped out into the courtyard. My guess was someone using either a candle or a shuttered lantern. It was up on the first floor above what used to be the ballroom. I watched for a moment and it disappeared. I was about to come back inside as it was quite gloomy and cold. Then suddenly I saw a figure dressed in a long black gown or cloak appear and move quickly, gliding almost across the grass towards the house. I was in such a state I came inside and closed the door.'

'Then it could have been a servant or one of the guests?' Kitty suggested.

'That was what I thought, but no. I made discreet enquiries amongst the staff and no one would own up. To be honest, Kitty, they tend to avoid that wing. They believe the stories and I don't think they would go there, not in the dark.'

'And your guests?' Kitty asked.

'Why would any of them go poking around there in the dark? Ralston has never been here before, nor has Moira or Calliope. Sinclair and Sandy visited here years ago with Rupert, before Rupert's uncle fell out with his father and disowned him. It seems an unlikely thing to do as a prank. And how would they get inside the wing? It's kept locked and I don't know of any entrances from inside the house.' Lucy's brow creased into a frown.

'So, what is bothering you most about this?' Kitty asked. She was certain there was something else, something Lucy hadn't said.

Lucy licked her lips. 'I can accept it might be a prank or someone not telling the truth, making some assignation or something. My head logically tells me that must be the truth, but Kitty, what if it isn't? What if there is some substance to this tale? What if Rupert is in danger somehow?'

Kitty stared at her cousin. 'Darling, why on earth would Rupert be in any danger? Who from?'

A tear rolled down Lucy's cheek. 'I don't know. It's ridiculous really and sounds even sillier now I've said it aloud. I haven't said anything to Rupert about what I saw, and I was discreet when I talked to the staff. I emphasised that the building was dangerous.

I don't know why I feel afraid, Kitty. I just do. I couldn't bear it if he were hurt. It was bad enough last June. I think that was when I realised how much I did care for him when he was almost killed by that beastly man.' She pulled out a handkerchief and dabbed away her tears.

'Why don't you tell him about what you saw?' Kitty could see her cousin was deeply worried.

'I can't. He's so superstitious and he has enough on his plate right now. There's the wedding and he's trying to get the estate business in order before we leave for France. Kitty, I know this is a big ask, but do you think you might be able to try and find out something? I know you'll be discreet. If I knew what and who it was then I could relax.' Lucy looked at her hopefully.

'Well, I suppose I can try but it's the wedding in a couple of days' time. Your parents will be arriving and there are all the last-minute arrangements to make.' Kitty wasn't quite sure what Lucy expected her to achieve.

'I'm certain Matt will help you when he gets here. Like you said, there must be a simple, rational explanation. Please, Kitty,' Lucy implored, placing her hand on Kitty's arm.

'Very well. I'll do a bit of poking about, but honestly, Lucy, I'm sure you're getting het up over nothing.'

There was a rustle from the direction of Alice's room, and she guessed her maid would have something to say on the matter after Lucy had gone.

'I know. I agree it's absurd, but I can't help it. Thank you, Kitty darling. I knew I could rely on you. I feel better for having told you. At least you didn't laugh at me.' Her cousin rose from her chair and clicked her fingers for Muffy to follow her. 'I'll let you get some sleep. Goodnight, Alice.'

Kitty walked her cousin to the door and closed it behind her.

'And what did you make of all that?' she asked her maid.

Alice had taken the opportunity to change into her night attire while Lucy had been visiting. She bustled forward to tidy up the used crockery ready to return the tray to the kitchen in the morning.

'It sounds to me as if Miss Lucy has got herself in a stew. Mind you, living in this place 'tis no wonder she's thinking she's seeing ghosts and the like,' Alice remarked with a sniff.

'Yes. You know what struck me too, Alice? Why was the front door open? Ghosts don't need to open doors or use candles or lanterns. No, the mysterious figure in black was human. I'd bet my last shilling on it.'

CHAPTER FIVE

Matt had a lot on his mind as he boarded the steam train bound for Yorkshire early the following morning. He had received an unsettling telephone call from Lord Medford, Lucy's father and Kitty's uncle, the previous evening. He had been keen to ascertain Matt's thoughts on rumours circulating in London about some of Rupert's guests, and to a small extent what this might mean for his son-in-law to be.

Matt had been unable to offer much advice as he didn't know the men concerned but assured Lord Medford that he would learn what he could ahead of Kitty's uncle's arrival for the wedding. On the other hand, the court case in Torquay had been successful and both he and Inspector Greville had been pleased with the outcome.

He settled back in his seat in the carriage and opened up the newspaper he had brought with him to read on his journey. The headline on the second page caught his eye. Inspector Greville had raised the same point with him as they had been leaving the courtroom the previous day.

Public unease about the continued failure of the police to capture Ezekiel Hammett had been rising for some time. Matt knew that Kitty had asked Inspector Greville to keep her informed of any new developments. There had been open criticism in the press from various high-profile people and even a question raised in Parliament. The competency of the police in Exeter and Torquay had been questioned.

Both Matt and Kitty had some sympathy for both Inspector Pinch and Inspector Greville. Their own encounters with Hammett had proved him to be elusive and highly dangerous. This was compounded when he was working under the directions of his sister, Esther, who had proved to be equally evasive.

'Pinch has assured me that they are genuinely very close to apprehending Hammett this time,' Inspector Greville had told him as they had walked back through the town together after the case.

'Forgive me for saying so, Inspector, but we have thought Hammett to be close to capture several times before.' Matt had been inclined to think that Inspector Pinch had been merely trying to reassure the public. Several officers had been dismissed recently when corruption had been brought to light. Matt had assumed the press release about Hammett had been intended to deflect further attention and criticism of the force.

'This time it is more certain. Pinch has a man on the inside. When the time is right the trap will be sprung,' the inspector had assured him.

'And Esther Hammett?' Matt had asked. He and Kitty were certain that it was Esther, rather than her brother, who was the mastermind of the two.

The inspector had sighed, his frustration evident in his demeanour. 'She is more difficult. She has money and a few powerful friends. Anyone who could give any kind of evidence of wrongdoing against her is either missing, dead, or seemingly suffering from amnesia.'

'Do you know where she is?' Matt had been concerned that Esther might have remained in the locality. She had been the prime mover in a failed attempt to kill Kitty only a few weeks earlier.

'London, we believe, and let us hope she remains there.' The inspector had bidden Matt farewell and turned off towards the police station, leaving Matt to continue walking to where he had left his motorcycle.

Matt closed and folded the newspaper, placing it on the seat beside him. Directly below an article discussing a recent political rally in Hyde Park, was a society piece informing readers of the *Torbay Herald* of Miss Lucy Medford's imminent wedding.

He sighed and gazed out of the carriage window at the scenery rushing past. Robert's words from the previous morning sounded in his mind. It was true that one wedding always seemed to spark interest and expectations of more to follow. Perhaps it was the time of year with spring flowers blooming and birds building nests.

Ever since he had discovered Kitty lying cold and apparently lifeless in her car after the brake cables had been cut, his feelings had been all over the place. Seeing her like that had brought back the grief and devastating sense of loss he had suffered after his wife and child had been killed towards the end of the Great War.

He had thought he had become more reconciled to that loss. That he was recovered and able to commit to another relationship again. Instead, it had raised doubts in his mind about whether he was being fair to Kitty. This vied with the pleasure he found in her company and the depth of his growing feelings towards her. Something his mother had remarked upon yet again during their last conversation.

His parents, despite their friendship with Kitty's grandmother, had left him in no doubt that they considered Kitty an unsuitable match. Then again, they had not approved of Edith, his first wife, who had been some ten years older than him at the time of their marriage.

Kitty's independence and forthright views didn't sit well with his parents' more traditional views of marriage and a woman's place in society. As for the depth of Kitty's own feelings towards him, well, he was uncertain of those too. Perhaps time spent at the wedding would make things clearer between them.

*

Kitty had woken quite early despite her fatigue from the previous evening. Alice had made her a cup of tea to drink in her room before she ventured back down the handsome oak staircase in search of breakfast. In daylight the castle turned out to be a veritable warren of corridors and odd little turns and steps and she was relieved when she found herself back in the vast square entrance hall.

She paused for a moment to get her bearings. The large space had more corridors leading from it than she remembered, and she was unsure which one she had taken the night before to reach the dining room.

Rupert's elderly butler appeared from the other corridor and Kitty was about to ask him for directions when she realised he was accompanied by a stout, middle-aged man carrying what seemed to be a medical bag.

She waited until the servant had shown the man out through the front door before approaching.

'Excuse me, I'm still finding my way around the castle. Is the dining room down that corridor over there?' If he was a doctor, she wondered who he could have been to see.

'Yes, Miss Underhay, you will find breakfast is all prepared. You take the turn past the portrait of the late Lord Woodcomb and follow the hallway to the end.' The man inclined his head politely.

'Forgive me, but was that the doctor I just saw leaving? I do hope no one has been taken seriously ill?' Kitty couldn't help herself. It would be too awful if someone became very unwell right before the wedding.

'Mr Galsworthy was unwell during the night; his wife was concerned so his lordship sent for the doctor as a precaution. I believe Mr Galsworthy is now recovering.' The butler's tone suggested that he considered Moira had overreacted.

'Oh dear, poor Sandy, how dreadful. Past the portrait you said?' She smiled at the butler and returned her attention to the promise of breakfast. Sandy must have seriously overdone the wine and port last night if a doctor's visit had been warranted. Still, after Lucy's confidences last night she was relieved to hear that it wasn't Rupert who was unwell.

'Yes, miss.'

Kitty left the man to continue about his duties and headed towards the dining room. She paused at the corridor entrance to look at the picture of the late Lord Woodcomb, Rupert's uncle.

She studied it for a minute and decided she could see little family resemblance between the rather disagreeable looking, dried-up elderly man in the picture and her cousin's handsome fiancé.

She took in more of her surroundings as she walked along the corridor. The castle looked different in daylight now she could see her way more clearly. The previous evening the poor lighting had made the rough stone walls adorned with the heads of long dead animals even more unnerving. Now in the light of day she could see they were rather forlorn, and moth-eaten. Kitty wondered how long it would take before Lucy had them all removed.

'Miss Underhay, up bright and early I see,' Mr Barnes greeted her from the breakfast table as she entered the dining room.

'Yes, I'm afraid I usually rise early for my employment and the habit is hard to break,' Kitty replied with a smile as she took a seat at the table.

A maid appeared and placed a fresh pot of tea in front of her and a silver toast rack filled with toast.

'I understand that Sandy was taken ill during the night?' Kitty poured herself a cup of tea.

'Yes, you probably noticed that my son-in-law had overindulged a little. A regular occurrence, I'm afraid.' Mr Barnes dabbed at the corners of his mouth with the white linen napkin. 'I'm sure you'll understand my sentiments, Miss Underhay, if I say that my daughter's marriage to Mr Galsworthy was not perhaps my first choice for her.' His tone was wry as he spoke. 'Moira tends to worry over things and you'd have thought Sandy had been poisoned, with all the commotion and fuss. The doctor's visit was just a precaution.'

Kitty was unsurprised by Ralston's feelings towards his son-in-law. After witnessing how much wine he had consumed and Sandy's behaviour towards Sinclair, she could see why Mr Barnes might have preferred Moira to make a different match. She went and helped herself to some scrambled eggs and bacon from the vast silver cloche-covered dishes on the side table.

'Kitty, Ralston, good morning.'

She turned to discover Rupert had entered the dining room.

'It seems you've joined the early-risers club. I take it preparations are all in hand ready for the wedding?' Mr Barnes asked as Rupert helped himself to a large plate of food and joined them at the table.

'I believe so. Lucy is terribly efficient, and Hattie and Daisy have been assisting her with everything. Lord and Lady Medford should be joining us tomorrow too, they have already set off I believe from London. Kitty, I take it Matt is expected to join us too this evening?'

Kitty blushed. 'I believe so. He anticipated that his case would be finished yesterday.'

'Kitty's young man is a private detective,' Rupert explained to Ralston.

The older man's moustache twitched, and his expression grew thoughtful. 'So I understand. Miss Merriweather had said something of that nature yesterday evening.'

'Yes, and jolly good at it too, and Kitty isn't a bad sleuth herself.' Rupert grinned at Kitty and nudged her elbow with his in a playful gesture.

'Really, Rupert,' Kitty admonished him. 'Like I said before, Mr Barnes, I've really only been involved in some of Matt's cases by chance.'

'Now she's being modest, Ralston. Kitty is as sharp as a tack when it comes to solving crimes and catching wrongdoers.' Rupert winked at her. 'Admit it, you give poor old Inspector Greville a run for his money.'

Kitty merely shook her head at Rupert's nonsense and applied herself to her eggs.

'I have a meeting later with Aubrey and my estate manager, but if you'd like, Kitty, I can give you a quick tour of the old pile after we've finished breakfast. Ralston, would you care to join us? I think you missed out when I took the others round the other day,' Rupert offered.

'That sounds like fun and I think it might help me to find my way. I got hopelessly lost this morning,' Kitty agreed. She knew the dress fitting was to take place mid-morning so there would be plenty of time. Plus, she might learn more about Lucy's mysterious ghost.

'By all means. This place is fascinating; we have nothing like this back home. Moira had told me when we received the invitation that it was old, but I had no idea it was so ancient.' Ralston drained his teacup.

Rupert beamed at them. 'Splendid.'

Lucy arrived just as they were finishing and took her seat next to Rupert.

'We're just about to go around the house, darling.' Rupert leaned in to kiss his fiancée's cheek.

'So long as you return Kitty in time for the dress fitting at eleven.' Lucy grinned at her cousin.

'I promise I'll be on time,' Kitty said as Lucy pinched the last piece of bacon from Rupert's plate and fed it to the ever-eager Muffy.

'I'll meet you in the hall then, Kitty darling.' Lucy ignored Rupert's frown at losing the last bite of his breakfast.

'Get Rupert to show you where the nun appears,' Lucy murmured in Kitty's ear as she rose ready to follow her host and Ralston on the impromptu tour.

Kitty nodded and followed Rupert out of the dining room and back along the corridor to the entrance hall, where she took her place beside Ralston under the morose gaze of the late Lord Woodcomb.

She was intrigued to discover more about the house and to try and solve Lucy's mystery for her. She was sure that Rupert would prove to be an entertaining guide.

'I used to visit here when I was young, before my father and his brother had their final disagreement. Sinclair and Sandy came here too for a couple of weeks the one year to join me. I think we were ten. You can imagine how much mischief three ten-year-old boys could have in a place like this.' Rupert's expression was wistful.

'I sure can, what with all those suits of armour and corners to hide in.' Ralston looked round at his surroundings appreciatively. 'This place is quite something.'

'This hall is one of the oldest parts of the house. When it was first built the fire would have been in the centre, with the smoke going up through a hole in the roof and all of life would have been in this space. Then over time the house evolved. The crenellations to turn it into a fortified manor house or castle took place in the fourteenth century. The roof and battlements are under repair at the moment, we're reusing the stone from the damaged wing,' Rupert explained. He waved his hand in the direction of the portrait. 'My uncle rather neglected the fabric of the house. He was a bachelor and concentrated his interests on his collections instead.'

Ralston nodded his head. 'I believe he had an extensive coin collection.'

Rupert gave a wry smile. 'Indeed. He donated it in his will to the British Museum. A pity as the sale of even some of those coins would have made a huge difference to supporting the costs of maintaining this house.'

Kitty decided that this probably explained some of the issues with the lighting. She followed Rupert and Ralston over to the fireplace.

'The other thing that fascinated us as children in this house was this.' Rupert placed his hand on a stone behind one of the suits of armour. There was a grating sound and, to Kitty's astonishment, a section of the wall retreated leaving a small space just large enough for a man to enter inside.

'Would you look at that?' Ralston leaned forward to put his head inside the opening, peering around it.

'It's one of a number of hiding places or priest holes. There are probably some we haven't even discovered yet,' Rupert explained. 'There are also some passages.'

'Good heavens. The space is so small. I've heard of them, of course, but never seen one before.' Ralston appeared suitably impressed as he stood back to allow Rupert to conceal the space from view once more.

Kitty tagged along behind the two men as they headed up the main staircase. She couldn't help wondering what else might be concealed about the castle. Stairs, rooms, tunnels, or corridors? It seemed to her that anything might be possible in such an old place.

Rupert paused once more, and she realised they had taken a turn off the corridor she had come along that morning. They were now in a long gallery similar to the one at Enderley but not so wide. The one wall had diamond leaded pane windows in a much larger size than she had seen elsewhere in the castle.

'The windows were made larger here in the eighteenth century to replace the old arrow slits, and here is the entrance to the chapel.' Rupert opened a beautifully carved oak door set on massive iron hinges.

The chapel was clearly being made ready for the wedding in two days' time. Maids were scrubbing and polishing as if their lives depended upon it. It was a fairly small space containing about thirty wooden chairs, but very beautiful with ornate woodwork and fine statuary. A beautiful stained-glass window spilled light into the room.

'We were a Catholic house for many years but converted some centuries back.' Rupert closed the door to allow the staff to continue their wedding preparation work undisturbed.

'Are there any more secret tunnels or entrances we can see?' Kitty asked as Rupert led them back downstairs. She was thinking of Lucy's mysterious nun.

Her host laughed. 'Of course. Come on and I'll show you one.'

Rupert took them back downstairs and into a room next to the dining room.

'Mighty fine library,' Ralston remarked appreciatively as he looked around at the floor-to-ceiling bookshelves all fully laden.

'Indeed. Now, come over here.' Rupert walked over to one of the bookshelves and indicated a volume on the shelf about halfway down.

'*Discoveries of Antiquity,*' Kitty read the title from the gold-embossed spine of the dark-red leather-bound book.

'Take it off the shelf,' Rupert urged.

Kitty placed her hand on the book and pulled it forwards. As she did so there was a very faint click and a section of the bookcase swung towards her.

'Very clever,' Ralston remarked.

Kitty stepped forward and at Rupert's urging pressed a small lever in the wall. To her astonishment she discovered she was in the drawing room beside the wall tapestry.

'We think this was a newer conceit installed when the house was last worked upon in my great-great-grandfather's time.' Rupert smiled at her surprised face.

Ralston was clearly enjoying the tour. He looked as pleased as a small boy when Rupert encouraged him to try opening the

connection for himself, showing the notch on the wall at the edge
of the tapestry in the drawing room to reverse the process.

'Amazing. What a place.' He shook his head as the bookshelf
in the library clicked back in place showing no trace of any kind
of door. 'Moira said there was some kind of a ghost story to do
with the castle?'

Kitty's ears pricked up. She was interested that Moira had heard
of the story and mentioned it to her father.

'The nun's story. I expect Sandy told her about our resident
ghost. As boys we would try to prank one another pretending to
be the ghost.' Rupert led them outside through the ancient front
door and into the courtyard.

The sun was already climbing in a clear blue sky and Kitty wel-
comed the heat of its rays through the thin silk of her pale-blue blouse.

The extent of the damage from the fire to the wing was more
evident in daylight. Very little glass remained in the windows; the
leading that had once held the diamond panes in place had clearly
melted and sagged in the heat of the flames. The creamy-yellow
stone was blackened and stained with soot. As they drew closer
Kitty could see the blue of the sky through the exposed timbers of
the roof on the top floor as she gazed upwards.

'The fire took hold some twenty or so years ago but was merci-
fully confined to this wing. It's thought a servant left a candle
burning and some of the drapes caught the flame. They managed
to save some of the paintings and furniture.' Rupert frowned at
the ruins. 'We're taking down the uppermost floor as it's become
unsafe in places and reusing the stone to repair the crenellations
over on the main house.'

Kitty glanced back and could see that high on the roof above
the front of the house, masons were hard at work repairing the
battlements. The sounds of hammers and chisels ringing out over
the courtyard.

'That must have been quite some blaze.' Ralston peered at the ruins.

'It took an army of people from the village to try and get things out via a human chain, whilst others pumped water from the moat to try to douse the flames.' Rupert's expression was grim.

'Where does the ghost come into all of this?' Kitty asked. She had heard Lucy's version of the story but hoped Rupert would be able to add more detail.

She listened while he repeated the information she had heard from Lucy and studied the building in front of her. Her cousin had said she had seen light on the first floor above the ballroom. From the appearance of the ruins, she could see that one end of the ballroom – the part nearest to the main house – appeared less damaged.

'Some of the staff believe the nun's ghost caused the fire. Family legend says that the nun appears shortly before a death in the house,' Rupert finished his tale.

Ralston appeared to be suitably impressed. 'Are there any stories to support that? I mean, not to be melodramatic or anything but has anyone ever seen her?'

Rupert nodded. 'One of my ancestors reported having seen her back in the sixteenth century, the next day he fell from his horse and died. Then one of the ladies of the house about one hundred or so years ago encountered her and passed away only a few minutes later, while recounting the tale to her husband.'

Kitty began to see why Lucy was concerned for Rupert. They turned away from the ruins and started back across the courtyard towards the front door.

'Oh, and, of course, my late uncle is reported to have seen the nun too. He told Beck, the butler, shortly before he passed away,' Rupert remarked as they re-entered the house.

A shiver ran along Kitty's spine even as she told herself that this was all nonsense. 'It's a wonder you've managed to retain your staff.

I know all too well what it's like once they get an idea in their head about anything like this. Many of my staff try to avoid the entrance in the cliff face at the rear of the Dolphin, which leads to the old smugglers' tunnels.' Kitty was keen to discover from Rupert if he believed his staff would avoid the ruined part of the house.

Rupert laughed. 'My uncle only kept a small number of staff but, yes, the servants tend to avoid going anywhere near the ruins especially after dark. We always make sure that the door that used to lead into that part of the house is kept firmly locked and bolted too.'

Kitty was intrigued to learn that there was still a door that led to the ruined wing. Lucy had said that she thought there was no entrance from inside the house and Kitty had assumed that any such access would have been bricked up following the fire. She hadn't noticed a door during their tour, but then the castle was so large that they hadn't seen every part of it.

A tall, thin manservant with sallow skin and slicked-down jet-black hair approached Ralston.

'Excuse me, sir, but there are some business matters requiring your urgent attention.'

'Thank you, Evans, I'll be right there.' Ralston turned his attention back to Kitty and his host. 'Thank you for the tour, I really enjoyed it. It's a fascinating old place you have here.' He bowed his head towards Kitty in a gesture of old-world courtliness. 'And made all the more pleasurable by your company, Miss Underhay. Now, I am afraid you must excuse me, duty calls.' He followed after his manservant.

'I'm afraid that I must dash too, Kitty. I must see my estate manager to finalise everything before Lucy and I leave for France.' Rupert glanced at his watch.

'Thank you so much for the tour. Mr Barnes was right, Thurscomb is quite fascinating.' Kitty smiled at her host.

Rupert grinned back at her before hurrying away to go about his business. Kitty checked the time on the slim gold watch adorning her own wrist and decided there was just enough time for her to go poking about in search of the door to the ruined wing before she had to meet Lucy for the dress fitting.

CHAPTER SIX

It seemed reasonable to Kitty that the door Rupert had mentioned was most likely to be found on the ground floor. Since they had already ventured along two of the corridors leading from the hall during the tour and she hadn't noticed a door, she decided to try the third corridor.

This corridor appeared to lead towards the ruined wing. The view from the windows out onto the courtyard on the one side of the passage appeared to support her supposition. However, after passing a couple of closed carved oak doors she was forced to halt.

Barring her route was another heavily carved wooden door set in an arch topped stone frame. This door was secured with massive iron bolts set into the stone and a thick metal bar running across the width of the door and sunk into the walls. It was clear that no entry or exit could be made through that portal.

Kitty made her way back to the main hall and decided to try from the first floor. There had been a corridor near the chapel that they hadn't explored that seemed to mirror the one she had just gone along downstairs.

This time her journey along the upper passage was stopped by a solid stone wall. It seemed that the late Lord Woodcomb had deemed the upper floor to require a more permanent barrier to the ruined wing. Kitty crossed to the windows and peered outside.

The courtyard was empty of people for the moment. A horse and cart stood near what she assumed was the trade entrance but was presently unattended. Kitty glanced around the deserted passage and released the catch on the window.

She turned so her back was to the ledge and hopped up, so she was seated backwards on the broad stone windowsill. She took care to ensure she was secure and holding firmly to the frame as she leaned out backwards in order to peer inside the exposed top floor above the ruined ballroom.

Fortunately the window on that floor had completely fallen away and she could see that although there were burnt patches and gaping holes in the centre of the floor there was sufficient amounts of solid wood left to allow someone to walk if they were careful.

Satisfied with her discovery she slid back down into the corridor and prepared to refasten the window.

'My dear Miss Underhay, whatever are you doing?'

Heat crept into Kitty's cheeks as she turned to face an astonished-looking Moira.

'Oh, nothing really. There was a small bird trapped and exhausted, poor thing. I just popped him out on the ledge. He seems to have flown away now.' Kitty crossed her fingers behind her back to offset the blatant lie.

'I must confess my heart was in my mouth when I came out of the chapel and saw you getting down from the ledge with the window open so wide. You could easily have fallen.' Moira looked appalled.

'I was quite safe, I assure you.' Kitty smiled at Moira to soften her words and to reassure her fellow guest. 'How is Sandy now, by the way? I met the doctor in the hall earlier this morning and your father mentioned he had been taken ill in the night.'

Moira walked beside her as they made their way back downstairs together. 'He seems to have recovered although he does appear quite pale. I'm hoping he will agree to come for a stroll with me and Father this afternoon. The weather appears so pleasant some air would do him good. Your cousin mentioned an historic folly along the river path.'

They reached the foot of the staircase and Kitty spied her cousin waiting to escort her to the dress fitting.

'I'm glad to hear he is recovered. I expect we shall see you both later at lunch?' Kitty waved at Lucy.

'Of course, we shall look forward to it.' Moira walked away towards the drawing room and Kitty went to meet her cousin and the ever-present Muffy.

'What perfect timing.' Lucy beamed. 'The dresses are at Daisy's apartment. She kindly agreed to keep everything at her house. I didn't want Rupert accidentally stumbling upon anything. Superstitious nonsense I know.'

'Where is Hattie? Is she not joining us?' Kitty asked as they crunched across the courtyard gravel towards the gatehouse.

'No, Mother is keeping her on her toes with constant telephone messages. Errands about ribbons and flowers and corsages and heaven only knows what. I'm sure Mother is more interested in the floral arrangements than my wedding dress.' Lucy gave a wry smile as they halted in front of a black painted door set in the creamy-yellow stone of the gatehouse.

She reached up and rang the large black angel bell suspended from a bracket beside the door.

A young maid in a black uniform answered and let them inside.

'Mrs Watts is expecting you, Miss Medford.' The girl led them through the small hall and into a long, narrow drawing room furnished in the modern style. Daisy was seated beside the fireplace talking to a plump older lady wearing a blue floral cotton print frock and a straw hat. A large, worn leather work bag rested at her feet.

Adalia was reclined elegantly on the black leather and chrome chaise longue with her eyes half closed.

Daisy had jumped to her feet when they entered. 'Lucy, Kitty. I've requested tea for us all. I thought we would take it in the other room while Mrs Challoner makes the adjustments. Adalia is unwell so I thought it would be less disruptive.'

'Of course. I'm so excited, I can't wait to show you both my dress and to see you in yours.' Lucy's face glowed with anticipation. Muffy, as if sensing her mistress' glee gave a woof of agreement.

This immediately drew a groan from Adalia. Daisy's cheeks reddened in embarrassment and she frowned as she led them out of the drawing room to one of the spare bedrooms. Mrs Challoner followed, carrying her work bag.

'I swear I shall murder that wretched woman if she doesn't go home soon,' Daisy muttered once the door was safely closed behind them.

'Has she said when she intends to leave?' Lucy asked.

Daisy shook her head and Kitty could see that tears were brimming in her friend's expressive blue eyes. 'No, and worse still she keeps hinting at Aubrey for him to invite her to live here permanently with us.'

'Oh dear.' Kitty went to assist the seamstress with their gowns. She could see that would be a recipe for disaster if Aubrey were to agree. From the expression on Lucy's face, she could tell her cousin was of the same opinion.

'I'm sure she'll leave soon. I intend to ask Aubrey to speak to her after the wedding.' Daisy gave a defiant sniff.

'Good for you, darling.' Lucy gave her sister-in-law to be a hug. 'Now, I'm dying to see if your dress fits you, Kitty. Daisy's is almost ready.'

Lucy had taken Kitty's measurements and given them to her dressmaker. Kitty crossed her fingers and hoped there wouldn't need to be many alterations so close to the big day.

The style her cousin had chosen was a pretty, modish dress in figured pale-blue satin with a modest neckline, chiffon sleeves and mid-calf in length. She slipped into the dress in the nearby bathroom and returned for her cousin and the dressmaker's approval.

Daisy was seated on a small chenille-covered chair in the window and Lucy was perched on the end of the bed. Muffy lay down at her feet.

'Oh, Kitty, you look marvellous. I knew that colour would suit both you and Daisy.' Lucy clapped her hands together in glee as Mrs Challoner scrutinised the fit.

'Just a bit off the hem I think, miss,' the seamstress pronounced and knelt in front of Kitty to begin applying pins to the handkerchief style hemline.

'It's always the hem. Alice usually has to adjust all my clothes for me.' Kitty turned obediently for the dressmaker to continue her work.

Daisy suddenly leaned forward in her seat and peered past Kitty to stare at an object in the corner. A puzzled frown creased her forehead. 'What on earth is that and how did it get in here?'

Kitty turned her head to see what Daisy was looking at. The bedroom, like the drawing room, had clearly been redecorated in the modern style with light fabrics and a few carefully chosen small ornaments. On a side table in the corner was the largest and ugliest vase Kitty had ever seen. It appeared to be Chinese, decorated in shades of pink and green, and totally out of keeping with the rest of the room.

'That's one of the vases that usually stands on the telephone table in the hall of the castle. It's vile, isn't it? I'd wondered where it had gone. There's only one there now and I assumed someone had broken one of them.' Lucy looked at Daisy.

'Well, I can assure you that I didn't take it.' Daisy's frown deepened. 'How has it ended up in here?'

Lucy giggled. 'I don't want it back, Daisy, so please do keep hold of it with all my love. It's probably worth tons of money, ugly things like that usually are, so if you'd like the other one too, do let me know.'

'I'll put it in the attic. If it does turn out to be worth lots of money, I have witnesses that you gifted it to me and please do keep its partner,' Daisy said, laughing as she spoke.

Mrs Challoner had completed her handiwork, so Kitty rotated around for Lucy's approval before going to change back into her skirt and blouse. She took Lucy's place on the end of the bed and waited for her cousin to change into her wedding gown for the final fitting.

She was surprised by how emotional she felt when Lucy reappeared to stand shyly before them, a vision in white lace.

'Oh, Lucy, that is gorgeous.' Kitty admired the delicate beadwork on the bodice as the seamstress made the final tiny adjustments, her tape measure about her neck and pincushion strapped to her wrist.

'It's wonderful. The bouquet will set if off beautifully.' Daisy produced her handkerchief and dabbed at her eyes.

'Mother has Hattie running all over organising lilies, pink rosebuds and gypsophila. I must say that despite Hattie's love of anything shiny she has really been a godsend organising everything with Mother having to be in London.' Lucy raised her arms for Mrs Challoner to check the side seams of her dress.

'Hattie wouldn't have moved the vase, would she?' Daisy asked.

Lucy laughed. 'No, Hattie loves silver things, she has no interest in porcelain. I swear she's a human magpie.'

Once the dress fittings had been completed to Mrs Challoner's satisfaction, Daisy led them out of the room to allow the woman to work in peace and took them into a smaller reception room, still furnished in a more old-fashioned manner.

'It's quite awful to feel one can't relax in one's own home but with Adalia claiming the couch…' Daisy shrugged somewhat helplessly as the maid entered with the tea trolley.

'Your drawing room is quite lovely.' Kitty smiled at the maid and took over dispensing tea.

'Adalia disapproves. She likes this room better. I need hardly say that this is the next room I intend to refurbish,' Daisy remarked wryly. 'She is constantly moving things around and criticising my choices.'

'Maybe she is the one who appropriated the vase,' Lucy suggested. 'She has already appropriated some of the staff and that's why the car was late coming to collect you and Alice, Kitty dear. Adalia had sent the chauffeur into Harrogate on some errand, unknown to Rupert. He was mortified when he discovered you were still at the station.'

'I'm so sorry.' Daisy's cheeks were crimson with embarrassment. 'I'll ask Aubrey to speak to her.'

'It's all right, no harm was done.' Kitty passed her one of the delicate floral-patterned china cups.

'Let me make it up to you. Come back after lunch, you too, Lucy darling, and bring Hattie. I'll organise some chairs in the garden and we can sit and have a nice chat in the sunshine and watch the swans on the river. We can have drinks. It's such a heavenly day.'

'That sounds lovely,' Kitty agreed as Lucy nodded. It would be nice to spend time together before everyone else arrived and the wedding preparations stepped up a gear. It would also be one of the last opportunities she would have to spend time with her cousin while she was a single woman.

It seemed clear to Kitty that once Lucy married Rupert, being mistress of Thurscomb would undoubtedly occupy most of her cousin's time.

*

Lunch back at the castle was a cheerful affair. Kitty was relieved that much of the tension she had sensed the previous evening appeared to have dispersed. Moira, Sandy and Ralston all expressed their intentions of taking a stroll along the river to visit one of the follies in the grounds.

Sinclair stated that he had discovered some interesting papers in the library and Calliope also seemed to have plans. Rupert and Aubrey were finalising business and visiting one of the tenant's cottages on the estate. Hattie's plump face lit up with glee when Lucy told her of Daisy's invitation.

'Oh, how kind. I must confess, Lucy dear, a little break before your parents arrive will be most welcome. I think everything your mother has asked for is in hand now at any rate.'

'I know both Mother and I are very grateful to you, Hattie. I think we're entitled to a little relaxation.' Lucy smiled affectionately at the older woman.

Kitty joined Hattie and Lucy after lunch was finished ready to walk back over to the gatehouse. The sun was quite strong now and she could feel the heat on her arms through the thin silk sleeves of her blouse. She hoped the fine weather would continue so she and Matt could enjoy exploring the countryside together during their stay.

Daisy had arranged some wicker steamer chairs with cushions and rugs to the side of the gatehouse overlooking the moat. Some nearby trees cast dappled shade and the sunlight reflected off the water in the moat as it rippled along, fed by the river.

Muffy ran on ahead of them barking excitedly when she spotted Adalia already positioned in the prime seat. This promptly caused Adalia to flap her hands ineffectually at the little dog as it tried to lick her.

'Really, can you not control this animal?' Adalia lowered her black circular-lensed sunglasses to glare at Lucy.

'Muffy darling, come here.' Lucy took a seat and called her dog. 'This all looks lovely, Daisy. We have a beautiful view of the water.'

Kitty agreed and took a chair in between Daisy and Hattie. The feel of the sun was pleasant on her face and she soon started to feel quite drowsy as they chattered between themselves about the wedding. The swans were gliding over the surface of the water and a large dragonfly floated aimlessly near the reeds at the water's margin.

Presently, Moira, Sandy and Ralston passed by on the opposite bank walking towards the small folly further downstream. Ralston waved his hat in greeting as they passed. Kitty thought that Sandy still appeared pale under the brim of his panama hat, and Moira carried a small Japanese-styled painted parasol to shade her from the sun.

'It really is too disagreeable in this heat,' Adalia complained. 'I think I must return inside.'

No one attempted to dissuade her since Kitty was certain Daisy had never invited her to join them in the first place. Once she had gone a maid arrived bearing a large glass jug of iced lemonade, which she placed on the table.

'This really is so lovely and restful,' Lucy said as she stroked the top of Muffy's head. The dog had found a shady nook beside her chair and seemed quite content to lie in the long grass.

Daisy poured them all a drink just as Ralston's manservant appeared hurrying along the path in the direction of the folly.

'It must be something urgent to send him at such a pace.' Lucy shaded her eyes with her hand and peered at the rapidly retreating figure.

'Ralston is a terribly busy man. I expect that's how he's been so successful. Unless, of course, it's Sandy that is required. His new role as a junior cabinet minister is quite a step up.' Daisy settled herself back down on her chair.

'Such a nice man, Mr Barnes, very interested in the arts too, you know. I read him a couple of my poems and he was most appreciative.' Hattie sipped her drink and Kitty tried to hide a smile at the idea of poor Ralston having to endure Hattie's verses.

'I would have thought they would be on their way back by now. Unless they have decided to rest for a while at the folly.' Lucy adjusted the cushion behind her head.

In the distance Kitty heard the loud and unmistakeable sound of a shot.

'What on earth was that?' Lucy promptly sat up. 'It sounded like a gun, but surely no one is out shooting crows or rabbits at this time of day.'

'It sounded as if it came from the direction of the folly.' Daisy's face was pale.

'Look, it's Mr Barnes.' Hattie pointed and they watched as Ralston stumbled into view having clearly run all along the path.

'Telephone for a doctor and the police. There's been the most terrible accident. My man, Evans, has been shot,' he shouted across to them.

Daisy's face immediately paled, and she appeared as if she were about to faint.

'Goodness. Stay there, Daisy, I'll go.' Lucy hurried inside the gatehouse, Muffy at her heels to make the telephone call.

Hattie started to tend to Daisy as Kitty headed over the draw-bridge to meet Ralston and to discover what had happened.

CHAPTER SEVEN

'Mr Barnes, we heard the shot! You say your man is injured?' Kitty ran to meet up with Ralston as he tottered across the drawbridge towards them. His face was clammy with perspiration from the exertion of running back to the castle for help. 'Where are Moira and Sandy? Are they hurt?' She put her hand to his elbow to support him as she guided him over the grass to the steamer chairs so he could take a seat and recover his breath.

Ralston removed his panama hat and fanned at his face as Kitty hastily poured him a cold drink. 'We were strolling on the river path having just turned to walk back towards the castle. We saw my man, Evans, hurrying to meet us. I assume he must have been bringing me an urgent message. As he drew to within a few feet of us, there was a shot. I don't know where from, then he crumpled to the floor at Sandy's feet. Blood, blood on his shirt,' Ralston gasped out the report and clutched at his chest.

'Mr Barnes, can I get you something?' Kitty was alarmed at the grey colour creeping into the face of the older man.

'My heart pills, in my coat pocket. Be quick.' He plucked limply at the front of his coat.

Kitty swiftly rummaged in the inside breast pocket of his linen jacket and retrieved the small pot of tablets. She opened the lid, and he gratefully took a pill from her, placing it under his tongue.

After a moment the colour began to return to Ralston's cheeks and his breathing began to improve.

'Sandy and Moira are with Evans. I fear any medical attention may be too late,' Ralston panted.

Kitty pressed the glass of lemonade to his lips. 'Here, try and take a sip. Did you see anyone nearby who may have fired the shot?'

Ralston sipped obediently. 'No, no one. I couldn't tell where it came from. Moira thinks that the shot was aimed at Sandy.'

Daisy had also now recovered a little of her colour. 'You think whoever shot your man was deliberately aiming at Sandy?'

'I'm afraid so. There were threats, you see, before he left London.' Ralston leaned his head back on the chair, his lips still tinged with blue. He appeared greatly shocked.

'Then are Moira and Sandy safe? The assailant may try again,' Hattie asked, her eyes wide at the drama unfolding before her.

'Rupert and Aubrey have just set off along the footpath,' Daisy said. 'Rupert had his shotgun with him.'

'I telephoned and the doctor and the police are on their way. Fortunately the doctor was at the police station when I telephoned,' Lucy said when she came to join them. In the distance they heard the sound of a motor car approaching along the lane. She stood on tiptoes to try and identify the vehicle. 'It's the doctor's car. Ralston, will you be all right if I send him to attend to your man first?'

Ralston nodded weakly. 'Of course. I hope he may be saved but he looked in a bad way.'

Lucy hurried over the drawbridge to stop the doctor's car to direct him after the others along the path. He had barely collected his bag and set off when another car pulled to a stop and the police quickly followed in the same direction.

Kitty itched to be able to get to the other side of the river so she could find out first-hand what was happening.

'Allow me to get you a little brandy, Mr Barnes,' Hattie suggested as Ralston closed his eyes. 'A restorative may aid your recovery.'

She quickly bustled inside the house and returned with a crystal tumbler containing a generous measure of the spirit. She proffered Ralston the glass and he took a grateful sip. 'Thank you, Miss Merriweather, most kind of you.'

The sun disappeared behind a cloud and a shadow fell across the river. It had become more overcast as the day had gone on and the air was starting to cool with the loss of the sunshine.

'We should all go inside. There is nothing more that we can do out here and I expect Rupert or Aubrey will be back soon with Moira. I do hope she's all right, what a horrid event to be caught up in.' Daisy began to gather her things together and the others followed her cue. Hattie offered Ralston her arm and they moved to the drawing room.

Kitty was the last to leave the riverside. She wondered exactly what had happened on the path down by the folly. Surely no one had followed Sandy all the way to Yorkshire to make an attempt on his life. Yet Ralston had sounded certain that the shot had not been an accident and it seemed implausible that anyone would want to murder a manservant.

Aubrey, Rupert, Moira and Sandy were making their way towards the drawbridge. Sandy and Aubrey were supporting Moira between them, while Rupert strode along behind them, his shotgun breached over his arm and a grim expression on his face.

Kitty went to meet them as they drew nearer to the entrance to the gatehouse.

'Everyone has gone inside the house, Daisy said to go on in.'

Sandy's normally ruddy complexion was pale. Kitty noticed the sleeve of his jacket and the front plackets were spattered with blood. Something that sent a shiver along her spine.

'Moira needs to sit down and rest, she's had the most frightful shock.' Aubrey looked anxiously at Kitty.

'Of course, Daisy has the brandy on standby.' Kitty could see that Moira was physically shaking and that it was all she could do to support herself. 'Ralston is waiting for her.' She followed them inside the house as Sandy assisted his wife into an armchair and Hattie clucked across the room bearing another glass of brandy.

Kitty loitered near the door beside Rupert. 'How is Mr Evans?' she asked in a low voice.

'Dead. The bullet entered his back and went straight through his heart. I gather it just missed Sandy.' Rupert's lips were compressed into a grim line.

'That's awful. How did it happen? Was it an accident of some kind?' Kitty asked.

Rupert glanced at her. 'Between you and I, Kitty, I don't believe it was. An accident would be a poacher shooting at rabbits or someone aiming at crows. This looked to me like a shot from a handgun. Much more like a cold-blooded execution.'

Kitty suddenly felt quite shaken at the image Rupert had presented. 'Do you think that Sandy may have been the target?'

Rupert placed his hand on her elbow and drew her a little way out of the drawing room into the hall. 'Sandy has told me that he received some letters before he left London. They arrived at his constituency offices and were making threats on his life. I regret to say he didn't take them seriously and threw them in the fire. Now, with this terrible incident, he's seriously concerned. He also believes his illness last night was not merely due to the alcohol he had consumed.'

Kitty stared at him in astonishment. 'Surely not. He thinks someone poisoned him? Then that would imply that he thinks whoever killed poor Mr Evans must be someone with access to the castle.'

Rupert shrugged. 'I know, it sounds ridiculous. It's like a nightmare especially with the wedding so close. Moira is in a terrible state. She suffers with her nerves anyway and this is bound to make her worse.'

Kitty peeped into the drawing room where Hattie was ministering to Moira. 'I take it she is giving some credence to this idea of poison then?'

Ralston was comforting his daughter while Sandy sat nearby, nursing a large tumbler of brandy.

'I'm not sure. If Sandy was the target today, then he's had a very lucky escape. Evans may have been simply in the wrong place at the wrong time.' Rupert scrubbed at his face with his hand. 'Kitty, would you keep your eyes and ears open. If there is anything, anything at all untoward then come and let me know. I'll speak to Matt too when he arrives this evening. I'm sure the police will do their best but if there is danger inside the castle, then I'd like to have you and Matt on the case.'

Kitty swallowed and nodded. This was a far more serious request than Lucy's ghost hunt. She slipped back inside the drawing room while Rupert went to ascertain the police progress.

Moira and Ralston had just begun to recover, thanks to Hattie's generous dispensing of the contents of Daisy's cocktail cabinet, when Rupert returned to introduce the local police inspector to his guests.

'If I may have everyone's attention, please, this is Inspector Lewis, he will be investigating the circumstances of Mr Evans' shooting. Unfortunately, poor Mr Evans has passed away as a result of his injuries and I know you will all be keen to assist the inspector with his enquiries.'

Inspector Lewis was a lean man in his forties with sharp dark eyes and an air of restless energy that reminded Kitty of a Jack Russell Terrier that Mickey, her maintenance man, had once owned. A nasty tempered little beast, he had been very good at catching rats but prone to snapping at people without warning.

'Thank you, Lord Woodcomb. Obviously, I will be speaking to Mr and Mrs Galsworthy,' he paused and consulted his small black notebook, 'and, of course, Mr Barnes. However, Lord Woodcomb has informed me that the rest of the party were outside at the time of the shooting and had a view of the river path. So, I would ask that if any of you noticed anyone on either side of the river, then please let me or my constable know. I will be seeing all of you at some point to obtain statements.' He waved his hand towards the door and Kitty noticed a uniformed constable was stationed in the hall.

The inspector went around the room taking their names and adding them to the notes in his book. 'May I ask if this is all of the party staying at the castle, my lord?' The inspector looked at Rupert.

'No, not quite, another guest, Sinclair Davies and his wife, Calliope, are in the main house and then there is my sister's mother-in-law, Mrs Adalia Watts, who is staying with my sister and brother-in-law here at the gatehouse.'

'Thank you, sir.'

Kitty was rather surprised that Adalia had not been disturbed by the sudden influx of people entering the house. She had expected her to have appeared by now to complain about the noise.

'I shall make my study available to you, Inspector. Now, I rather think we have trespassed upon my sister for too long. Shall we all return to the castle? This has been the most terrible shock for everyone and I'm sure Moira and Ralston could use a little rest.' Rupert looked at the inspector.

Ralston patted his daughter's hand, Moira responded with a wan smile as if trying to reassure her father.

'Yes, certainly, Lord Woodcomb. If you could show us the way.' The inspector stood aside, and Rupert led the party back across the courtyard to the main house. Daisy and Aubrey remained behind at the gatehouse.

Kitty followed at the back of the group with Lucy and Hattie beside her.

'What an awful thing to happen. So close to the wedding too.' Hattie managed to look both horrified and thrilled at the same time.

'Perhaps it will turn out to simply be the most dreadful accident. A stray shot from someone shooting crows, perhaps. They may not even know they have hit someone,' Lucy suggested hopefully.

Kitty doubted this very much but felt it better not to disillusion her cousin from clinging on to her theory. She wondered how much Mr Barnes knew about his manservant and how long he had been in his service. Not that she could see why Evans would have been the target, if the shooting were deliberate. Surely that fatal bullet must have been intended for Sandy. There would be a lot to tell Matt when he arrived, that was certain. And the sooner he arrived the happier she would be.

Rupert arranged for coffee to be served in the drawing room and everyone gathered to await an invitation from the inspector to attend the study. Sinclair entered the room just as the drinks were being served.

'I say, there's a police constable in the hallway. Has something happened?' He directed the question to Rupert who took him aside and appraised him of the recent events.

Kitty watched closely over the brim of her coffee cup to see how Sinclair took the news. She wondered if Sinclair had spent his afternoon in the library or had he somehow managed to leave the castle unseen with a gun in an attempt to dispatch his former friend?

Sinclair certainly appeared shocked by Rupert's information. Sandy had left the room at this point to change his bloodstained clothes. There was still no sign of Calliope. Kitty felt for Rupert and Lucy, such a tragedy was bound to cast a shadow over the wedding celebrations.

She glanced at her cousin who seemed to be attempting to comfort Moira. Thankfully Lucy possessed a great deal of common sense, although Kitty would be glad when her aunt and uncle arrived. Lord Medford's cheerful calm demeanour would certainly help to reassure everyone.

Ralston was called through for his interview with the inspector and Kitty went to take his freshly vacated seat on the other side of Moira.

'Oh, you poor thing. It must have been the most terrible shock,' Kitty said. She noticed that Moira had her lace-edged handkerchief clutched so tightly in her hand her knuckles were white.

'Oh, Miss Underhay, it was awful, quite awful. We had walked to the old folly. Such a pretty spot, and we stopped and rested for a while in the shade. Sandy still felt weak from being so ill during the night and Father has a bad heart. We had just turned to walk back when we saw Evans hurrying towards us.' She broke off to dab at her eyes with the handkerchief.

'What happened then?' Kitty asked gently once Moira had composed herself.

'I thought he must have received an urgent message that he needed to give to my father. Daddy's business interests are quite extensive, and he often receives telephone calls or telegrams requiring a swift response. Evans drew closer until he was just a few feet in front of us.' A tear escaped to run down the side of her face. 'He was right in front of Sandy and there was this cracking noise and he fell forward onto the path.'

Lucy gasped. 'Oh, Moira!'

'I know, Lucy. We couldn't think at first what had happened, then I noticed the blood spatters on Sandy's coat, and I realised what the sound must have been. Sandy had knelt down to try and help Mr Evans, but it was too late.' Moira shuddered. 'There was so much blood.'

'And you didn't see anyone else at all while you were out?' Kitty asked.

Moira sniffed and shook her head. 'No. Daddy looked all around while Sandy tried to help Mr Evans. There was no sign of anyone else at all.'

Lucy looked anxiously at Kitty. 'There are a lot of trees around that part of the estate so someone could conceivably have been in one of the glades.'

'Do you know if Evans had been working for your father for a long time?' Kitty asked. 'If he had any family at all?'

Moira dried her eyes once more. 'I think he must have been with Daddy for about six months or so. He always appeared a very solitary kind of person, not given to chatter, you know? I suppose Daddy would know if he had any family. They'll need to be informed, won't they? Oh, it's all too horrid. I'm sure whoever it was hoped to kill Sandy and poor Mr Evans happened to be in the way.'

She dissolved back into tears leaving Lucy to look despairingly at Kitty. Moira swallowed a sob. 'I'm so terribly afraid, Miss Underhay. What if whoever did this tries again?'

Kitty was saved from responding when Ralston returned to say he would accompany Moira to see the inspector. With Moira having gone from the room, Lucy moved closer.

'This is awful, Kitty. What do you make of it? I'd convinced myself it had to be an accident but now…'

'I'm sure the inspector probably has men out combing the estate for whoever did this. They are bound to catch them soon and then we shall get to the bottom of it.' At least Kitty hoped that was what the inspector had been organising.

Lucy glanced around the room, then put her head closer to Kitty's and murmured in her ear. 'You don't think this is anything to do with the sighting of the nun? I know I'm probably being ridiculous, but suppose it is?'

Kitty stared at her cousin wondering if she had been too generous in crediting Lucy with common sense. 'Of course not, darling. The police are bound to catch whoever did this quite quickly. If someone has followed Sandy here from London, then someone will have seen them. Either when they arrived or if they are staying locally. The castle is a good mile from the village and it's unlikely that they would have local knowledge.'

Lucy leaned back on the sofa and rubbed her temple. 'I know. You're quite right, Kitty, I'm being foolish. I think perhaps pre-wedding nerves are getting the better of me. It just all feels so unreal. One minute we were outside enjoying the air and then this.' She shuddered.

The door to the drawing room opened and Calliope entered, a frown marring her pretty features. 'The police constable in the hall said everyone was in here. What's going on?'

Sinclair broke off his conversation with Rupert to greet his wife. 'Calliope, my dear, it seems there has been a terrible accident. Mr Barnes' manservant, Evans, has been shot dead.'

Calliope's elegant brows raised. 'How extraordinary. An accident, I presume?'

'I'm afraid it seems as if it may be murder,' Rupert interjected and Kitty heard Hattie give a small squeak of alarm.

'Moira believes that Sandy was the intended target,' Sinclair added.

Calliope placed her hand over her heart and Sinclair led her to a vacant seat. 'That is truly shocking. When did this happen? And where? I was asleep in my room this afternoon.'

'On the path leading back from the folly, by the river. I only found out myself a moment ago from Rupert. I was in the library and never heard a thing.'

'Moira believes someone may have followed Sandy here from London. He had received threatening letters at his constituency office.' Rupert placed his coffee cup and saucer down on the mantelpiece.

'What was in the letters? It must have been something quite extraordinary for someone to have followed him into Yorkshire to try and kill him,' Calliope said.

'He burned them. Apparently, it's not unusual for a man in his position to receive strange or threatening missives from the public.' Rupert frowned.

Kitty could see from her cousin's face that if this were true then Lucy was relieved that Rupert had abandoned his political ambitions in favour of managing his estate.

'Was Sandy hurt at all?' Calliope asked.

Sinclair looked at Rupert.

'No, just shocked, obviously, as were Ralston and Moira. He went upstairs to change, I believe. He may have gone to join them in talking to the inspector.' Rupert looked at Lucy. 'I'm sure Inspector Lewis will soon have the culprit. He seems a very sharp fellow.'

Kitty hoped he was right.

CHAPTER EIGHT

Kitty's own interview with Inspector Lewis was short and, in her opinion, not very sweet. She barely had a chance to take her seat in front of Rupert's battered mahogany desk before the inspector was firing questions at her.

What had she seen? When did she hear the shot? What happened next? Five minutes later the constable was showing her to the door. By the time she had mounted the stairs to her bedroom to change for dinner she had worked herself into a state of indignation. Wait until Matt heard about it all.

She discovered that the seamstress had delivered her bridesmaid's gown to her room. Alice was examining the newly turned hem with a critical eye when Kitty entered.

'Well, what a day! I presume you've heard about poor Mr Evans?' Kitty took a seat on one of the fireside chairs and slipped off her shoes. She knew that word travelled swiftly in the servants' quarters of such a large establishment.

'Yes, indeed, miss. 'Tis the talk of the servants' hall. No one can understand such a thing happening.' Alice frowned at the dress.

'What was the staff's view of Mr Evans?' Kitty knew he had only been at Thurscomb for a few days, but she also knew that his fellow servants would have wasted no time in making an assessment of his character.

Alice tore her attention away from the stitching on the bridesmaid's dress to answer Kitty's question. 'He kept himself to himself mostly.'

The crease on Alice's forehead returned. 'Although, Maud, Mrs Galsworthy's maid, said as he were one of them who liked to know things. A bit of a snoop. She caught him a couple of times reading through Mr Galsworthy's papers as he'd left out on his desk. She thought as perhaps Mr Barnes had asked him to keep an eye on Mr Galsworthy.'

Kitty was not surprised by that titbit of information. She doubted that Mr Barnes could have become so wealthy or done so well in business if he had not been alert to everything around him. It was also plain that Ralston had little affection for his son-in-law.

'I have just had the most aggravatingly short interview with Inspector Lewis, the man in charge of the case. Every time I attempted to ask something, or to propose something, he dismissed me. I swear I was scarcely in the study for five minutes.' Kitty drummed her fingertips on the arm of the chair.

'I suppose as the police might do things a mite different here to how they do things at home. Do you reckon as this shooting has anything to do with Miss Lucy's ghost?' Alice asked as she busied herself gathering towels ready for Kitty to take her bath.

'I don't know, Alice. I can't see why it should but at the same time I can't dismiss a possibility that the two things may be linked in some way.' She would have to find out how anyone could get inside the ruined wing.

She knew there was one small door on the outside of the ruined wing that the builders used for access, but she presumed that it was normally locked. No doubt Lucy would know where the key was kept and who was likely to be able to get to it.

'Captain Bryant will have a surprise waiting for him when he gets here in a bit. Up to his neck in a murder and barely off the train,' Alice observed.

Kitty sighed. 'It seems I can't even attend a wedding without murder following me.'

'I expect as that inspector will soon catch whoever did it. Mrs Galsworthy's maid says as her mistress is convinced as Mr Galsworthy were the target. He'd had nasty letters, something about treachery and demanding money. She overheard Mr Galsworthy and her mistress arguing about them before they come here. Mr Galsworthy lost his temper and threw them in the fire, she said.'

Alice's account appeared to support what Kitty had learned already from Moira. 'It seems a big step though to follow him into Yorkshire. Why not simply wait and bide their time until he returned to his constituency?'

Her maid shrugged her slim shoulders. 'Who knows what some of these folk get into their heads, miss.' Alice picked up Kitty's wrap. 'Shall I draw the bath, miss? Only the water takes an age to hot up.'

'Yes, thank you, Alice.' She smiled at her friend and the girl scurried off down the hall to the bathroom. Kitty hoped it would prove less draughty than it had on the previous evening.

Alice had only been gone for a minute when there was a tap at her door and Lucy popped her head in.

'I had to come and talk to you, Kitty.' Muffy trotted into the room at Lucy's heels and settled herself down with a sigh on top of Kitty's discarded shoes.

'Do you know if the police have found anyone yet?' Kitty asked as Lucy perched on the chair opposite hers.

Her cousin shook her head. 'Not that I've heard. There is so much land around here, it would be relatively simple for someone to lie low. I believe the inspector has asked the railway stationmasters to look out for people attempting to return to London.'

'I take it he thinks that Sandy was the target then?' Kitty said.

Lucy nodded. 'It seems so. It makes sense after he received threats. No one seems to know of a reason why Mr Evans would have been targeted. Inspector Lewis is insisting that a constable remain in the castle until Mr Evans' killer is caught. At least that will reassure Moira. She is convinced this person may try again.'

'Oh, Lucy, I'm so sorry. This has cast an awful cloud over your wedding.' Kitty leaned forward to squeeze her cousin's hand.

'Oh, I'm all right, really. Rupert has said he will drive the motor himself to meet Matt from the train this evening. He'll tell him what has happened. Perhaps, as an outsider looking in, he may have some ideas to assist Inspector Lewis.'

Kitty snorted at her cousin's optimism. 'I doubt the inspector will listen. He certainly was not keen to hear anything that I might have had to say.'

Lucy gave a wry smile. 'Then I hope you and Matt may prove him wrong.'

Her cousin caught sight of the bridesmaid's dress hanging from the corner of the wardrobe and her expression brightened. 'Oh, she finished the hemming. Do try it on again and if you or Alice think it needs anything else then let me know.'

'I'm sure it will be perfect. Alice has already scrutinised it.' Kitty laughed. 'I'm sure the wedding will go off perfectly. Your parents are due to arrive tomorrow, you said?'

'Yes, they should be here in time for dinner and then, all being well, the day after I shall be Lady Woodcomb.' Lucy smiled at Kitty.

'I'm so pleased for you both. I refuse to allow this terrible murder to spoil your big day.' Kitty could see that the new more mature Rupert was the perfect match for her cousin.

Lucy admired her engagement ring and gave a happy sigh before lifting her gaze to Kitty. 'Thank you. And when do you think I might have the pleasure of standing up in church for you and Matt?' she asked, a mischievous note in her voice.

Heat flooded into Kitty's cheeks. 'I think we're some way off that step.'

Lucy laughed and rose to take her leave. 'I won't tease, I promise, well at least not much.' She clicked her fingers for Muffy to follow her.

'By the way, I forgot to ask you, when we were talking about the ruined wing, who has keys to the external door? The one in the courtyard that the builders use?' Kitty asked.

'Oh, that would be Rupert, the works foreman, and I believe there is a spare key in Rupert's desk drawer. Oh, and there will be one in the butler's pantry, on the hooks. There are spare keys for most of the castle on a board in there.' Anything else her cousin may have added was lost when Lucy realised that Muffy was attempting to steal Kitty's shoe.

'I'm so sorry, Muffy, you wretched dog.' Lucy prised the shoe from her pet and returned it to Kitty just as Alice came back along the corridor.

'Your bath is all ready now, Miss Kitty,' Alice said.

'I must go and change. I'll see you at dinner, Kitty.' Lucy smiled at Alice and walked away with Muffy capering on ahead of her.

'Is Miss Lucy all right now?' Alice asked.

'Yes, I think so, despite this awful murder. Let's hope the wedding goes off without anything else unpleasant happening.'

*

Matt was surprised to find Rupert waiting for him on the platform at the small station.

'I thought I would come for you myself. Something dreadful has happened.' Rupert's face was grim beneath the brim of his hat.

'Kitty? Lucy?' Matt asked quickly. He was well aware of Kitty's propensity to find trouble.

'No, nothing to do with them. I'm rather afraid this is a murder.' Rupert kept his voice low as Matt strode beside him to the waiting car.

'A murder?' Matt asked as Rupert stowed his bag on the back seat.

'Yes, and I rather fear the assailant got the wrong man.' Rupert climbed into the car behind the wheel.

Matt got in the passenger side and settled in his seat as Rupert started the engine. 'What on earth has been happening?' he asked.

Rupert filled him in on all the details on the drive to Thurscomb.

'What does Sandy have to say about all of this?' Matt asked as Rupert drove through the gatehouse and into the castle courtyard.

His host halted the car outside the front door to the castle. 'That's just it, Sandy is saying very little about the whole thing. Moira is quite distraught, weeping and wailing about how he's going to die. Ralston, his father-in-law, is concerned for Moira. There is very little love lost between Ralston and Sandy. Ralston begged Moira not to marry him and I'm pretty certain, from what Sandy has said to me, that Ralston has urged Moira to apply for a divorce.'

'Has Sandy said much about these letters? The ones that threatened him?' Matt asked.

Rupert sighed. 'Only that there was some vague accusation of treachery and a demand for money. Nothing specific. He doesn't even recollect if they were signed, and he burned them so that isn't much help to the police.'

'Do the police think the threats are credible? That this man Evans was killed in error?' Matt wondered what Kitty had discovered about all of this. He was pretty certain that she would have been investigating.

'It would seem to be the most likely theory. Evans knew no one here except for Ralston, Sandy, Moira and Moira's maid. He may have encountered Sinclair and Calliope before at Sandy's home, oh and myself, of course. But there seems no motive for killing Evans.' Rupert switched off the engine. 'Come on, it's almost time for dinner. Leave your bag and I'll see that it's taken upstairs. Kitty will be waiting eagerly for you no doubt.'

Matt followed his host into the huge square hall of the castle and handed his outdoor wear to one of the maids.

'Quite a place.'

Rupert laughed. 'Indeed. It's taking up a lot of my time to try and sort out the mess my uncle left behind. He lived here alone for years and begrudged spending anything at all on the upkeep of the house or the estate.'

'I wouldn't care for your coal bill.' Matt grinned back at him.

Rupert clapped his hand on Matt's shoulder. 'I'm glad to have you here, come, the others will be in the drawing room and we may have time for a quick drink before dinner.'

The drawing room was indeed full of people. He was greeted warmly by Lucy and Hattie, before Daisy and Aubrey also came to greet him.

'No Adalia this evening?' Rupert asked.

'Mother is unwell. The murder of Mr Evans has unsettled her nerves.' Aubrey gave a faint smile. Matt thought he detected a look of relief on Daisy's face.

'I'm sorry to hear that. Adalia is Aubrey's mother, she is staying with them for a while,' Rupert explained as he pressed a tumbler of whisky into Matt's hand.

'Now, do allow me to introduce you to Sinclair and Calliope.'

Matt had noticed the exotically beautiful woman seated on a low chair near the French windows and the tall man with receding hair standing beside her. He thought they made an unlikely pair.

'Delighted to make your acquaintance.' Matt nodded to both of them as Rupert performed the introductions.

'Sandy and Moira Galsworthy and Mr Ralston Barnes, this is Captain Matthew Bryant.'

The older man with the silver-grey hair shook his hand. 'Ah yes, the charming Miss Underhay has told us about you. You're a private investigator, I believe.'

'Yes, sir.' Matt shook hands with Ralston and then with Sandy.

'Talking of Kitty.' Rupert beamed as a familiar petite blonde in a pale-green evening gown made her way over to their group.

Matt's spirits lifted as she approached, and he greeted her affectionately with a kiss on her cheek. He was amused to see colour bloom on her cheeks at his greeting.

'My ears were burning.' Kitty smiled up at him.

'All good, my dear lady, I assure you,' Ralston said. 'I was just remarking to Captain Bryant that you had appraised me of his skills as a private investigator.'

'One of those gumshoe Johnnies, eh?' Sandy knocked back the remains of his tumbler of whisky. 'Perhaps you can assist Inspector Lewis to discover who's been trying to kill me.'

Moira's face paled and she seemed to flinch at her husband's tone. 'Darling, please, the police will have their man soon, I'm sure.' She looked towards her father as if anxious for his reassurance on the matter.

'Let us hope so before whoever tried to murder me tries again. It might be third time lucky next time.' Sandy scowled at the bottom of his empty glass.

'The shooting was not the first attempt then?' Matt asked.

'Someone nearly succeeded in poisoning me the other evening.' Sandy's complexion had darkened to a ruddy plum colour.

Moira looked as if she was about to burst into tears.

'Oh, what if that was Evans? He could have been paid to try and kill you, then when he failed, whoever it was shot him before he could go to the police,' Hattie suggested brightly, having clearly overheard their conversation.

'Hattie darling, I think that may be a little melodramatic,' Lucy said as Sandy gave a snort of derision at this theory.

The gong in the hall sounded bringing an end to the conversation. Kitty slipped her hand through the crook of Matt's arm so he could walk with her to the dining room.

'I rather fear this will be something of a busman's holiday for you,' Kitty murmured as they followed Sinclair and Calliope along the corridor.

'You must tell me everything you've discovered after dinner.' He knew she would have already been asking questions.

Had anyone tried to poison Sandy? If they had, and then had tried and failed to shoot him, then that pointed to someone inside the castle and not a discontented voter.

Rupert and Lucy between them kept the conversation over the clear soup and lemon sole, followed by Queen of puddings, firmly away from all talk of murder.

Matt was keen for the post-dinner ritual of port and cigars amongst the gentlemen to be over. He wanted to talk to Kitty to find out her thoughts on both the shooting and Sandy's assertion that someone had attempted to poison him.

It wasn't long after the ladies had withdrawn to the sitting room that the conversation amongst the gentlemen swiftly returned to the subject of Mr Evans' demise.

'What I'd like to know, Sandy old bean, is what it is that you've done that might provoke someone to travel to Yorkshire in an attempt to kill you,' Sinclair remarked as he blew out a thin blue plume of cigar smoke.

Ralston, who had declined a cigar, surveyed his son-in-law over the brim of his port glass. 'Indeed.'

'Why should it be assumed that I have done anything? These people are deranged. There is no rationality to be ascribed to the actions of madmen,' Sandy blustered.

'No disgruntled constituent or cuckolded husband that you may have upset?' Sinclair's tone was bland.

'That is an outrageous suggestion!' Colour climbed in Sandy's already ruddy face.

Ralston merely raised an eyebrow as if Sinclair's suggestion that Sandy was unfaithful to Moira was not something of which he wasn't already aware.

'Gentlemen,' Rupert's mild rebuke was ignored.

'Well, let's face it, your amorous activities are the talk of London.' Sinclair made a show of studying his fingernails. 'Not to mention the various payments you receive from various sources.'

Sandy slammed down his empty port glass so hard that Matt thought it might shatter. 'That, sir, is a vicious lie as well you know.'

'Gentlemen.' Rupert's tone was much sharper now. 'Please can we stop this petty squabbling. A man is dead, and we don't know who did it or why. Bickering between ourselves is not helpful. Plus, my dear friends, I am getting married the day after tomorrow.'

'Hear, hear,' Aubrey added his assent to that of his brother-in-law.

'Perhaps we should go and rejoin the ladies,' Ralston suggested, rising from his seat.

Sinclair extinguished his cigar and followed Ralston to the door. Sandy remained standing, glaring into the fireplace as if it, rather than Sinclair, had been the cause of offence. Matt took his cue from Rupert and strolled out after the others. He was keener than ever now to go and talk to Kitty.

CHAPTER NINE

Kitty was seated beside Daisy when Matt and the rest of the gentlemen returned to the drawing room. She noticed that Sandy had not accompanied them and was unsurprised when Moira immediately darted away, presumably to look for her husband.

Sinclair looked smug she thought, and Ralston grave as they joined Lucy, Calliope and Hattie beside the fireplace.

'I'm afraid I'm not good company for you this evening, Kitty dear,' Daisy said as Aubrey and Matt crossed the faded Turkish carpet towards them. 'I have the most terrible headache. I think perhaps the sun and then the shooting have all been a bit much.'

'You'll both excuse us if I take Daisy home?' Aubrey asked as he extended a hand to his wife to assist her from her chair.

'Of course. Do go home and rest, Daisy,' Kitty urged.

Once Daisy had gone Matt moved swiftly into her seat. 'Now then, darling girl, tell me everything.'

Kitty glanced around to ensure no one was in earshot before quickly appraising Matt of everything that had happened since her arrival at Thurscomb. In return he passed on the conversation that had just been held amongst the male half of the house party.

'Whatever is Rupert thinking asking Sandy to be his best man?' Kitty asked. 'I know that Sandy and Sinclair were his best friends when he was younger, but neither of them appear to be terribly pleasant people. Sandy is a drunk and has a reputation for being a ladies' man and Sinclair seems to have unsavoury political leanings.'

'Rupert said he was best man for Sandy and Moira so perhaps that may explain his choice there. Sinclair was his political mentor, although he is very radical, and I have heard whispers that he has shifted politically to favour Oswald Mosley. Rupert was unaware of the extent of this about-face in Sinclair's views.' Matt's tone was sober.

'The Blackshirts?' Kitty struggled to keep her discomfort from her voice. 'But Rupert has always been opposed to them and their ideals.'

'And still is. Very much so. I doubt that Sinclair will ever be invited again to Thurscomb if the rumours are true,' Matt said.

'Daisy had said Rupert had only heard the rumours after Sinclair arrived. But how do you know all this?' Kitty asked.

'Your uncle has heard some talk whilst he has been in London. There are ugly rumours abroad about Sinclair and his involvement with Mosley's movement. There are rumours of more rallies planned for London. He telephoned me at home before I left for Yorkshire. I think he wished to be assured that Rupert was not influenced by Sinclair.'

'Surely it might be perilous for Sandy too, as a member of the Labour Party and a junior cabinet minister, to fraternise with Sinclair?' Kitty could not imagine the prime minister looking favourably on the connection.

'There is no love lost between Sandy and Sinclair, whatever their boyhood friendship may have been,' Matt said and leaned back in his seat.

Kitty noticed the dark shadows beneath his eyes and guessed he was fatigued from the journey. 'It is a long way from Torquay to Thurscomb. Shall I get you another drink?' she offered.

'Thank you.'

Kitty rose and walked across the drawing room to the drinks table and poured a generous measure of whisky into a glass, before pouring a gin and orange juice for herself. She was surprised, and more than a little displeased, to discover that Calliope had taken her place next to Matt while she had been gone.

Calliope was dressed in another expensive gown, this time of an unusual shade of dark-amber silk. Kitty handed the whisky to Matt and took a seat on an upright carved mahogany chair nearby.

'What kind of private investigating do you undertake, Captain Bryant?' Calliope asked as she inserted a cigarette into the slender ebony holder she favoured.

Kitty sipped her gin. She had obviously arrived a little after the start of this conversation.

'All kinds of things. Fraud, theft, murder,' Matt responded as he obliged Calliope with a light. To the casual observer he would have appeared indolent and relaxed, but Kitty knew that under the façade he was alert to Calliope's probing.

'Really? Then arriving here to this dreadful news will not have overly distressed you. Unlike poor dear Moira, she is a martyr to her own imaginings.' Calliope's gaze slid over to the drawing room door where Moira and Sandy had just entered. She blew out a thin stream of smoke.

'I take it, Mrs Davies, that you don't feel that Moira should be concerned that her husband might be the intended target of a murderer?' Matt's tone held a faint note of amusement.

'Do you think he is that important that someone might try to kill him? I'm sure the police will discover poor Evans' death was nothing more than an unfortunate accident. Someone taking potshots at crows, no doubt.' Calliope dismissed Matt's question with a casual shrug of her elegant shoulders.

'You don't give any credence then to Sandy's assertion that someone has attempted to poison him?' Kitty asked.

Calliope laughed. 'My dear Miss Underhay, you saw how much Sandy drank that night. Really, the man is too full of his own self-importance.'

'Of course, you have known him for a long time, I believe?' Kitty asked, refusing to be deflected by the scornful note in Calliope's tone.

She could see Matt watching Calliope closely from beneath his half-closed eyelids.

'We were close once, many years ago, before Sandy met Moira and I met Sinclair. In fact, I met Sinclair through Sandy at a party at some embassy or other in London.' Calliope glanced at her husband who was deep in conversation with Rupert and Lucy. She took another pull at her cigarette.

'Sinclair mentioned that Sandy has something of a reputation as a ladies' man,' Matt murmured and took a sip of his drink.

'Sandy likes a pretty face, but he also likes Moira's bank balance. Poor Moira, she chases him around all over the place and believes everything he tells her. She's desperate for a baby you know, and, of course, Ralston would like a male heir in line for the Barnes fortune. Although I think he would prefer Moira to be married to someone else first.' A small smirk played along Calliope's crimson-painted lips.

'If Evans' death wasn't an accident and someone was attempting to kill Sandy, what motive do you think they might have?' Kitty asked. Calliope obviously knew the Galsworthys and Ralston much better than she did.

'Oh, darling, it could be anything. A cheated husband, someone who has lost at cards with Sandy. A disgruntled voter. Who knows?' Calliope shrugged again as she stubbed out her cigarette.

'Your husband seems to dislike Sandy,' Kitty remarked in a casual tone.

Calliope shot her a glance. 'Disliking someone's political stance is a long way from murder, Miss Underhay. Besides, Sinclair was in the library all afternoon and I was resting in my room. I don't think either of us would have crept out of the castle to hide in the woods in the hope of taking a potshot at Sandy. And if we did harbour any desire to shoot him, I doubt we would have missed and hit Evans. My husband and I are both excellent shots.'

'Good to know,' Matt said, raising his glass slightly in Calliope's direction.

A delicate flush mounted in Calliope's cheeks. 'I suppose the inspector may wish to consider that Ralston and Moira have more than enough money to hire someone to murder Sandy if they wanted to. I should go and rejoin Sinclair. I think, Captain Bryant, that if anyone were to consider people closer to home who may wish to kill Sandy, then there are better suspects than either myself or my husband.'

Kitty watched Calliope stroll away to stand next to Rupert. 'Gosh, she's a bundle of fun, isn't she? That's quite the most conversation I've had out of her since I arrived.'

Matt grinned. 'I think Calliope may be described as a man's woman.' His smile broadened and the dimple in his cheek flashed as Kitty glared at him.

'Is there anyone else Calliope was hinting at as a suspect for wanting Sandy dead? Daisy and Hattie were with Lucy and I. Aubrey and Rupert were with the estate manager, so who does that leave?' Kitty frowned. 'Adalia was in her room but I can't see Adalia firing off a potshot at Sandy. I don't even know that she knows him. I suppose Calliope has a point that Ralston or Moira could have paid someone, but it seems unlikely. I mean, why do that here? Right before Rupert and Lucy's wedding?'

'I suggest we let Inspector Lewis stew over this one for a while. Your aunt and uncle arrive tomorrow and then it's the day of the wedding. I daresay Calliope may be right when she says it's an outsider who shot Evans. After all, we've only Sandy's assertion that someone tried to poison him.' Matt raised his hand to his mouth in the attempt to stifle a yawn.

'True, the doctor I met in the hall who had examined him didn't raise any concerns.' Kitty looked at Matt. 'You should retire upstairs, I think. Then perhaps you can at least consider the mystery of Lucy's ghost with me tomorrow.'

Matt rose and kissed her cheek. 'Very true. A ghost hunt sounds fun. You must show me these secret passages too. Goodnight, Kitty, I'll see you at breakfast.'

Kitty settled back in her seat and watched as Matt said goodnight to his hosts and accompanied one of the maids out of the drawing room. She glanced around the room. Ralston and Hattie were seated on the sofa and engaged in examining some photographs in a book. Lucy and Rupert were talking to Calliope and Sinclair.

At least Sinclair was talking, his thin, clever face alert as he made some point or other. Calliope looked slightly bored. Lucy wandered off to fix herself another drink and came to join Kitty.

'Matt has gone upstairs. I think he found the early start and the journey quite tiring. He's been so busy the last few weeks too with the court case and wrapping up various jobs.' Kitty took another sip of her gin and shuddered, discovering she hadn't mixed it as well as she'd thought.

'I know how he feels. Planning this wedding and hosting all these house guests has been exhausting,' Lucy said. 'Thank heavens for Hattie. She really has been quite marvellous. Daisy has helped too but the poor darling has been under the weather this last week. I rather think Adalia has consumed most of her time and energy.'

Kitty abandoned her gin. 'Your parents will be here tomorrow and then the day after is the big day.'

Lucy swirled the drink in her glass making the ice cubes chink together. 'I know, it's all a little daunting as well as exciting. I think Mother and Father will be here just after lunch. They set off early yesterday and were staying with friends overnight on the way here.'

'It will be lovely to see them again. So, Lady Woodcomb, how terribly grand. I shall have to practise my curtseys,' Kitty teased, grinning at her cousin.

Lucy laughed and pretended to hit her with a cushion. 'Nonsense. You and Matt will be very welcome here at any time, you do know that, don't you? I can't imagine not having you in my life, Kitty. I always wanted a sister and ever since we met, well, that's how I feel about you.'

Kitty hugged her. 'I shall expect the best suite and lots of fuss whenever I visit.'

Lucy smiled. 'Of course.'

'You have Daisy for company too,' Kitty reminded her.

'I know. I am so lucky. Daisy is such a dear.' Lucy swallowed a large sip of her cocktail.

'I rather think I'm going to head for bed too, Lucy darling. It's going to be a hectic few days.' Kitty embraced her cousin once more and called her goodnights to the rest of the party.

On her way to her room, she glanced out through the windows overlooking the courtyard in case there was any sign of Lucy's ghost. All was still and quiet, however, and she wondered if the presence of a police constable stationed in the hallway might prove a deterrent to any spooky goings on.

Alice was engrossed in her film magazine beside the fire when Kitty entered the bedroom.

'You'm up a bit early tonight, miss.' Her friend immediately set her magazine aside and jumped up to turn off the big band music that was playing quietly on the wireless.

'I feel rather tired, Alice, and this murder is playing on my mind.' Kitty took a seat on the chair opposite the one her maid had occupied and unbuckled her shoes.

''Tis a right puzzle, miss. The constable were telling us as they hadn't found nobody in the woods and the fields on the estate.

Although there is a lot of ground to cover so that might not mean anything.' Alice collected up Kitty's shoes ready to polish them and return them to their box.

'What else did the constable say?' Kitty was sure that Alice would have been paying attention to anything said downstairs.

'The inspector checked all of Mr Evans' things. He had a daughter living on the Isle of Wight apparently. Married to a farmer, but she's not in the best of health the constable was saying. The inspector found letters from her in Mr Evans' drawer. Large doctor's bills to pay. Poor lady, and now she's got the loss of her father to contend with.' Alice shook her head as she encouraged Kitty to stand so she could unbutton her from her dress.

'That's terrible.' Kitty turned around so Alice could help her with the tricky side fastening. 'So, what else did you discover?' Kitty's gown slithered to the floor in a pool of satin around her feet and she stepped out of it so Alice could gather it up.

'Not much, miss. Everybody is of a mind to think as poor Mr Evans was shot by mistake. The constable said as that was the line the inspector was taking.' Alice collected up Kitty's dress ready to place it on one of the padded hangers.

'Sandy is convinced someone tried to poison him,' Kitty said as she continued to prepare for bed.

'Oh dear, I know as they had the doctor out, but nobody mentioned poison. More like he'd drunk too much. He's known for being fond of the bottle, so the staff say.' Alice hung Kitty's dress on the outside of the wardrobe ready for her to inspect in the morning.

'I just hope this doesn't spoil Lucy's wedding. I'm a little worried about Daisy too. She seems so frail at the moment. I thought she would pass out when Ralston came back telling us about the shooting,' Kitty mused as she brushed her hair.

'Well, that's to be expected I suppose for a lady in her condition,' Alice remarked placidly.

Kitty swivelled around from her perch on the dressing table stool. 'I beg your pardon? Do you mean?'

'Miss Daisy is in the family way.' Alice continued tidying.

Kitty was about to ask how Alice knew but then as Alice had seven younger brothers and sisters, she probably knew the signs.

'The seamstress has had to adjust her frock for the wedding. I expect she'll start to show in the next few weeks.' Alice stood behind Kitty to unfasten the catch on her necklace.

'Well, what a lovely surprise,' Kitty said. She was pretty certain that Lucy was unaware of her almost sister-in-law's condition.

'I don't think as Miss Daisy has told anyone yet, miss. The seamstress only guessed because of where she had to adjust some parts of the dress.' Alice moved away to tidy up her magazine.

'I wonder how Adalia will receive the news. She may go into a permanent decline.' Kitty smiled at her friend.

'Now there's a lady the servants will be pleased to see the back of. Runs them ragged and they aren't even her staff. By rights they work for his lordship. Miss Daisy has one maid, and the food comes over from the castle mostly, except if Miss Daisy is hosting a dinner party and then she borrows some staff from her brother. That Miss Adalia is forever asking people to fetch and carry for her.' Alice's lips pursed in disapproval.

'Rupert said that was why the car was late collecting us from the station.' Kitty was unsurprised that the staff were not keen on Adalia.

'They also say, miss, as she has a habit of moving things.' Alice whisked the last of Kitty's belongings into their proper place.

'Moving things? What? You mean like Hattie?' Kitty was confused.

'No, Miss Hattie is like a magpie, she just collects shiny things. 'Tis more of a habit with her. Miss Adalia, well, she moves furniture and ornaments. She takes things from the castle and puts them in Miss Daisy's apartment.'

'Ah!' Kitty suddenly realised that this must be the explanation for the mysterious appearance of the ugly vase.

'It isn't right.' Alice shook her head, disapproval written large on her pretty face.

'No indeed, it's very odd behaviour. I wonder what she means by it.' Kitty yawned and jumped into her bed. 'We had better get to sleep, Alice. Tomorrow will be very busy.'

*

Matt was awake early and headed downstairs for breakfast. He knew Kitty would not be far behind him, as she too was usually an early riser. He was, however, somewhat surprised to discover that Sandy was already installed at the breakfast table.

'Good morning,' Matt greeted him as he headed for the side buffet to inspect the contents of the silver chafing dishes.

'Morning.' The reply was a barely distinguishable grunt as Sandy continued to stare morosely at the dish of porridge in front of him.

Matt selected a generous helping of bacon and eggs and took the place opposite. 'Any news from the police yet?' he asked.

He wasn't expecting Inspector Lewis to have made much progress overnight, but it occurred to him that this might be why Sandy was downstairs so early.

'What? Oh, Lewis, the police, no. Not heard anything yet.' Sandy scowled at his dish and poked at the congealing mass of oatmeal with his spoon.

'It's the big day tomorrow. I expect you have your speech all ready.' Matt applied a little salt to his egg.

'Yes, decent sort, old Rupert.' Sandy gave up on his porridge and pushed the bowl away as a maid appeared and placed a fresh pot of tea and a rack of toast before them.

'He said you'd been friends for years, you, Rupert and Sinclair,' Matt remarked in a conversational tone.

Sandy raised his gaze to look directly at Matt as if seeing him properly for the first time. Matt was shocked at how bloodshot the whites of his eyes were and at the dark shadows on his face. 'Yes, we were at school together as boys. First came here years ago for a couple of weeks when we were young. It all seems like a long time ago now.'

'And he was your best man when you married Moira.' Matt put down his cutlery to pour himself a cup of tea. He waved the silver pot towards Sandy's cup and the man muttered an assent.

'Yes, he was.' Sandy added sugar to his tea.

'It's nice that you've all stayed in touch.' Matt offered Sandy the milk jug.

Sandy snorted. 'Hardly. Oh, Rupert and I have but not so much Sinclair.'

Matt stayed silent and reapplied himself to his breakfast hoping Sandy might fill in the gaps.

Sandy, however, lapsed back into moody silence.

'Good morning.' Kitty bustled into the room and Matt thought how well the soft cornflower-blue print of her summer frock suited her.

Sandy rose abruptly from his seat and mumbled a good morning at Kitty before hastening from the room.

'Gracious, was it something I said?' Kitty asked, her brows arching upwards in surprise at Sandy's rapid exit.

'I doubt it was anything to do with you, old thing. He appears to be a man with a lot on his mind.'

Kitty helped herself to eggs and came to join Matt at the table. 'Did he say anything about what happened yesterday?'

Matt shook his head. 'Nothing at all. Trying to get any conversation flowing was like trying to draw blood from a stone.'

The maid reappeared to bring fresh tea and toast curtailing their conversation for a moment.

'What are your plans for the day?' Matt asked as Kitty patted the corners of her mouth with the white linen napkin.

'Well, I'm free for the morning. I tried on my dress for tomorrow, and it fits, plus my aunt and uncle are not expected until lunchtime.' She smiled impishly at Matt. 'How about a nice walk, perhaps along the river path?'

CHAPTER TEN

Kitty collected her straw hat and a pale-blue cardigan to match her dress as the morning air was still cool. Matt remained downstairs waiting for her in the hall in front of the portrait of the late Lord Woodcomb.

'Remind me to show you the secret passages and hiding places later that Rupert showed me.' Kitty smiled and tucked her hand into the crook of his elbow.

'Just so long as you don't plan to send me into any more dark and enclosed spaces.' Matt gave a mock shudder, but Kitty knew there was a serious note underlying his jest. The Great War had left Matt with a morbid terror of being trapped. Unfortunately several of their adventures so far together had involved just such places.

He had seen too many deaths in the suffocating, muddy trenches of the battlefield when the shoring had failed. He had witnessed the loss of men and horses buried under the sticky mud. Even now, so many years later, he would occasionally awake from a nightmare to discover he had wrecked the room in his sleep or walked about the house.

'I think you will be quite safe on the riverbank,' Kitty said as they strolled out into the wide courtyard.

Despite the early hour the square was already busy with tradesmen's vans and carts delivering supplies for the wedding.

'I think the weather forecast on the radio said that it's set to stay fine and dry for the next couple of days,' Kitty remarked as they skirted around a stationary horse and cart with what appeared to be huge floral arrangements placed in the back.

'That's good. It would be a shame for the weather to turn. It can be unpredictable at this time of year.' Matt looked about him with interest as they walked through the gatehouse opening and out onto the drawbridge to cross the moat.

Kitty glanced back at the gatehouse in time to spot a face at one of the narrow leaded windows. She raised a gloved hand in a friendly wave and saw Adalia duck out of sight.

'Who was that?' Matt asked.

'Adalia.' The woman's behaviour really was most peculiar.

'Which direction are we taking?' Matt asked.

Kitty paused for a moment to get her bearings. She hadn't ventured out of the castle since her arrival so only had what Lucy and Rupert had told her about the estate to guide her.

'Rupert said the moat which surrounds the castle is formed from the river. His ancestors diverted it so the part we have just crossed is the river itself, while the water at the rear of the castle is a kind of backwater.' She looked about her.

With the play of the early sunlight on the water and the fresh spring green of the meadows it looked a pleasant and peaceful place to be. There was certainly no indication that a man had been shot dead here less than twenty-four hours ago.

'Where was Evans shot?' Matt asked.

'Along this path. It leads to one of the follies, according to Lucy.' Kitty studied the landscape. Unlike most castles that were built high up, Thurscomb was hunkered down as if hiding from any potential enemies.

On the drive in to the castle the buildings had not been visible until they were quite close. The water meadows were surrounded by woodland and as she looked along the path towards the distant ruins of the folly, she could see there were several strands of trees. Any of which could have provided cover for whoever had shot Evans.

'Where were you when Evans was killed?' Matt asked.

'Just over there, see the terraces and the wooden jetty where the swans are. We were seated there.' Kitty pointed to Daisy's small and pretty waterside garden.

'So you can't see the whole of the drawbridge but can see the river path leading to the folly from there?' Matt surmised as he studied the garden.

'What are you thinking?' Kitty asked. She guessed it was probably what she herself had already thought. That someone could have left the castle via the drawbridge and potentially have gone around the moat behind the castle in the other direction. They could then have hidden in the woods unseen by the party outside the gatehouse.

'That it would be useful to know if the path goes around the castle at any point.' Matt grinned at her and she knew she had been correct.

'Let us go and explore,' she suggested, and they set off along the narrow dirt track toward the folly ruins.

The swans accompanied them for a short time, paddling along the river margin next to the reeds. Overhead the clear blue sky promised another warm day and the twitter of birdsong sounded from the trees at the edge of the field.

'We must be approaching the spot soon. Moira said they had reached the ruins and rested before they had turned to walk back when Evans approached them.' Kitty could see the ruins of the folly clearly now. A stone archway and a small tower covered in ivy were visible further along the path in the distance.

Matt halted to take stock of their position. 'The path splits here and so does the river. If you look back, Kitty, you can see the other side of the castle quite clearly.'

Kitty could see what Matt meant. 'So we were right, someone could have left the castle and gone the other way around to hide in any of these pieces of woodland.'

A shiver ran along her spine and her pleasure in the loveliness of the countryside speedily began to dissipate. They continued on towards the folly until they reached a spot where the grass appeared to have been flattened by the trampling of feet.

Kitty suppressed a shudder when she spotted a dark reddish-brown patch staining the green of the grass.

'I think this is the place,' Matt said.

Kitty turned so that her back was to the folly ruins. 'They would have been walking in this direction to return to the castle. Mr Evans would have been approaching them. Then the logical place for someone to have been hiding, ready to shoot would be where?' She narrowed her eyes and scrutinised the surrounding landscape.

Matt straightened up from where he had been examining the crushed grass at their feet. 'I would have thought somewhere over there in that copse of trees.'

Kitty looked in the direction he was indicating. 'Shall we go and take a closer look?'

They set off across the field towards the strand of trees. Kitty was slightly surprised that they had not encountered any kind of police presence during their walk. Unless the inspector considered the castle to be so isolated that it was unlikely to attract a rush of onlookers.

The ground became increasingly uneven, and Kitty was glad of Matt's support. She had no desire to turn an ankle before she followed Lucy up the aisle. They reached the start of the woods and walked under the shade of the trees.

Kitty realised the woods extended further than she had thought and were filled with scrubby shrubs and bushes under the tree canopy. She avoided a large patch of nettles and looked back across the field to where the shooting had occurred.

'Here, Kitty.' Matt indicated another area of grass and weeds that had clearly been trampled underfoot.

'It looks as if the police have been here,' Kitty remarked.

In the distance she heard the faint rumble of a motor. 'I suspect this piece of woodland backs onto the road leading to the castle. I suppose someone could have come that way if they had come from the village,' she suggested.

'That's possible.' Matt frowned.

'But how would they have known that Sandy would be walking to the folly?' Kitty asked.

'A tip off,' Matt suggested.

It was true that there had been a lot of chatter during lunch about everyone's plans for the afternoon. That would still imply that the shooting was orchestrated from inside the castle. There was no sign of a fire or of anyone having been rough sleeping in the wood, so it was unlikely that whoever had shot Evans had simply been waiting around for an opportunity.

They made their way back towards the castle and encountered the brisk figure of Inspector Lewis walking towards them.

'Miss Underhay, sir.' He tipped his hat politely to Kitty, but she could see the spark of annoyance in his eyes as he greeted them. 'I do hope you have not been poking around the scene of yesterday's shooting?'

'Not at all, Inspector, merely taking the air beside the river.' Kitty's tone dared him to challenge her.

'There is a dangerous man still at large, Miss Underhay. For your own safety I would recommend that you remain within the castle.' Inspector Lewis' eyes narrowed.

'I daresay we shall be kept very busy for the next day or so with my cousin's wedding, Inspector. I'm sure there will be little opportunity to view the estate.' Kitty attempted to disarm him with a smile.

'Lord Woodcomb has made me aware of your reputation, Miss Underhay, as some kind of amateur sleuth. Whatever they may tolerate in Devon, I can assure you it is not the same here in Yorkshire. I would suggest you leave any idea of investigating to the professionals.' The inspector tipped his hat once more, glared at Kitty, and marched away from them towards the folly.

'Oh dear, and I never even had the chance to introduce you.' Kitty shook her head before flashing an impish grin at Matt. 'It's a good thing that Rupert must have neglected to inform him that you're a private investigator.'

Matt chuckled. 'I don't think we shall enjoy the same cordial relationship with Inspector Lewis that we have with Inspector Greville.'

'Then we shall have to hope he catches whoever shot Evans quickly. In the meantime, we can concentrate on the mystery of Lucy's ghost.' Kitty replaced her hand on Matt's arm, and they continued their stroll.

'I suggest then that we have a restorative cup of tea and then you can show me these secret passages.' Matt winked at her.

The castle was a hive of activity on their return both inside and out. Delivery carts and vans were at the side door and the sound of hammering still rang out from the roof. After finding a quiet corner away from the hustle and bustle in the library, Kitty rang the bell and requested some tea. The day had warmed up considerably after their early start and Kitty removed her hat, using it to fan her face.

Matt sprawled out in one of the dark-green button-backed leather chairs opposite her. 'Well, it appears everything is gearing up ready for tomorrow. Are you and Daisy all set?'

'Of course, Hattie has been most thorough in instructing us. She has attended a great many weddings and been a bridesmaid on several occasions.' Kitty and Daisy intended to assist each other to dress for the wedding and Alice was to assist Lucy.

This was something that Alice was delighted to do and had gone about the bedroom humming happily to herself when Kitty had asked the question. She regarded it as a great honour that Lucy had asked for her and Kitty guessed she would spend a great deal of time boasting about it when they returned to the Dolphin.

The door of the library opened, and a maid entered carrying a polished silver tray of tea things, which she set down carefully on the small round walnut burr table next to Kitty.

'Begging your pardon, sir, but there is a letter come for you.' The girl reached inside her apron pocket to extract a small white envelope, which she passed to Matt. As soon as the girl had gone, Kitty leaned forward to pour the tea.

'Mail already?' she enquired.

Matt frowned at the envelope, which appeared to have been addressed in an old-fashioned hand.

'I rather fear that this is a missive from my aunt Euphemia.'

Kitty's eyebrows arched in a mute enquiry as she passed Matt his tea.

He sighed and set down his teacup so he could open the envelope. Kitty sipped her own tea and watched as he read the contents.

'Bad news?' she asked when he set the letter aside with a groan.

'Aunt Euphemia is my father's older sister. She lives some ten miles from here and is apparently invited to the wedding tomorrow. She was an old friend of Rupert's late uncle.'

Kitty surveyed him with a level gaze. 'And why has that information elicited a groan?'

Matt shook his head. 'Perhaps you should read it for yourself.' He picked up the letter and passed it across to her.

Kitty set aside her tea and applied herself to deciphering the crabbed handwriting.

Dear Matthew,

Your father has informed me that you are staying at Thur-
scomb Castle for a few days in order to attend the wedding of
the late Lord Woodcomb's nephew, Rupert. Bertie Woodcomb
was a dear friend, and I shall also be attending the wedding.
I understand that the young woman you have been walking
out with is related to the bride and will be acting as one of
her bridesmaids. I shall, of course, expect to be introduced
so that I may form my opinion of the girl. Your parents I
gather are not entirely convinced of the suitability of a match
between you. Although I know they are both longstanding
friends of the girl's grandmother, who I believe to be in
business in Dartmouth.
  I look forward to seeing you tomorrow.

Your affectionate aunt

'Oh,' Kitty said as she handed the letter back to Matt. 'I see. At least she didn't mention the murder.' She was unsurprised about Matt's parents continuing to disapprove of her walking out with him. They had not approved of Matt's first marriage either.

Matt gave a wry smile. 'I'm not sure how swiftly that news will travel. I suspect that your uncle and Rupert will combine forces to keep it under wraps until after the wedding at least.'

'So it seems that I am to be inspected by your aunt tomorrow? What is she like?' Matt's father was a very upright ex-military man with old-fashioned views on the roles of women. She suspected from his aunt's handwriting and Matt's reaction to the note that his aunt might be of a similar mind. Kitty wasn't sure how she felt about it. Had Matt more serious intentions towards her? Or did his parents disapprove of her so much?

Matt refolded the note and returned it to its envelope before tucking it inside the breast pocket of his jacket.

'Aunt Euphemia is a, well, like a female version of my father, minus the moustache, although I must confess, I think that is only because she has removed it.'

Kitty burst out laughing and leaned forward to give him a playful tap on his knee. 'Oh dear. In that case, I shall endeavour to behave and be more ladylike than usual.'

Matt merely smirked and took another draught from his cup.

'Matthew, Kitty, oh, thank goodness I've found you both.' Hattie bustled into the room, her plump face heated and bearing a flustered expression.

'Hattie dear, do come and sit down and have a cup of tea. The pot is still fresh and there is an extra cup.' Kitty was concerned about the older woman who looked quite exhausted.

'I really shouldn't, there is so much to do and, of course, Lucy's parents will be arriving this afternoon.' Hattie however subsided into a vacant chair and accepted the tea, which Kitty had hastily poured and pressed upon her.

'Now, do have a drink and then tell us what we can do to help you,' Kitty suggested.

Hattie sipped her drink gratefully. 'There is so much to be done before tomorrow. Lucy asked me if you would mind taking Muffy out for a short walk this afternoon. I have to go over the arrangements once more with the staff. Lord and Lady Medford are arriving, and Lucy has her final dress fitting, and the flowers will need to be checked.' Hattie paused for breath.

'It's quite all right, Hattie dear. We can walk Muffy, and I don't mind checking the floral arrangements and the seating in the chapel,' Kitty said.

'Thank you so much, my dear, and for the offer of your maid to assist Lucy to dress tomorrow. I offered myself as I know the staff will be very busy and dear Lucy doesn't yet have a maid of her own.' Hattie swallowed the rest of her drink.

'Alice is delighted to be able to help.' Kitty picked up the almost empty teapot in case Hattie needed a drop more tea.

'Thank you so much, no more tea for me. I must get on, as it will be lunchtime soon. I do feel much better for that little break. If you could collect Muffy from Lucy after lunch,' Hattie suggested.

'Of course,' Matt agreed, and Kitty noticed the silver teaspoon disappear from the saucer into one of Hattie's capacious pockets.

Once Hattie had gone, Kitty showed Matt the secret openings that Rupert had demonstrated to them during the tour of the house.

'Incredible. I wouldn't mind betting there are more of these,' Matt said thoughtfully as the secret door in the hallway clicked shut.

'It seems very likely,' Kitty agreed. 'I had wondered if a passage such as this might be the answer to Lucy's ghost.'

'Hmm.' Matt rubbed his chin. 'It could be a possibility.'

'Perhaps while you are exercising Muffy this afternoon you might wish to take the other path around the castle?' Kitty asked, an innocent smile playing at the corners of her lips. 'I cannot see how Inspector Lewis could raise an objection.'

Matt grinned. 'And I take it you might be looking into a few other things whilst assisting Hattie with her chores this afternoon?'

CHAPTER ELEVEN

After a light luncheon of cold cuts and boiled potatoes followed by plum tart, Matt departed with Muffy trotting happily on a leash at his side. There had been several faces missing from around the table as Calliope and Sinclair had decided to walk into the village and take lunch at the local hostelry. Daisy had remained at the gatehouse and Adalia had not appeared either.

Kitty was presented with a list of tasks by a grateful Hattie and resolved to use the opportunity to see what she might learn either about the so-called ghost, or about anyone in the castle who might wish to harm Sandy.

Sandy himself had made a glum appearance during lunch, rebuffing any attempt at conversation. Kitty looked at Hattie's list and set off up the main staircase to the chapel. She slipped inside through the half open door intent on her instructions.

The chapel was devoid of occupants except for a familiar female figure, head bent seemingly in prayer as she sat on one of the chairs on the front row. Kitty had no desire to disturb Moira so checked the large standing floral arrangements at the rear of the chapel first. The flowers at the ends of the rows of chairs also appeared to be in order. The delicate white blooms contrasting against the dark polished surfaces of the seats.

Kitty glanced at her list once more. Hymn books, apparently, she had to ensure that they were all in place along with orders of service. She started checking quietly from the back as she made her way along the red-carpeted aisle towards the altar.

The air in the chapel was cool and smelt of beeswax and lilies. Sunlight shining through the stained-glass window made the stone flags of the floor sparkle with multi-coloured jewel tones. Moira appeared oblivious to her presence.

Once Kitty had reached the top of the aisle, she could see why Moira hadn't noticed her arrival in the chapel. The woman's eyes were tightly closed in an attempt to prevent her tears from streaming down her face.

'Moira? Are you all right?' Kitty realised that was a ridiculous question since she could see that the woman was patently not all right.

Kitty took a seat on the chair next to her. 'Can I help you in some way? Fetch someone for you?'

Moira's silk-clad shoulders shook and she pressed a sodden lace-edged handkerchief to her lips. 'No, thank you. I shall be perfectly fine in a moment.'

'May I take you back to your room? Perhaps a lie down might help you.' Kitty was unsure what to suggest. She felt quite awkward, as if she were somehow intruding into something private.

'Thank you, no, really, I'm quite all right. It was just a moment of foolish sentiment, the wedding, you know.' Moira dabbed fiercely at her eyes and gave a determined sniff.

'You have had a distressing time. I mean seeing that poor man killed right in front of you would be enough to unsettle anyone,' Kitty sympathised.

Moira shot her a glance from under tear-soaked lashes. 'Yes, it was quite terrible. It came from nowhere. One moment he was striding towards us calling my father's name and then he, well, crumpled. Sandy rushed forward to try and catch him. I think the sound of the shot must have alerted him. I was rooted to the spot. I simply couldn't move. At first, I thought he must have tripped, or it was some kind of practical joke.' Moira shivered, her face pale under what was left of her foundation. 'Then I saw the blood, all red and sticky on his shirt.'

'I wonder if the inspector has managed to find the person responsible yet,' Kitty voiced her thoughts aloud.

'I hope so, Miss Underhay, but somehow I doubt it. I have such bad feelings about all of this, you know. Sandy says that I'm being foolish, but I can't shake them off.'

'What feelings are those?' Kitty asked.

'Ever since those letters arrived at the constituency offices, I've had this awful sensation that Sandy is in some frightful danger. Not that he will agree to taking any sensible precautions. Although that poor man dying at his feet has certainly unnerved him. He says he doesn't know why anyone would want him dead and that Evans' death must have been an accident.' Moira dabbed at her eyes again. 'But I know there is more to it than that, Miss Underhay. A wife knows her husband.' Moira rose from her seat and hurried away, out of the chapel before Kitty could ask any more questions.

Kitty sat frowning for a moment. There had to be some reason why Moira was so convinced that Sandy was in danger. She refused to believe it was merely instinct. No, there was something else at work here, Kitty was certain.

By the time she had completed the rest of the jobs on Hattie's list, her aunt and uncle had arrived at the castle. Kitty entered the main hall just as her uncle's Bentley pulled up and Rupert's butler went out to greet them.

Once Lucy had greeted her parents and Rupert had shaken hands with his future in-laws, the party moved to the drawing room where Hattie ordered tea.

'Now, my dears, tell us what has been happening? We were most upset to hear that one of the servants had been killed.' Kitty's aunt, a tall and stately woman carefully removed her hat and set it to one side. She patted her neatly curled grey hair to ensure it was in place before turning her attention to Lucy and Rupert.

Rupert confirmed the report he had apparently given to Kitty's uncle the previous evening by telephone. As he finished speaking Matt entered the room with Muffy.

The little dog made a beeline for her mistress, while Matt greeted Lord and Lady Medford.

'What do you make of all this then, you two?' Kitty's uncle asked, looking first at Matt and then at Kitty. 'Is this Inspector Lewis chappie up to the mark, do you think?'

Matt took a seat on one of the armchairs and accepted a cup of tea from Hattie. 'I don't know, sir. He seems to believe that Sandy Galsworthy was the intended victim and is searching the estate and nearby village. I met some of the searchers just now while I was walking the dog.'

'Hmm, and what say you, Kitty m'dear? You usually seem to know what's what.' Her uncle beamed at her affectionately, appearing more than ever like a genial grocer than a lord of the realm.

Kitty blushed. 'Inspector Lewis seems to believe he has everything in hand. I don't think he is keen on amateurs interfering with his cases.'

'Then let us hope he is successful, eh. Now, we have a wedding to celebrate tomorrow. Hattie tells me the champagne has arrived, so I think we can commence our celebrations this evening, Rupert dear boy, if that is agreeable to you?' Kitty's uncle's eyes twinkled.

'Certainly, sir, that's most generous of you,' Rupert agreed.

'Oh yes, everyone is coming for dinner tonight and it will certainly help to lift the mood.' Lucy beamed at her father and slipped Muffy a shortbread biscuit from the trolley.

'If you'd care for a tour of the castle, sir, I'm sure the ladies are eager to discuss the plans for tomorrow,' Rupert suggested.

Lord Medford was happy to agree. 'I could do with stretching my legs after all that time in the motor. Are you accompanying us, Matthew?'

Matt agreed and placed his cup back on the trolley. 'Kitty has shown me some of the surprises in the castle but I'm sure there are more.' He followed Rupert and Lucy's uncle out of the drawing room.

Kitty then spent a pleasant hour or so with her aunt, cousin and Hattie reviewing the arrangements for the next day. It made a nice change to think of something other than murder and suspicion and Kitty's spirits were high when she went upstairs to change for dinner.

Alice had laid out a pretty, pale-pink dress with a finely knitted silver evening shawl ready for the evening. Of Alice herself, however, there was no sign. Kitty was slightly surprised as she knew Alice usually made herself available at this time of day in anticipation of Kitty's return to dress for dinner.

Kitty had scarcely begun to gather her things ready to take a bath when Alice reappeared, rosy-cheeked with indignation.

'I'm so sorry, miss. I went to run your bridesmaid's dress over to the gatehouse ahead of tomorrow when that Mrs Watts collared me. Wanted me to help her and Miss Daisy's maid move a round table in Miss Daisy's drawing room.'

'Why was she moving Daisy's furniture?' Kitty asked.

'She said it was a surprise for Miss Daisy. I reckon she'll be surprised all right, 'tis a right ugly old thing.' Alice shook her head knocking her fancy lace cap askew.

'Oh dear.' Kitty thought her friend was probably right and she suspected that Rupert was probably now missing a table.

'I'll go and draw you a bath, miss.' Alice briskly removed the towels from Kitty's arms and headed out of the room.

Kitty was prepared to follow her until a noise from outside caught her attention. Her room had a view over the courtyard, and she peeped out from behind her curtain to see what the commotion was about.

Sandy stood near the front entrance smoking a cigarette. He appeared to be arguing with the police constable that Inspector Lewis had insisted should remain at the castle. Kitty tried to hear the conversation but knew if she opened the window any wider it would call attention to her presence.

'It's quite unnecessary. I shall speak to your superior.' Sandy's face was flushed, and he was strutting up and down like an enraged turkey cock.

Kitty couldn't make out the police constable's reply, but she guessed he was attempting some kind of conciliatory remark. At that point Sinclair approached, arm in arm with Calliope. The two of them evidently returning from their day out walking, as they were both still clad in their tweeds and wearing walking shoes.

Sinclair made a remark that Kitty didn't catch. Instead, she heard Calliope's distinctive smoky laugh. This seemed to enrage Sandy even more as he ground out the stub of his cigarette underfoot with some force. Sinclair and Calliope then passed into the castle and after a moment Sandy followed, leaving the constable at his post outside the front door.

'Your bath's all ready, Miss Kitty,' Alice called from the doorway.

'Thank you, Alice.' Kitty went off to lie in the rose scented water while she tried to puzzle out what was going on at Thurscomb.

*

Matt followed Rupert and Lord Medford around the castle. Once the tour was completed, the three men ended up in Rupert's study where he produced a cut glass decanter of whisky.

'I think we have time for a quick drink before we dress for dinner,' Rupert suggested.

Lord Medford had installed himself on a worn brown leather club chair. 'Excellent idea, dear boy. Most interesting place you've got here. I visited once a good many years ago when your late uncle had the house. Before Lucy was born, in fact.' He accepted a crystal tumbler from Rupert.

Matt took the other vacant chair next to the window and declined Rupert's offer of a cigar to accompany his drink. 'You may know my aunt Euphemia then, sir. She was an old friend of the late Lord Woodcomb?'

'Effie, yes, by George I do, haven't seen the old girl in years.' Lord Medford accepted a cigar.

'We've invited her to the wedding tomorrow. I think we were rather afraid not to ask her.' Rupert gave Matt a wry smile. 'I hadn't realised you were related. It's a small world.'

Matt grinned. 'My father's older sister, and, yes, she is rather formidable. She sent me a note this morning. She intends to inspect Kitty.'

Rupert's brows raised and Lord Medford coughed. 'Hmm, does Kitty know?'

'Yes, sir.' Matt swallowed a sip of whisky and tried not to grimace at the heat when it hit the back of his throat.

He noticed Rupert and Kitty's uncle exchange a look.

'I saw the constable patrolling earlier. Is he remaining at the house until whoever killed Evans is caught?' Matt asked.

Rupert sighed. 'Yes, or until Sandy sets off back to London, whichever comes first. The inspector is convinced Sandy was the intended target.'

'Hmm, a most unfortunate event, right before the wedding.' Lord Medford blew out a plume of smoke from his cigar.

'Indeed, sir. Ralston, Sandy's father-in-law, is most upset. Evans was his right-hand man. I think they all intend to leave the day after tomorrow. As do Sinclair and Calliope,' Rupert said.

Lord Medford looked meaningfully at Matt at the mention of Sinclair's name. 'Heard some rum stuff about that Sinclair fellow while I was in London.'

Rupert sighed. 'I'm not surprised, sir. At one time we were all very close as friends, Sinclair, Sandy and myself. Now though, Sandy seems to have lost his way, becoming far too fond of the trappings of his position, and Sinclair, well, frankly, sir, once he leaves Thurscomb I do not foresee our friendship continuing.'

Lord Medford refrained from commenting, contenting himself with his cigar, but he appeared satisfied by Rupert's response.

The oak door to the study opened unexpectedly and Sandy glowered at them from the doorway. 'Rupert, have you any idea what that confounded inspector is up to? That wretched constable is dogging my every move.'

Rupert's shoulders stiffened but his voice was calm. 'I've no idea, old bean, he's not confided in me. All I know is that the constable is for your protection. Moira and Ralston seem quite happy for him to remain.'

Sandy scowled. 'Moira would be. Brain of a hen that woman, constantly nagging.'

'Come and join us, we were just having a quick drink before dinner. Tonight and tomorrow are a celebration after all.' Rupert stood and lifted up the decanter.

Sandy entered further into the room and came to sit on a small wooden chair beside the marble fireplace. Rupert pressed a glass into his hand. 'Thank you. Sorry, Rupe. This business is getting to me. It's not a pleasant feeling to think someone may be trying to kill you.'

'And you have no idea at all, sir, who that person might be?' Matt asked. He couldn't believe that Sandy truly had no one in mind. No one that he had somehow wronged or annoyed.

Sandy rubbed a large hand over his florid face. 'Dash it all, a fellow is bound to upset a few people as one goes through life but not enough to drive them to murder. I gave a few names to that inspector chappie, Lewis. A couple of disgruntled constituents, a few people I owe money too, a fellow who blames me for his losses at cards and a chap whose wife took a bit of a shine to me.' He picked up his glass and took a large swallow of whisky. 'Nothing serious.'

Matt was certain that Sandy wasn't telling them the whole truth. His body language and the awkward flitting of his gaze away from Matt's told a different story.

'Perhaps the inspector will inform us of his progress later,' Lord Medford suggested as he finished his cigar.

Sandy gave a snort. 'Sinclair said they had seen him in the village interrogating the publican at the local hostelry.'

'The Plume of Feathers?' Rupert murmured.

Sandy nodded and dashed back the last of his whisky. 'That's the place. After some Johnny who'd been staying there apparently.'

'Perhaps that's the man?' Matt suggested.

Sandy shrugged his large beefy shoulders. 'I don't know. Sinclair didn't get the name. Calliope seems to find the whole thing amusing for some reason, like it's a giant game.' A shadow crossed his face. 'Well, I'm not laughing.' He stood abruptly. 'Thanks for the drink, old boy, hit the spot marvellously. I'll see you all at dinner.' He gave them all a farewell nod and left to change.

'Perhaps the inspector has found his man after all.' Rupert waved the decanter at them but both Matt and Lord Medford refused a top up.

'Let us hope so,' Lord Medford said.

Matt could only agree. If whoever shot Evans was not caught quickly and it was not someone from outside the castle, then he feared Lucy and Rupert's wedding would be forever overshadowed by the murder.

Matt bathed quickly, mentally cursing the castle's antiquated and ineffectual hot water supply and dressed for dinner. He hoped to have a quiet word with Kitty before everyone assembled downstairs so they could exchange information.

For once his luck was in and Kitty was standing in the main hall in front of the fireplace frowning at the suits of armour. His breath caught in his throat and his steps slowed as he descended the stairs towards her. The pale glittering material of her gown and the silver shawl combined with her short fair hair so that she resembled a sparkling Christmassy angel. Incongruously out of place in the vast bare space of the castle's hall.

She turned to him and smiled as he advanced towards her. 'What marvellous timing. I have things to tell you.'

'And I you.' He drew her to the side of the fireplace, so they were out of the main eyeline of anyone descending the stairs, and they quickly exchanged information.

'Sandy's conversation with you seems to confirm what I saw and heard from my bedroom window,' Kitty said.

'Let us hope this mystery guest at the public house is the man who killed poor Evans.' Matt could see that Kitty didn't look convinced.

'Perhaps. Anyway, I refuse to think any more about it for now. All I care about is Lucy and Rupert's wedding.' Her eyes sparkled. 'Now, let's go and find the others and join the party.'

The evening passed surprisingly well. Lord Medford's generous donation of champagne appeared to lubricate away the frictions and tensions between the guests. There was no more talk of the murder and all focus was now cheerfully upon Lucy and Rupert's upcoming nuptials.

Matt and Kitty were amongst the last of the party to retire upstairs, having stayed to enjoy one last dance together before the evening ended. Kitty shivered as they walked together into the hall. 'Brr, there is a draught from somewhere in here.'

'It was quite warm in the drawing room.' Matt noticed the front door was slightly ajar.

Kitty glanced at him. 'Lucy's ghost?' she murmured.

They crept over the stone flags to the door and peeped out into the dark and silent courtyard. The only thing of any notice was the crimson dying flare of a discarded cigarette butt, which winked and went out even as they spotted it. Of the person who had smoked it, there was no sign at all.

CHAPTER TWELVE

The morning of the wedding dawned bright and clear. The house was awake early as the staff completed the preparations for the ceremony, which was to take place at eleven.

Alice had woken Kitty with a cup of tea and had set out her things for the day.

'Do have a cup of tea yourself, Alice. You will be rushed off your feet in a minute assisting Lucy.' Kitty shuffled over in her bed and patted the pink-satin coverlet beside her.

Alice frowned and looked at the time on Kitty's small leather-cased travel clock. 'Very well then, miss, but I don't want to be late. There's a lot to do.'

Kitty grinned. 'I know. It's terribly exciting. I'm going over to Daisy's after breakfast to change and then we are coming back across to collect our flowers and to wait with Lucy until they are ready for us in the chapel.'

Alice poured herself a cup of tea from the small silver pot on Kitty's tray. 'All of the staff are to watch the service from the gallery. It will be very exciting to see. 'Tis a shame as Enderley's staff will miss it, but his lordship has arranged for them to have a party to celebrate. Miss Lucy's gown and veil is beautiful, I'm fair excited to be helping her dress.'

'Thank you so much for assisting her. I know my aunt is very grateful. It would have been different if she had married from Enderley, but here I think my aunt and uncle don't wish to embarrass Rupert by offering money to pay for all of the costs. Something about it being indelicate after he has offered to host the wedding. The Thurscomb estate was not in a good way when he inherited, however, and from what I've heard and seen money is, well, not as plentiful as one might think.' Kitty took a sip of tea.

'I can believe that, miss. You know as how the car smelled a bit funny when we was collected from the station? Well, apparently the late Lord Woodcomb used to keep his chickens in it.' Alice's nose crinkled.

'Golly. I had wondered what that smell was.' Kitty's lips quirked.

'Well, Miss Lucy will look lovely, I'm sure. Your aunt has brought the family tiara for her veil.' Alice gave an approving nod.

'I suppose that must be her something old?' Kitty asked with a smile.

'Yes, miss, her dress is the something new. Miss Daisy has loaned her a pair of pearl and diamond drop earrings for her something borrowed,' Alice confirmed.

'Her something blue?' Kitty asked.

'The dressmaker said as she'd put blue ribbons on Miss Lucy's shoes and sewn a couple in the underlay of her dress for good measure. And her father has given her a nice shiny new sixpence for her shoe.' Alice smiled happily, clearly feeling that all the proper measures had been taken to ensure the bride's good luck.

Kitty finished her tea. 'It sounds wonderful.'

'I'm sure it will be. I have heard too as Miss Lucy's intended has arranged for a sweep to come from the village to bring them good luck. Now you'd best get a wiggle on, Miss Kitty. Breakfast is only on for a short spell this morning as they'll be preparing the dining room for the wedding.'

'Yes, and Daisy will be expecting me.' Kitty set down her cup and gave her friend a quick hug. 'Have a lovely time helping Lucy and you can tell me everything later.'

*

Kitty made her way across the courtyard to the gatehouse after breakfast. The castle was a hive of activity with the main hall being dressed with elaborate floral arrangements of white roses and lilies and side tables and chairs ready to receive the wedding guests for a pre-ceremony sherry reception.

She rang the large brass angel bell beside the wooden studded front door to Daisy and Aubrey's home. To her surprise Aubrey opened the door himself already attired in his morning suit.

'Kitty, do come in. Daisy is expecting you.' His pleasant bespectacled face looked a little harassed.

'I hope I'm not too early.' Kitty followed him into Daisy's beautiful modern lounge.

The table Alice had told her about was nowhere in sight and Kitty wondered what had happened to it. Adalia was half reclined on the couch, still in her housecoat.

'Miss Underhay, I do apologise. My health you know is not the best and mornings are something of a trial for me. I am without a maid to assist me as well this morning.' Adalia fluttered her half-opened eyelids as if too weak to fully focus on Kitty.

'Nonsense, mother, you're as strong as a horse,' Aubrey remarked mildly. 'I'll tell Daisy you're here, Kitty.'

A pink patch of colour had appeared on Adalia's cheeks at her son's rebuke, and she pulled herself into a sitting position. 'You must be looking forward to standing up for your cousin, Miss Underhay?'

Kitty was studying a rather lovely figurine on the side table. 'Oh yes, Lucy is such a dear.'

'Perhaps it will be you next, Miss Underhay. Weddings seem to be rather like omnibuses. None at all, then several of them all at once. At least your cousin will have her family present at her wedding, unlike my own poor dear son.'

Kitty was uncertain how to respond to this rather barbed remark of Adalia's so stayed silent.

'You know that Daisy persuaded Aubrey to elope? I cannot tell you how that was a dagger to my heart, Miss Underhay. No one understands or has sympathy,' Adalia continued apparently misconstruing Kitty's silence for interest in her cause.

'I try my best to help. To make this… this empty space a proper home, and I receive no thanks at all. No gratitude.' Adalia was working herself up nicely now and Kitty guessed this must be to do with the table and the various other appropriations that Adalia had made.

'I think this room is perfectly lovely. So light and airy. Daisy has wonderful taste.' Kitty smiled at Adalia, keen to nip the stream of complaints in the bud.

Adalia's lips puckered as if she had sucked on something sour. Kitty was relieved to see Aubrey return.

'Do go on through, Kitty. Daisy is all ready for you.'

Kitty murmured a hasty farewell to Adalia and made her escape along the hall to the spare room where Daisy was waiting.

'Kitty, oh I am so glad to see you. Adalia is lying around like a dying swan in my sitting room and poor Aubrey is trying to get ready so he can receive the guests along with Sinclair.' Daisy looked pale and tired. She had left the party early the previous evening accompanied by Aubrey, pleading a headache and Ralston had escorted Adalia across the courtyard at a later hour.

'I'm sure that everything will be fine. Now, let me assist you first and then you can do my buttons. Alice has gone to Lucy and I think the first cars with the guests will be here soon.'

Kitty helped Daisy into her dress, noticing for the first time the gentle swell of her friend's abdomen and the extra fullness around her bust.

'Thank you, Kitty dear.' Safely fastened into her gown, Daisy returned the favour for Kitty as she hastily changed.

'Let me do your hair,' Kitty instructed, and Daisy took a seat obediently in front of the dressing table mirror. Lucy had chosen ornamental combs for them to wear covered in flowers to match those of the bouquets.

'I am so very grateful for your help, Kitty. I just haven't been very well lately, and this is all… well, with Adalia, it's been a lot.' Daisy's blue-eyed gaze met Kitty's in the mirror's reflection.

'With the baby you mean?' Kitty said gently as Daisy's blue eyes rounded in surprise. 'It's all right, your secret is safe with me. Alice guessed it and told me.'

Daisy blushed. 'Yes, only Aubrey knows about it at the moment. I didn't want to take attention from Lucy and Rupert. We thought we would tell them later, once Sinclair and Sandy had all gone back to London and it was just family in the house. Before Lucy and Rupert go on their honeymoon.'

'That will be lovely. Lucy will be thrilled.' Kitty smiled at her and secured the comb in Daisy's artificially blonded curls.

She swapped seats and Daisy repaid the favour so both girls were ready when Aubrey knocked at the door to say the bouquets had arrived and he was to escort them to Lucy's room.

The courtyard was now full with motor cars and carriages and a hubbub of chatter reached Kitty's ears as she entered the hall of the castle clutching her huge bouquet of white roses, lily of the valley and trailing ivy.

Aubrey guided her and Daisy swiftly through the crowd and up the stairs. Kitty glanced about her as she walked looking for Matt or anyone who might be his aunt Euphemia. She reached the halfway point on the staircase and spotted his dark head bent over listening to a diminutive older lady with silver-white hair. There was no time to notice anything more as she had to get to Lucy's room.

Her aunt and Alice were standing with Lucy as Kitty and Daisy entered. Lady Medford was in peacock-blue shot silk with an impressive hat that had been dyed to match. Alice's cheeks were pink with pleasure as she tweaked Lucy's diaphanous floor-length veil with its scalloped embroidered border.

'Oh, Lucy, you look gorgeous.' Kitty blinked back tears that threatened to fall at the sight of her pretty, dark-haired cousin in her wedding finery.

'My brother is a very lucky man,' Daisy agreed, her bright blue eyes also sparkling from unshed tears.

'I must go now and take my place in church, your father will be here for you shortly.' Lady Medford kissed Lucy's cheek and slipped out of the room, leaving the girls alone for a brief moment.

'You do look fabulous, Lucy.' Kitty admired the white satin embroidered gown trimmed with fine lace and the bandeau style diamond tiara sparkling on Lucy's chestnut curls.

'Alice has been a gem.' Lucy smiled at the maid who blushed and excused herself so she could join the other servants in the gallery to watch the proceedings.

Lord Medford knocked on the door, resplendent in his morning suit, and kissed his daughter tenderly on the cheek. For a moment Kitty envied her cousin her closeness with her parents. With Kitty's own mother dead and her father in America, there was only her grandmother and great-aunt Livvy left, besides Lucy's family. Until the previous June she had been unaware of the connection until her father had returned to her life and told her that his estranged sister was Lady Medford.

Daisy and Kitty withdrew to a tactful distance while Lord Medford spoke privately with his daughter. Then the knock came once more at the door to say that all was ready, and they were to make their way to the chapel.

Lord Medford looked at his daughter and Lucy gave her father a tremulous smile before taking his arm. Kitty and Daisy followed behind taking care to ensure the short satin train of Lucy's gown and her floor-length veil were displayed to full advantage.

The doors of the chapel were open and the small congregation standing as the harpist in the gallery played 'Greensleeves' and they began their short procession down the aisle. From her vantage point behind Lucy, Kitty could see the bright jewel colours of the stained-glass window and the look of love and adoration on Rupert's face when he set eyes on his bride.

They halted at the top of the aisle and Kitty and Daisy stepped aside. Kitty blinked furiously, her heart full at being part of the small, intimate occasion and she was glad of the clean linen handkerchief that Matt passed to her from his position at the end of the row.

Before long the ceremony was over, and they were all being ushered outside to the courtyard to have photographs taken. Kitty's jaw had begun to ache from smiling and holding her pose.

'Champagne, darling.' Matt handed her one of the crystal flutes from a tray being carried by a passing maid.

'Oof, thank you.' Kitty chinked her glass against his and took a sip, savouring the cold, fizzing sensation against her lips.

'I think the photographs are all completed now.' Matt smiled at her and she wondered how his wedding day to Edith, his first wife, had compared to this one. They had been married at short notice in the middle of the war. Matt's parents had disapproved of Edith also, and even more so when baby Betty had arrived an unseemly few short months after the ceremony.

The guests were milling around, some inside the hall of the castle, others were taking the air in the courtyard. Kitty longed to set aside her large bouquet of flowers. The scent of the blooms was starting to irritate her nose and they were surprisingly heavy.

'Here, let's place those in the shade here for now.' Matt could see her problem and took them from her, putting them in the shade of a stone wall buttress.

'Thank you.' Relieved of her burden, Kitty drank some more of her champagne and started to relax.

Rupert and Lucy were with Lord and Lady Medford. Ralston, Moira and Sandy were talking to Hattie, who looked quite resplendent in emerald-green chiffon. Sinclair and Calliope were listening to Adalia and another guest. Everyone seemed to be having a splendid time. Kitty guessed that Daisy had remained inside with Aubrey to rest in the cool.

The village sweep had arrived with his cart in his sooty regalia and was duly wishing good luck to the bride and groom.

'Good afternoon, Miss Underhay, Captain Bryant.' Kitty turned to see Inspector Lewis looking quite dapper in a smart grey suit. 'Lord Woodcomb informed me you are a private investigator.' Lewis nodded to Matt. 'Well, you'll be pleased to know there won't be any need of your services this time, sir, we have our man.'

'Really? You've made an arrest?' Kitty asked. 'That is good news. Was it the man at the Plume of Feathers?'

'He's under lock and key. The gun was found in his room, concealed in a chest of drawers.' Lewis rocked up onto his toes and back down onto his heels, clearly delighted at having captured his man.

'And has he admitted the murder? Was it Sandy he was attempting to kill?' Matt asked.

'He's refusing to talk at present, apart from saying he's never set eyes on the gun before, but I daresay he'll crack in the end. They always do. Cocky fellows murderers, always like to let you know how clever they've been. That's what it does for them all in the end, you know.' Inspector Lewis helped himself to a flute of champagne.

'Well, jolly well done, Inspector. Sandy will be pleased, and you can have your constable back now too, I suppose,' Matt said.

'I've asked Mr Galsworthy to pop into the police station tomorrow before he leaves. See if he recognises the fellow. I would have asked him to go today but seeing as he's the best man and all.' Inspector Lewis frowned. Clearly he would have liked nothing better than to haul Sandy away from his duties.

'Very thoughtful, Inspector. I'm sure Lord and Lady Woodcomb will be most grateful,' Kitty said.

The sonorous sound of the dinner gong sounded from inside the castle and everyone began to file back inside ready for the wedding breakfast and the speeches. Kitty and Matt excused themselves from the inspector and followed the crowd.

'Well, that was a turn up for the books,' Kitty murmured to Matt. He wondered if she was convinced by the inspector's claim.

'Quite, but a welcome one. The less welcome news is that my aunt is in attendance and wishes to speak to you after lunch.' Matt gave a wry smile and the dimple in his cheek quirked at Kitty's low groan.

The wedding banquet was a superb affair. At least thirty guests had been accommodated with the extensions put on the table, which groaned under the weight of the brilliant white linen, sparkling silverware and fresh white flowers and greenery.

Sandy proved to be an excellent speaker and made a funny, touching and lovely speech that did a great deal to redeem him in Kitty's eyes. Lord Medford was clearly much moved at parting with his only child. Something Ralston Barnes appeared to empathise with.

Rupert himself gave a nice toast and Kitty and Daisy were both presented with small jewel cases containing a lovely fine gold bracelet each as a gift from the bride and groom. Kitty was also presented with a small gift wrapped in tissue paper from Lucy, especially for Alice.

Once the rich iced fruit cake had been cut and slices dispensed with – the top tier being preserved for any future christening – the formalities were over and everyone was once more free to mingle, chat and dance as the gramophone was started and music began to play in the great hall.

Kitty watched with tears in her eyes as her uncle led Lucy onto the dance floor and completed a circuit with her, before handing her over with great ceremony to her new husband to complete the dance.

'Are you all right, old thing?' Matt asked.

'Weddings always make me emotional,' Kitty reassured him as her uncle and aunt then joined the couple on the dance floor along with Daisy and Aubrey as Hattie cued up the next song.

She was about to suggest to Matt that they too should take a turn when she spied the small, elderly woman she had noticed earlier heading at speed towards them.

'Aunt Euphemia, may I present Miss Kitty Underhay,' Matt made the introductions.

A pair of sharp grey eyes scoured her from head to foot. 'Good afternoon, Miss Underhay. Perhaps, Matthew, we should all move to those seats over there where it is a little quieter so we may converse without having to shout.' The elderly woman glared at Hattie who appeared to have taken charge of the entertainment.

Kitty and Matt dutifully accompanied his aunt to the seats in a quieter corner of the hall.

'Hmm, so you're Elowed Underhay's girl. I've heard about your father.' Matt's aunt Euphemia settled herself on one of the club chairs, which had clearly been pressed into service for the wedding from the library.

'That's correct.' Kitty had selected one of the smaller bentwood seats.

'And you run the hotel in Dartmouth with your grandmother? Matthew's father has told me about you.' Aunt Euphemia held up an autocratic hand to stop one of the footmen as he passed. 'A pot of tea for three, young man.'

Matt gave Kitty an apologetic look.

'Yes, I manage the Dolphin with my grandmother. My father is in New York.' She was determined to simply answer the older woman's questions as briefly and politely as possible.

'A modern young woman. Matthew's father said as much.'

Kitty could imagine what Matt's father had said. He was very traditional in his views of women and what they should and should not do. He was fond of referring to Kitty as a popsy, even when she could hear him.

The footman returned with a tray of tea and set it down on the table before them.

'Would you continue in your employment if you were married?' Aunt Euphemia continued her questions as the footman served their tea under Matt's aunt's gimlet gaze.

'I expect so. My grandmother is not getting any younger and the hotel has been in the family for a very long time,' Kitty replied calmly as the footman made good his escape.

Aunt Euphemia stirred several spoons of sugar into her tea. The diamonds in her numerous rings sparkling in the light spilling into the hall through the open front door. 'And what are your views on the matter, Matthew? Your first wife had no such inclination, I believe, to continue in her employment after marriage.'

'You know that it would have been impossible, Aunt Euphemia, even if Edith had wished to do so. There was a war on and, besides, she had Betty to think of.' Matt's tone was light, but Kitty noticed his grip had tightened around the bone china handle of his cup.

'Perhaps, Matthew dear, you might wish to make yourself scarce for a few minutes. Go and fetch us some cake while I talk to Miss Underhay privately.' Euphemia waved her hand dismissively in Matt's direction.

Kitty bit the inside of her lip to stop herself from laughing as Matt was sent away like a naughty schoolboy.

'Now, Miss Underhay, we can speak frankly. Matthew is a dear boy and whilst his marriage to his first wife was not what the family would have chosen for him, there is no doubt that he loved Edith dearly. When she and Betty were killed, he took it very

badly. Indeed, it has taken years for him to recover from their loss.'
Euphemia's sharp grey eyes were fixed on Kitty's face. 'He is not a
man to give his affections or his loyalty lightly.'

Kitty swallowed. 'May I also speak frankly?' she asked.

Euphemia nodded.

'Very well. I am a modern woman, meaning that I earn my own
money and I have employment. The role of women should not be
simply to have babies or to iron shirts. I am not, however, modern
when it comes to my relationships. I am not flirtatious, nor do I
trifle with the affections of anyone that I hold dear.' Kitty met the
older woman's gaze and held it.

Euphemia studied her for a moment and then, to Kitty's surprise,
she nodded her head decisively and rose with a struggle from her
seat. 'Very well, my dear, you'll do.' She went to move away but as
she did so she placed a hand on Kitty's shoulder and murmured,
'Just remember, Miss Underhay, the hand that rocks the cradle is
the hand that rules the world.'

Kitty stared at Euphemia's retreating back and saw her stop to
speak to Matt, who had been on his way back to their table bearing
a small plate of cakes. She saw his aunt was speaking and watched
as she slipped something small into his jacket pocket.

Matt took his seat beside Kitty and placed the cakes on the
table. 'That went well, then?'

CHAPTER THIRTEEN

The wedding guests took their leave after tea, including Matt's aunt Euphemia. Rupert had given the staff the evening off to celebrate the wedding, having arranged for a cold collation to be served in the dining room at eight.

By mutual agreement everyone retired for a few hours to rest and change, before returning to the drawing room later to continue the festivities. As she wrote a note to her grandmother full of the wedding details, Kitty felt quite exhausted. The meeting with Aunt Euphemia had resembled a job interview and since Matt hadn't advertised a vacancy for a new Mrs Bryant, she couldn't help feeling it was all a little premature.

Alice had also returned to their room to change from her uniform into her best light-pink print dress.

'There's to be music, miss, and a nice spread. Lord Medford has sent champagne downstairs for us too and we're to all have a bit of cake.' Alice was beside herself with glee at the idea of a proper party.

'Lucy has given me a gift for you. She wanted to thank you for all your help this morning and with assisting the house staff to prepare for the wedding.' Kitty presented Alice with the small package wrapped in layers of tissue paper.

'Oh, that's very kind of Miss Lucy. She looked so lovely in her gown, like an angel in that veil. She didn't need to give me anything. It was an honour to be asked to help her dress.' Alice's face flushed with pleasure as she carefully unwrapped the layers.

Kitty watched as her maid opened the small box contained within the papers. 'That is lovely, Alice. What a nice thing.'

It was a small, beautifully engraved silver-plated photograph frame in the modern style. 'It's smashing.' Alice was clearly delighted by Lucy's thoughtfulness. 'It's been a lovely day.'

'Yes it has. I survived meeting Matt's aunt Euphemia, and, best of all, Inspector Lewis has made an arrest for Mr Evans' murder. Some man staying at the Plume of Feathers in the village. Apparently, they found the gun hidden in his room.'

'That is good news, miss. I reckon as the staff will be glad to see the back of that constable and all. He's been eating them out of biscuits in the kitchen.' Alice put away her present and came to assist Kitty with the tiny satin covered buttons on the side of her bridesmaid's gown.

Kitty stepped out of her dress as the satin puddled around her feet. 'Now we can put our glad rags on and have some fun.' She beamed at her friend.

'About time too, miss. It'll be nice to be doing something without any shenanigans overshadowing it all.' Alice slipped Kitty's new pale-green gown from its hanger.

Once dressed for the evening the two girls left the room together. Alice to take the back stairs down to the servants' hall where the party was to occur for the staff, and Kitty to head for the drawing room.

Hattie and Ralston were the first to arrive downstairs, where Ralston was engaged in demonstrating the art of cocktail making to an admiring Hattie.

'Miss Underhay, may I offer you a cocktail?' He brandished the silver shaker.

'They really are delicious,' Hattie encouraged. Her eyes were suspiciously bright and shiny, and Kitty wondered how many she had consumed all ready.

'That sounds delightful,' Kitty agreed. With her bridesmaid's duties dispensed with she intended to relax and enjoy herself.

Adalia and Aubrey were next to arrive. Adalia dressed in a black evening gown that did little for her wan features.

'No Daisy?' Kitty asked.

'She's still rather tired so may join us later,' Aubrey said.

'I practically had to force myself to come. These occasions are always exhausting, and my health is not good,' Adalia announced to no one in particular, before taking a seat on the most favourable chair and looking to Aubrey to supply her with a drink.

Kitty noticed Ralston hiding a smile at this statement and Hattie's carefully pencilled brows rose into her hairline. Her own heart gave a small flutter at Matt's arrival, tall and dapper in his evening wear, he always had a rakish edge to his appearance.

'Music, my dears, we must have music.' Hattie applied herself to the wireless finding a dance band programme. 'It's too bad that there is no piano in this room. I could have sung for you all.'

'I'm sure that would have been delightful, my dear. Here, permit me to refresh your glass,' Ralston offered. Hattie responded with a girlish giggle.

Sinclair and Calliope were next to arrive. Calliope looked more exotic than ever in a dark-red figure-hugging sheath gown with a low back. Her sleek black Louise Brooks style bob accentuating the dark kohl lines around her eyes. Sinclair seemed oddly colourless beside her.

Sandy and Moira were accompanied by Lord and Lady Medford. Kitty noticed Moira's sharp eyes looking at Calliope with a faint hint of revulsion at the other woman's appearance. Moira herself was almost matronly in her plain modest style of dress.

Kitty could see her aunt still looked fatigued and immediately went to greet her to offer her a seat while she fetched a drink for her.

'Thank you, Kitty dear. Lucy and Rupert will be along shortly, I think. They were going downstairs to the servants' hall first to thank the staff and to raise a toast. I must confess, I'm looking forward to having a nice evening of celebrations with just a small group of us. All the travelling and stress of the preparations does affect one at our age.'

Lord Medford opened some more champagne and by the time everyone was in the room and nibbling on the tasty buffet set out for the evening, the party was soon in full swing. Daisy made her entrance a little later, still looking tired but pretty in a silver lace gown.

Kitty gave herself up to pleasure, dancing with Matt, then Rupert and Aubrey. Even with Ralston who was surprisingly light on his feet. The evening went on and Kitty and Matt were talking with Rupert, Lucy and Hattie when there was an unexpectedly loud noise from the front of the castle. Almost as if the ceiling had collapsed or some other calamity had occurred.

'What on earth?' Rupert hurried out of the room across the hall accompanied by Matt, Aubrey and Lord Medford.

The front door was slightly ajar, just as it had been the previous evening. Kitty was swifter than the others so was hot on Matt's heels as they all spilled outside into the inky blackness of the courtyard.

'What is it?' Lucy caught hold of Kitty's arm.

'Go back inside. Don't let the others come out,' Kitty said urgently. She could see a prone shadowy figure in the darkness. The glowing ember of a cigarette or cigar nearby and a large piece of masonry pinning whoever it was down on the gravel.

'Telephone the police and get the doctor urgently. There's been an accident.' Lord Medford came back towards where she stood blocking the doorway to prevent the others from seeing what had happened.

'I'll go.' Lucy promptly hurried away.

There was a hum of chatter behind Kitty as the rest of the party tried to see what had occurred.

'M'dear, what is going on? Has there been an accident?' Lady Medford's autocratic tones cut through the babble.

'I'm afraid so, m'dear, best all go back to the drawing room. Nothing to be done out here. Where is Mrs Galsworthy?' Lord Medford replied.

Someone shoved Kitty hard in her back, pushing her out of the way and forcing her way through. 'It's Sandy, isn't it? I know it's Sandy.' The woman rushed outside, and Kitty saw her pale figure sway as she caught sight of the body.

Someone must have alerted the staff because Rupert's butler, accompanied by the chauffeur, appeared carrying lanterns and blankets. An unearthly wail rang around the thick stone walls of the courtyard and Kitty realised it must be Moira.

'My poor girl.' Ralston's anguished gaze met that of Kitty's uncle as Aubrey and Rupert bore Moira's limp body towards her waiting father.

Kitty moved aside to allow them through, then, spying her chance she slipped outside to join Matt. By the light of the lantern, she could see what had happened.

'He must have come outside for some air and to smoke. It was a habit he had,' Kitty murmured to Matt.

'Then his killer must have been lying in wait up on the roof. I doubt this wretched piece of stone fell by itself just as Sandy was in the right spot. The builders did not strike me as careless men,' Matt replied in a low voice in her ear.

It looked as if a large piece of dressed stone had tumbled from above the main door battlements and had landed squarely on Sandy's head.

'It would have killed him outright.' Kitty swallowed hard and looked away from the slowly spreading small pool of blood oozing from under the stone.

Matt placed his arm around her shoulders. 'I think so, old girl. Come, let's go inside, there is nothing more to be done out here.'

Kitty was slightly surprised to discover she was shaking as Matt gently guided her back through the shadowy hallway. They had just reached the door to the drawing room when there was a fizzing sound and the lights failed, plunging everything into darkness. Shrieks of surprise came from inside the drawing room.

Matt reached inside his jacket pocket and struck a match to briefly illuminate the way.

'The lights will be back shortly. Rupert has been having difficulty with the fuses.' As Kitty spoke, the lights flickered and came back on.

Matt extinguished the match and Kitty released the breath she hadn't realised she had been holding. He opened the drawing room door to reveal a tableau of the occupants.

Moira lay sobbing on a couch as her father and Hattie pressed brandy upon her. Sinclair was beside the French doors smoking. Calliope was seated beside him clasping a large goblet. For once, even her cool composure appeared to be ruffled.

Lady Medford was seated with Daisy and Aubrey, whilst Adalia kept up a thin stream of complaint about her nerves from her position on the other couch. Kitty assumed that Lucy must still be telephoning or had been the one to alert the servants.

Matt pressed a glass into her hand. 'Have a sip of this, darling.'

'I wish we could go up onto the roof to take a look.' Kitty's teeth chattered slightly on the rim of the glass. The lovely champagne induced buzz from earlier in the evening was rapidly dissipating.

'I agree, but I don't think Inspector Lewis will be keen on that idea.' Matt gave a wry smile.

Someone had turned off the dance music and the room was fairly quiet with only the subdued hum of chatter and Moira's anguished sobs combining with the steady tick of the mantelpiece clock and Adalia's complaints.

Lucy returned to the drawing room, her lovely face pale beneath the glittering tiara she had continued to wear for the party.

'Inspector Lewis has arrived. I've asked for coffee to be sent up and the doctor is on his way. I thought that Moira might wish to see him.' Lucy looked at her mother and Kitty saw Lady Medford give her daughter a brief nod of approval.

'Oh yes, a doctor, perhaps a powder or something. I shan't sleep a wink tonight with a murderer on the loose.' Adalia pressed the back of her hand to her forehead.

'Mother, do be quiet.' Aubrey's tone was not unduly loud, but it was firm. Two spots of colour immediately appeared on Adalia's cheeks and she looked affronted at his rebuke.

'Lucy dear, this is dreadful. Is Rupert with the police now?' Kitty asked as she went to her cousin, guiding her to a seat close to Lady Medford.

Lucy nodded. 'Yes, I think they will be along shortly. He's taken the inspector up to the roof. Father is with the doctor.'

Kitty's gaze met Matt's and she wondered what the inspector would find up there. Whoever had killed Sandy had moved swiftly, leaving the party to go up to the roof and then somehow prising that great piece of stone free to tumble down onto its unsuspecting victim.

A pale-faced young maid with a frightened expression appeared with a trolley. The doctor and Lord Medford followed her into the room and Lucy prevailed on the girl to assist Moira up to her bedroom, where the doctor could attend her in private. Ralston accompanied them, the grey colour back in his complexion.

Lord Medford placed a comforting hand on his daughter's shoulder. 'Inspector Lewis should be joining us shortly, m'dear.

Hopefully he may be able to shed more light on what has happened this evening.'

Sinclair had begun to pace up and down in front of the window. He lit another cigarette and offered one to Calliope who inserted it in her elegant ebony holder.

'If you ask me, the fellow is incompetent. He told us this afternoon that he had the man who shot Evans. So how could this happen now?'

No one answered.

Kitty could see his point. She was trying to remember who was where when they heard the rock fall from the roof. She and Matt had been talking to Hattie beside the gramophone. Lucy and Rupert had been with them and Lord and Lady Medford had been seated beside the fireplace with Aubrey and Daisy.

Sandy had obviously gone outside for air and a cigarette. Kitty frowned, she had thought that Moira might have gone after him, but that clearly was not the case. Ralston had gone to collect more food from the dining room and Adalia had slipped away somewhere. Sinclair and Calliope had also been absent.

A shiver ran down her spine. No doubt Inspector Lewis would require statements from everyone saying where they had been at the time of the murder. Kitty was certain it was murder. She couldn't see how that rock could have fallen by itself just at the moment Sandy had stepped outside.

The servants had all been in the servants' hall enjoying their own party. It was unlikely that one of them would have been involved. Unless, of course, Calliope was right, and someone had been paid to harm Sandy.

Kitty assisted Hattie to serve coffee to those that wanted a cup. They had just finished when the drawing room door opened once more, and Inspector Lewis entered. Rupert followed behind him, his handsome face grave.

It was clear that the inspector was not in the best of tempers. 'I must ask all of you to remain here for now. Lord Woodcomb has once again granted me the use of his study and I will need to interview you all in turn about where you were when Mr Galsworthy was killed.' He glared around the room as if inviting them to argue with him.

'By all means, Inspector, we are hardly likely to vanish into the night, however I would remind you, sir, that it is my daughter's wedding day still.' Lord Medford stared at the policeman.

'I shall endeavour to complete the statements as quickly as possible.' From his expression, the inspector clearly resented the reminder. His usual pomposity deflating under Lord Medford's stern gaze.

A uniformed constable appeared behind Rupert as Muffy barrelled her way into the room, tail wagging. She had obviously escaped from the servants' hall where she had been spending the evening. Her white satin bow from the wedding was still attached to her collar, although it now looked rather crumpled.

Lucy hugged her little dog to her, uncaring of any possible damage to her beautiful silver filigree lace gown. 'Mother, why don't you and Father go first with the inspector. Most of us were in here so I'm certain this will not take long, and you have had a very tiring day.'

Lady Medford did appear fatigued, Kitty thought.

'As you wish, my dear.' Lord Medford helped his wife up from her seat, and they followed Rupert and the inspector from the room.

The door had scarcely closed behind them when Adalia erupted into speech. 'Well, really, this is most high-handed. Treating us all as if we are suspects or common criminals.' She glared at the constable who had remained inside the room barring the exit.

'The man has to do his job, Mother. I'm sure we shall be able to return home very shortly.' Aubrey patted Daisy's hand, a look of tender concern on his face as he answered his mother.

'We have nothing to hide.' Calliope lit yet another cigarette. 'Sinclair and I were together in the library when we heard the commotion.' She looked at her husband.

'The library?' Matt asked mildly.

'I had misplaced my stole earlier when I went there to find Sinclair. He helped me to look for it.' Calliope's eyes narrowed as if daring Matt to challenge her alibi.

'Well, I'm sure I have nothing at all to hide. I had gone to powder my nose.' Adalia gave a sniff.

Hattie clasped her hands together, a look of excitement in her bright eyes. 'Who else was missing?'

Lucy frowned. 'I'm not certain. Ralston and Moira, I think.'

'Well, there you are then,' Calliope scoffed. 'There are two people in this castle with more motive than anyone to wish Sandy dead.'

'They were both with him when Evans was killed,' Hattie pointed out.

Kitty wasn't so sure that they could clear Ralston and Moira of any involvement. Calliope did have a point, but Moira seemed to genuinely adore Sandy. And then, how had the gun that had killed Evans found its way to the Plume of Feathers? Was the man the inspector had arrested involved in some way after all? And why had someone desperately wanted Sandy dead?

CHAPTER FOURTEEN

Rupert popped his head around the door. 'Lucy darling, we're next.'

Lucy jumped up and slipped out of the room with Muffy trotting at her heels.

'This is quite ridiculous.' Adalia gave the constable a look of distaste.

'Aubrey, perhaps you and Daisy should go after Rupert and Lucy?' Hattie suggested. 'Poor Daisy looks quite exhausted, and you were both in here with us when it happened.'

Kitty thought Adalia was about to explode at Hattie's kindly suggestion. 'Nonsense, the younger people should see the inspector last. My own health, you know, is very fragile. I declare I shall have to rest for days after this ordeal in order to recover.'

Kitty ignored the older woman. 'Yes, Daisy dear, you and Aubrey go next. Matt and I don't mind waiting.' It might give them the opportunity to find out more information from Calliope and Sinclair. The story about the stole seemed very thin to Kitty.

Adalia was puce with rage but a look from Hattie seemed to force her into grudging submission.

Rupert returned quite quickly. 'The inspector is ready for the next person.' He looked anxiously at his sister, obviously noting her wan features.

'Daisy and Aubrey are coming,' Hattie said decisively, giving Adalia a pointed look.

Aubrey helped Daisy to her feet and steered her from the room.

Sinclair went over to the bar trolley and helped himself to another glass of brandy. 'Might as well have another; it looks as if this will be a long night. Anyone else?' He waved the decanter towards Matt and Kitty.

Kitty shook her head, as did Matt. She wanted a clear head so she could think. Adalia, however, accepted the offer and Sinclair poured her a generous measure.

'You must be exhausted, Hattie dear. You've done so much the last few days helping Lucy prepare for the wedding.' Kitty gave the older woman's plump hand a gentle squeeze.

'Oh, I'm all right. I've quite enjoyed being useful, truth be told. Lucy is such a dear girl and your aunt and uncle have always been very kind and generous to me.' Hattie patted Kitty's own hand in return and smiled at her. 'It's terrible that this has happened to spoil such a lovely day.' Her mouth drooped.

Calliope yawned and stretched. 'I do hope this won't delay our return to London. We have important commitments there in the next few days.'

'I expect you may have to remain for a short while, until the inspector gives you leave to go,' Matt remarked mildly.

'Will that inconvenience you, Mrs Watts? How long were you intending to stay with Daisy and Aubrey?' Hattie asked, turning round, innocent eyes towards Adalia.

Kitty pressed her lips together to hide a smile. She knew that Hattie was all too well aware that Daisy felt Adalia had outstayed her welcome.

'My plans are quite fluid. Clearly Aubrey may need me to remain here after such a dreadful event,' Adalia retorted stiffly and took a large swig of brandy from her glass.

'Let us hope that Inspector Lewis gets to the bottom of this matter quite swiftly then,' Matt said.

Hattie frowned. 'I wonder who the man was that Inspector Lewis arrested at the Plume of Feathers and how he came to have the gun. It's most peculiar, don't you think?'

'Very strange.' Matt leaned forward in his chair. 'Of course, it could have been placed in his room by the real murderer. Or he could have been working with someone else.'

Kitty noticed Adalia stiffen at this and Calliope and Sinclair exchanged glances.

'You had lunch at the Plume of Feathers the other day, didn't you? Did it seem like the kind of place that people could come and go easily?' Kitty asked, looking at Sinclair. She was keen that they shouldn't think she was hinting that they may have been responsible.

Sinclair lit up another cigarette and blew out a thin stream of smoke as he considered Kitty's question. 'It's in the centre of the village, on the green, so there is a lot of passing trade. Adalia, you were in the village too that day, with Ralston. I think you were coming out of the chemist's shop when we saw you.' He looked at Adalia.

'I may have been. Ralston kindly gave me a lift in his car. Everyone else was busy. Rupert's chauffeur has been running a few small errands for me but, of course, I couldn't possibly continue to impose with the wedding so close. All the staff were needed here. I'm sure that I would never go near a hostelry.' If looks could kill, then Kitty was certain Sinclair would have been the next victim if the murderer was Adalia.

The door to the drawing room opened again. 'Hattie, the inspector would like to see you next.' Aubrey turned his head and looked at Adalia as Hattie scurried from the room. 'I'm sorry, Mother, you'll have to wait. I'm taking Daisy home and I'll return to escort you over to the gatehouse when the inspector allows you to leave.' He ducked out before his mother could argue.

At first Kitty thought Adalia was about to try and follow her son but the constable placed his not inconsiderable bulk back in front of the door.

'I suggest you wait for Inspector Lewis to send for you, madam.'

'Well, when I do see him, he will receive a piece of my mind.' Adalia flounced back over to the couch and retook her seat. She drummed her fingers restlessly on the arms of the sofa and glowered at everyone in turn as if they were personally responsible for the wait.

Kitty was relieved when the door opened once more and this time it was the inspector himself. 'Mrs Watts, if you would be so good.' He indicated the corridor beyond and Adalia stalked over.

'About time too,' they heard her say before the door was closed once more.

'Just us four left. Do you suppose he will talk to Ralston tonight too? I expect the doctor will have given Moira some kind of sedative,' Calliope mused.

'Ralston has a weak heart. The inspector may decide to leave them both until morning,' Kitty replied. She thought Ralston had looked quite ill when he had accompanied Moira from the drawing room.

She shivered and rubbed the tops of her arms. The air in the room had grown cool while they had been waiting and the fire was almost out. She wrapped her shawl around her shoulders.

Matt rose and strolled about the room, stretching his legs. The clock on the mantelpiece chimed the hour.

'One o'clock,' Sinclair remarked.

'I hope this won't take much longer. What an end to such a lovely day.' Kitty suppressed a yawn. She really was more than ready for her bed and pretty tired of being penned in with Sinclair and Calliope.

The inspector returned and Kitty thought he looked quite tired after dealing with Adalia.

'Mr and Mrs Davies, if you would come through.' He stood aside allowing them to pass him. 'My apologies for the late hour, Miss Underhay, Captain Bryant. I shall be as quick as I can.' He flashed a quick – and to Kitty's mind – insincere smile.

With Sinclair and Calliope gone, Kitty felt as if a huge weight had been lifted from her shoulders.

'Do feel free to take a seat, Constable. I assure you we won't make a run for it.' Kitty smiled at the police officer.

He looked a little doubtful at first but succumbed to a small upright wooden chair beside the door. 'Thank you, miss. I don't suppose as it will hurt for a few minutes. It's been a long one today.'

'I can imagine. I'd offer you some coffee, but I fear it must be stone cold by now. Have you been here all day?' Kitty asked.

'Yes, miss. I was protecting poor Mr Galsworthy up till after the wedding when the inspector stood me down.' The constable shook his head, clearly upset that his charge had been murdered just a few hours later.

'Although I know Mr Galsworthy wasn't always entirely grateful.' Kitty gave a slight shrug of her shoulders. 'I think he said as much to you, Matt, didn't he? I think he considered that the danger to his person was perhaps overstated.' She decided to see what she could learn from the constable about the case. She doubted that Inspector Lewis would be very forthcoming when they finally saw him. He had made his views clear already about them involving themselves in the investigation.

'That's right, miss. Accused me of spying on him, and I was only performing my duties. Still, the poor man was not mistaken about the risks to his life.' The constable rubbed a large hand across his face.

'Sandy usually went outside the front of the house each evening to smoke and take the air. Such a hideous thing to have happened to him,' Matt said.

'Who would have thought it?' The constable shook his head. 'That great piece of stone, levered off the battlements like that.'

Matt exchanged a glance with Kitty. 'It couldn't have been an accident, not if a lever was involved.'

The constable blinked. 'No indeed, sir, the inspector found a tyre lever out of one of the motor cars up on the roof.'

'Oh dear, how awful.' Kitty's mind was busy. If a lever had been used, then no great pressure would have been required to move the stone. It could be a man or a woman who had sent it tumbling down onto Sandy's unsuspecting head.

It also spoke of premeditation and planning. Someone had placed the lever up there awaiting the right moment.

'I expect the inspector has had the cars checked to see which motor is missing its lever?' Kitty mused aloud.

'Lord Woodcomb's chauffeur accompanied me to the carriage house. It was from his lordship's own vehicle. Lord Woodcomb was most upset about it.'

The drawing room door opened, and the constable shot to his feet as the inspector's sharp features appeared.

'Miss Underhay and Captain Bryant, perhaps you would like to accompany me.'

Kitty raised an eyebrow at Matt as they followed the inspector along the dark and deserted corridor and across the hall to Rupert's study. She was relieved to find that at least the study was warm with a small fire in the hearth. The late hour and the chill from the castle walls had started to make itself felt.

She settled herself on a chair next to Matt and waited for the inspector to take his place behind Rupert's desk. It was a pity the inspector had called them just as she was about to try to discover more about the mystery man at the Plume of Feathers. The constable had proved a very valuable source of information.

Inspector Lewis steepled his hands together and surveyed them both from behind the desk. 'My apologies for leaving you until last but as you are an investigator yourself, Captain Bryant, I'm sure you can appreciate the difficulties involved in dealing with people in certain levels of society.'

Kitty gritted her teeth, the apology, half-hearted as it was, hadn't been offered to her. The rudeness of the man really grated on her, but she was determined not to give him the satisfaction of seeing her annoyance. Instead, she intended to learn what she could about the case.

'I must admit, Inspector, that I have never especially considered anyone's social standing during the course of my work be they a prince or a pauper.' Matt's tone was cool and called a mottled flush to the inspector's cheeks.

Kitty had an absurd urge to giggle but hastily swallowed it down.

'Well then, perhaps you would both be so good as to give me your accounts of the events of the evening, commencing with where you both were shortly before the alarm was raised.' Inspector Lewis picked up his pen and held it over his notepad.

Matt gave a succinct account with Kitty agreeing to his evidence. Presently the inspector set down his pen.

'Thank you. I think that will be all for now. The hour is late, so you are no doubt longing for your beds. I have requested that no one leave Thurscomb until I say so.'

'Of course.' Kitty rose from her seat and gathered her shawl, draping it about her shoulders. 'By the way, Inspector, what happened to the man from the Plume of Feathers? Is he involved in this somehow?' She strove to keep her tone light and casual.

'Mr Whitlock remains under lock and key until we have satisfactory answers from him about how he came by the gun that killed Mr Evans.' The inspector had also risen.

'Well, he cannot have killed Sandy if he was in custody,' Kitty observed. 'Unless you believe him not to be working alone?'

Inspector Lewis gave her a look of deep distaste. 'That may be a possibility, Miss Underhay. However, I will repeat what I said to you before, leave the detective work to the professionals.'

Kitty gave him what she considered to be her most disarming smile. 'Of course, Inspector Lewis, forgive me, it's very late and I was merely thinking aloud.'

'I'll walk you upstairs to your room, Kitty.' Matt gave her hand a warning squeeze, out of the inspector's view.

'Thank you, I must admit I feel quite nervous now within the castle. Good night, Inspector.' She flashed another smile at the policeman, and they made their exit back out into the empty corridor.

'Well?' Kitty asked as soon as she was confident that they were alone and couldn't be overheard. 'What did you make of all that?'

Matt grinned at her. 'All interesting stuff.'

'I wouldn't mind a quick look up on that roof,' Kitty said as they mounted the stairs towards their respective rooms.

'I am not going up there tonight, in the dark,' Matt said firmly.

'In the morning? Early? Before everyone is up for breakfast?' she suggested.

Matt heaved a long-suffering sigh. 'Very well, I'll come and tap on your door. Make sure you're ready, we shall have to be quick.'

They had halted outside the door to Kitty's room. She stood on her tiptoes to place a kiss on his lips. 'See you in the morning.'

CHAPTER FIFTEEN

Alice was waiting up, wrapped in a warm woollen blanket beside the fire when Kitty entered the bedroom.

'Oh, Alice, I'm so very sorry. You must be exhausted.' Kitty was immediately riddled with guilt at her friend's tired expression.

'It's all right, miss. I've been catnapping while I waited. Here, let me give you a hand with your frock.' Alice jumped up and began to assist Kitty to change into her night attire. 'I've a flask of cocoa here as well, miss. It should still be hot. I thought it might help you sleep.'

Kitty was grateful for the maid's thoughtfulness. 'You know me so well. Yes, a nice cup of cocoa would definitely hit the spot.' She snuggled under her covers and Alice poured them both a mug of cocoa from the travel flask.

'I heard as you was to be the last to be seen by the police before I come upstairs. I was a bit worried as time went on, so I went to the kitchen to make the cocoa. The constable said as you'd just been called through to the study. He was there collecting his bicycle ready to go home. The footman had put the blessed thing in the scullery as it shouldn't be on view for the wedding.' Alice perched on the end of Kitty's bed cradling her cup in her hands. Her long red curly hair swinging in a thick braid over her shoulder.

'Matt is calling for me before breakfast. We want to try and take a look up on the roof.' Kitty savoured a sip of the hot sweet milky liquid.

Alice gave her a doubtful look over the thick white porcelain brim of her mug. 'Do you think as that's wise, miss? It could be dangerous up there. The chauffeur said as whoever killed Mr Galsworthy pushed that rock off the roof with Lord Rupert's tyre lever. Since that was the one they found on the roof. That means as it has to be somebody here in the castle.'

Kitty drained the last of her cocoa. 'I know. We'd thought of that. Don't worry, Alice, we'll be careful.' She covered her mouth as she yawned. 'We'd better both get some sleep. I think it will be a very busy day tomorrow.'

*

Matt tapped on Kitty's bedroom door a little before seven o'clock. Alice opened the door and, after a quick glance to ensure that no one had seen them, admitted him inside.

'I'm all set.' Kitty had dressed in her tweed skirt, a print blouse and sturdy shoes.

'Let's go then before anyone else is abroad.' Matt knew that breakfast was to be later than usual as Lucy had anticipated that people would prefer it after the excitement of the wedding. She obviously hadn't anticipated someone being killed at her evening reception, however.

'You'll need to go up the servants' stairs to get to the roof. Go up to the attics where the staff bedrooms are. There won't be anyone there now as everyone should be at work downstairs. Then at the far end you'll see a cream painted door that leads into the attics and there is a trapdoor what goes onto the roof. I saw it when one of the housemaids took me around the castle and the builders was going up. Mary, that's the maid, is sweet on one of the stonemasons,' Alice explained.

'Thank you, Alice. You're a gem.' Matt grinned at the maid, sending her cheeks crimson at his praise.

They set off quickly along the empty corridors towards the green baize covered door leading to the staff stairway. All around them

Matt could hear the sounds of the castle rising to start the new day. Someone singing tunelessly in the bathroom, the clatter of metal on stone as the staff put the downstairs rooms to rights after yesterday's wedding and the faint hum of distant conversations.

He led the way through the door and onto the narrow stone stairwell used by the staff to service the floors and to reach their own quarters. They paused for a moment to listen and ensure that no one else was likely to be on the upper floor near the attic door.

Hearing nothing, they hurried upwards. As they reached the top of the stairs, Matt froze and placed a cautionary hand on Kitty's arm. He hadn't been sure if he'd heard a door close on the staff landing.

Kitty waited in place while he ventured up and had a quick look. The coast seemed to be clear, so he beckoned her to follow him. The door to the attic was exactly as Alice had described it.

'It's locked.' Kitty tried the handle.

Matt felt in his coat pocket for the small leather case of tools he carried with him for just such occasions. Within a few seconds of jiggling the narrow metal tool in the lock the door opened.

'You must teach me to do that. I have been practising with a hairpin but I'm not at your level of breaking and entering quite yet,' Kitty murmured, with a wide smile on her face.

'Come on, close the door behind you.' He had no intention of allowing her to go first for all her modern principles. They had no way of knowing what might lie ahead, or even if someone else might be up there already. Memories of their escapades on the roof of Elm House just a few weeks earlier were still fresh in his mind.

The attic was dark and full of the debris from centuries of one family living in the same house. Boxes, old paintings and discarded and broken furniture. The skylight to the roof, however, was framed by daylight all around the edges of the trapdoor and was easy to see.

Matt pushed the heavy wooden door open and stepped onto the rather rickety wooden steps that had clearly been used by both the builders and the police to access the roof. He climbed out onto a broad stone ledge, sealed at various points with lead flashing. A quick look told him it was deserted, and he reached down to offer Kitty a hand up.

She arrived looking disgruntled and brushing her blonde curls with her free hand. 'Yuck, I think I walked into a cobweb.'

Matt picked his way around a couple of pieces of dressed stone which were clearly waiting to be fixed in place to repair the crumbling parts of the battlement. He could see where the mortar had been freshly done and pointed on the repaired section.

'It's a long way down,' he remarked as he peered over the edge.

The rope and wooden planking that the builders had used to raise the stone up to the roof was dismantled and lying to one side, neatly stacked. Fine white dust from where the masons had chipped and shaped the stone littered the floor, but it was impossible to pick up any clear footprints.

'They must have levered it from here.' Kitty joined him and pointed out some fresh scrapes in the stone where one of the crenellations was missing. It left a gap like a missing tooth in the neat row.

The stone was directly above the spot that Sandy had favoured for smoking. A shudder ran along Matt's spine. Whoever had killed Sandy was cold-blooded and methodical. Viewing the roof confirmed for him that this was not an opportunistic murder.

'We had better go before we're seen. Inspector Lewis will not look kindly upon us if he discovers we have been nosing about,' Matt said as a familiar black car pulled into the courtyard, forcing both he and Kitty to duck down out of sight.

'In the nick of time. It seems the police are back,' Kitty said as she lowered herself back into the attic.

They hurried out and relocked the attic door behind them.

'Someone is coming,' Kitty hissed and grabbed at the sleeve of Matt's jacket, hauling him out of sight inside a nearby closet. They peered through a crack between the door and the frame.

He was somewhat surprised to see Moira peeping nervously around before putting her hand to the door to the attic. She appeared dishevelled and was still dressed in her night attire, as if she had woken and gone straight there. He felt Kitty's small frame tense next to him as Moira tried the catch and found it locked.

Her object thwarted, Moira hurried away back down the stairs the way she had come up.

'Moira?' Kitty breathed. 'Well, that was a surprise. Come on, let's get downstairs before we are found up here.' She slipped back out into the corridor and scurried to the stairs to check the coast was clear before signalling to him to follow her.

They made it down to the upper floor and through the baize door back onto the main landing without encountering any more of their fellow guests.

'Breakfast, I think. I'm starving.' Kitty grinned at him and together they headed for the dining room, lured by the faint scent of coffee and bacon.

Hattie and Calliope were already seated at the table. Calliope nibbling on a small slice of toast and Hattie tucking into a huge bowl of porridge.

'Kitty, have you seen? Calliope says the police are back here again,' Hattie said brightly after she had wished them both a good morning.

'I expect Inspector Lewis wishes to speak to Moira and Ralston,' Matt observed as he helped himself to eggs, bacon and devilled kidneys.

'Oh yes, of course, that must be it.' Hattie beamed happily at Matt.

'Or to arrest them,' Calliope said, before taking a sip of her coffee.

Hattie's eyes rounded. 'Oh, my dear, surely not. Moira was devoted to Sandy and poor Mr Barnes, well, I know he was not overfond of his son-in-law, but I doubt he would be fit enough to do him harm in such a way.'

Calliope shrugged her thin shoulders. 'I don't know but Moira was obsessed by Sandy. It was not a healthy kind of love, and such an affection can easily be turned into hatred in my experience.'

Matt took his place opposite Kitty who was busy applying butter to her toast. 'You feel that something might have happened to turn Moira's love to hate?'

He thought about Kitty's discovery of Moira crying in the chapel. Then, there was Moira's trip to the attic only a few moments ago. What had she been up to?

Calliope set down her cup leaving a scarlet smudge of lipstick on the china brim. 'The woman would have to be a saint to continue ignoring all his affairs with other women. Not to mention his gambling debts. Perhaps she snapped.'

'You seem to have been set on either Moira or her father wishing to kill Sandy right from the start when poor Mr Evans was shot,' Kitty observed.

Matt waited to see what Calliope's response to her remark would be.

'You must remember, Miss Underhay, that I have known them all for quite some time. Indeed, I knew Sandy before he met Moira. It's quite clear that Ralston has never wanted Sandy as a son-in-law and a divorce would be very costly. In fact, the marriage was costly. Ralston paid for all of Moira and Sandy's expenses. His salary as an MP was hardly enough to maintain them.' Calliope's delicately pencilled brows raised. 'It would no doubt have softened the blow had Moira been able to present her father with a grandchild.' Calliope placed her used linen napkin on the table beside her plate. 'You must excuse me, my husband is busy in the library again and I intend to force him out for some fresh air before we return to London.'

'I thought the inspector wished everyone to remain at Thurscomb for now?' Kitty said as Calliope stood to take her leave.

'He did but since we can have nothing to add to his investigation, I'm sure he will see sense and permit us to depart soon.' Calliope stalked out of the dining room.

Hattie leaned across the table as soon as Calliope had gone. 'Captain Bryant, you and Kitty are going to investigate Sandy's death, aren't you?'

Matt exchanged a glance with Kitty. 'Well, Inspector Lewis has made it quite clear that he disapproves of what he calls amateur investigators.'

'Poo, you are a professional, that surely doesn't apply to you. And, Miss Underhay, well look at what happened at Enderley at Christmas.' Hattie frowned.

'But we are in Yorkshire now, Hattie dear, they may not be as well disposed towards us as the police in Devon.' Kitty smiled.

'Rot, that inspector looks to me as if he needs all the help he can get. After all, it's clear that man at the Plume of Feathers didn't murder Sandy, so who did? And why?' Hattie dabbed at the corners of her mouth with her napkin.

Any more conversation on the subject was halted as the staff started to top up the breakfast dishes and clear away the used crockery. Matt noticed Hattie secreting a small silver cruet into her bag and smiled to himself.

*

Once breakfast was over Kitty took Matt's arm as they strolled out into the hall. The furniture was all back in place and apart from the abundance of fresh flowers everywhere all traces of the previous days wedding reception had disappeared.

'Captain Bryant, Miss Underhay.' The inspector came towards them with his usual sour expression. He was accompanied by Rupert.

'Good morning, Inspector Lewis.' Kitty smiled politely and was surprised to see Rupert wink at her from behind the police officer's back.

'Um, I have had a message, Captain Bryant, from the chief constable indicating that due to the, um, sensitive nature of Mr Galsworthy's death, and that of Mr Evans, of course, that, um, I am to invite your thoughts on the case.' Inspector Lewis looked as if he would like nothing less than to involve Matt in the investigation.

Rupert cleared his throat. 'Capital idea, and Miss Underhay too, I believe, isn't that so, Inspector Lewis?'

Rupert's eyes twinkled as he spoke and Kitty guessed that Rupert, and probably her uncle too, may have had words with Inspector Lewis' superiors in order to affect this change of heart.

'That's most kind of you, Inspector. I'm sure we shall have little to add to your enquiry and we will, of course, stay out of your way.' Kitty smiled at the policeman again.

'Absolutely, Inspector. We wouldn't wish to impede you at all,' Matt agreed.

The inspector's sharp gaze darted from Matt's bland countenance to Kitty's smiling one as if suspecting them of laughing at him. 'Hmm, well, I have to talk to Mr Barnes and Mrs Galsworthy this morning to establish where they were when Mr Galsworthy was killed.'

'Excellent, Matt and I were thinking of going to the village. I have to send a letter to my grandmother. She will be keen to hear about the wedding, and we intended to call at the Plume of Feathers.' Kitty glanced up at Matt and saw the corners of his mouth had lifted in a small smile. 'If you've no objection, Inspector? I know you have already been most thorough in your enquiries in the village but sometimes people may be more forthcoming to visitors.'

Inspector Lewis looked as if he would very much like to object to Kitty's errand, but a brief glance at Rupert seemed to change his opinion. 'Very well, Miss Underhay. I doubt very much that there is anything useful to be gained, but by all means if you wish to go there.'

'Ask my chauffeur to take you, Kitty. It's a decent walk and there may be thunder later according to the forecast on the wireless this morning.' Rupert grinned at her.

'Thank you, that's very kind.'

The inspector moved away with Rupert and Kitty released the small chuckle of amusement she had been holding inside throughout the conversation. 'Well, it seems we are on the team after all.'

'I wasn't aware we planned to visit the Plume of Feathers?' The dimple in Matt's cheek flashed.

'Really? And I thought you were the great detective? I'll just run and collect my things while you chase up the driver.' She patted his arm.

Matt shook his head in mock despair and went on his errand.

CHAPTER SIXTEEN

The bright blue sky of yesterday was rapidly fading into memory as they were driven towards the village in Rupert's elderly motor car. Angry dark grey clouds had already begun to gather menacingly overhead, and the air was still and oppressive.

The chauffeur halted outside the hostelry. 'I'll wait for you here, sir, miss. It looks as if we're due for a fine storm and you'll be drenched else.'

'Thank you, this is very kind.' Kitty was assisted from the rear of the car by Matt and she looked around her with interest.

The village was much larger and busier than she had anticipated. The Plume of Feathers was a substantial stone building, which she surmised must once have been a coaching inn on the route to Ripon. A village green lay before it with a tree-lined pond. A small group of ducks were settled on the grass near the water. There was a chemist's shop, a drapers, a blacksmiths and a small general store, newsagent and tobacconist and post office.

'Where shall we begin?' Kitty asked.

'Hmm, Adalia claimed to have been in the village to visit the chemist. Shall we try there first and see what we can discover?' Matt suggested.

Kitty nodded her approval. The chemist had been her thought too, especially as Sandy had claimed he had been poisoned. It would be interesting to discover who had visited from the castle. Then perhaps a trip to the post office and finally the Plume of Feathers to try and learn more of Mr Whitlock.

They crossed the street and entered the small chemist's shop, setting the brass bell above the door jangling. There were no other customers inside and it took Kitty's eyes a moment to adjust to the dimness of the interior after entering from outside.

The store was traditionally laid out with racks of carefully labelled wooden drawers on view behind the glass-topped counter. On top of the cabinets were various equally exotically labelled large porcelain storage jars. One of the other walls was shelved and housed various cosmetics, perfumed soaps and talcum powders next to more mundane items like bandages and corn plasters. The air smelt faintly of camphor and peppermint.

A young dark-haired girl was behind the counter. 'May I help you?'

'I hope so. I need a toothbrush, please.' Kitty smiled at the girl while Matt tried to look unobtrusive in the background.

'Certainly, miss.' The girl produced a selection for Kitty from a box under the counter.

'This one looks perfect, thank you.' Kitty took one from the box. 'My friend recommended me to call in here. We're staying at the castle for my cousin's wedding,' Kitty said chattily as she opened her bag to look for her purse.

'Would you be on the bride's side or his lordship's side, miss?' the girl asked as she stowed the box of toothbrushes back in their proper place.

'The bride's.' Kitty smiled hoping to encourage more conversation.

'I heard as the wedding was to be proper grand. I saw the flower arrangements go by on the cart and they looked beautiful, all them roses and lilies. Miss Medford has been in here a few times with Miss Merriweather. Proper pretty she is.' The girl blushed and placed Kitty's purchase in a small, brown paper bag.

'Lucy is a dear and she did look very lovely.' Kitty held out her money for the girl. 'My friend, Mrs Watts, wondered if she might have left her gloves here when she came in the day before the wedding? A tall, slim, older lady? She came to have some powders made up I think?' Kitty pretended to be vague as she made up an excuse to discover if Adalia had told the truth about her errand.

The girl beamed. 'Oh yes, miss, she did leave a glove. Pale-grey kid it was. Lucky I saw it and went after her when I got a chance. She's forgot I caught her as she was coming out of the Plume of Feathers. If she's misplaced them again since it's not been in here.'

Kitty took her change elated at her stroke of luck on hitting on such a plausible excuse to be nosey. 'She is so easily distracted.'

The girl's smiled widened even further. 'It was probably with the wedding being the next day and all the upset with that poor man being shot in that accident. Still, I could have given the glove to the other lady from the castle. The one having lunch at the Feathers with a gentleman.'

Kitty's ears pricked up. 'Which lady was that?'

'A tall, exotic lady, looked foreign, like a model.' The girl seemed quite awestruck.

'That must have been Calliope. She is very pretty,' Kitty agreed. 'It sounds as if all the ladies from the castle have given you their custom.'

'Oh yes, miss, and there was a Mrs Galsworthy, she had to collect a script a couple of days ago and it wasn't a name I knew. Took me a spot to find it. Odd mix of things it was from some London physician, so the chemist said.'

'Yes, Moira did say that she had been in here too now that you come to mention it. Thank you so much for this. You've been most helpful.' Kitty popped her purchase into her bag and she and Matt left the shop.

'Well, what do you make of that?' Kitty asked Matt as soon as they were back on the pavement outside the shop.

'Very interesting. What was Adalia doing inside the Plume of Feathers?' Matt scratched his chin thoughtfully. 'Especially as she was very keen to say she wouldn't go anywhere near a hostelry.'

'She wasn't at all happy last night when Calliope and Sinclair said they had seen her there.' Kitty frowned. 'And what was in Moira's mystery prescription?'

Matt looked up at the darkening sky. 'The clouds are growing thicker, there is hardly any blue sky left now. I think we had better hurry or we shall be soaked.'

'I must post this note to Grams. I scribbled it right after the wedding, but my hand is so bad she will struggle to read it.' Kitty turned towards the small stone-built post office. 'I've always found the staff of the post office to be very knowledgeable.'

Matt chuckled. 'So I believe.'

This time an older grey-haired lady was behind the counter when they entered.

'I need a stamp, please.' Kitty produced the letter from her bag.

'Certainly, miss.' The woman opened the drawer to produce a stamp for Kitty to apply to the corner of the envelope.

'My grandmother will be expecting an account of the wedding.' Kitty smiled at the woman hoping she would be willing to make conversation.

'You must be from the castle? Here for Lord Rupert's wedding?' the woman said as Kitty passed the letter over for the postmistress to add it to the bag behind the counter.

'Yes, my cousin, Lucy, was the bride.' Kitty pulled out her purse once more and eyed the tempting array of boiled sweets in various large glass jars on the shelf. 'Oh, you have barley sugars. May I have a quarter ounce, please?'

The woman lifted down the large glass jar of sweets and poured some into the weighing scales at the end of the counter. 'I bet as Miss Medford was a picture. Such a nice lady. We've had a few folks in the village from the castle.'

'Yes, the girl in the chemist said several of the party had been here.' Kitty nodded to accept the weight.

The woman tipped the sweets into a small, white paper cone and gave it a twist to seal it. 'The American gentleman came to post a whole bundle of letters and one of the other gentlemen came in to use the telephone.' She gave a nod towards a small alcove tucked away discreetly in the corner.

Kitty gathered from her tone that this was obviously a matter of great pride. 'How fortunate that you have all the latest appliances here.'

'Indeed, miss. Some would think we were a backwater being outside of the towns but no, Lord Woodcomb is very good at making certain as the village has all the opportunities and amenities of a bigger establishment.' The woman accepted Kitty's money and rang up the till to give her change.

'That's wonderful. I expect it would be Mr Davies who used the telephone. A tall, thin man with a very glamorous wife?' Kitty hinted.

'The very one, miss. Put through lots of calls to London.'

Kitty wondered why Sinclair had come to the village to telephone when he could have called for free from the perfectly good telephone at the castle. 'He is a very busy man I believe.' She popped her sweets in her bag.

'We must get going, Kitty. This rain is not likely to hold off much longer.' Matt peered out of the shop window frowning at the sky.

Kitty thanked the woman and they hurried out.

'Hmm, more information. I wonder what Sinclair was up to?' She pulled out her sweets, took one and offered the bag to Matt. 'Barley sugar?'

He shook his head, and she tucked the sweets back inside her bag. 'What do we want to know from the Plume of Feathers?' Matt asked as they walked back across the road.

Kitty adjusted the sweet in her mouth. 'I'd like to know if anyone saw Adalia the day before the wedding, and also which room that man, Mr Whitlock, was staying in.'

Matt glanced at her. 'Hmm.'

They let the driver know they would be back at the car in a few minutes and went inside the Plume of Feathers.

Kitty was pleased to find the hostelry was a bright and airy place, scrupulously clean and respectable. A man wearing thick-lensed glasses sat at a wooden table in the corner staring morosely into a glass of beer. Otherwise the room was empty with no one present behind the bar. A narrow cream-painted wooden staircase was visible at the far end of the room and Kitty guessed it must lead up to the bedrooms. A board with numbered keys hanging from brass hooks was to the side at the back of the taps.

Matt rang the small brass bell at the end of the counter. Within a minute a burly middle-aged man with a shock of thick fair hair appeared, drying his hands on his apron.

'Begging your pardon, sir, miss. I hope as you've not been waiting long. I were in't cellar.'

'No, not at all, my good man. I wonder if I might be able to get a beer and a small sherry for the lady?' Matt asked.

'Aye, take a seat.' The landlord took down a glass and began to draw a pint of nut-brown ale from the tap for Matt. 'I reckon as you'm from the castle then, sir?'

'Yes, Kitty is Lady Woodcomb's cousin. We came for the wedding,' Matt confirmed.

The landlord glanced at Kitty as he set the pint down on the bar for Matt. 'And now that there London bloke has got himself killed and all I hear?'

'Unfortunately, yes. We heard that one of your guests had been arrested for the murder of the other man?' Matt took a sip from his pint as the man poured Kitty's sherry.

The man set the bottle back behind the bar. 'Aye, that's him over there, Mr Whitlock. They found a gun in his room, but they reckon now as he couldn't have had owt to do with it.' The man took the money for the drinks from Matt. 'I could have told them that me sen. Bloke is as blind as a bat. You can tell that just by looking at him. He couldn't hit a barn door at fifty paces never mind shoot somebody from across a field.'

'Oh dear, it sounds as if someone must have placed the gun amongst his things on purpose,' Kitty said as Matt handed her the sherry.

'Aye.' The landlord shook his head. 'I dunno what the world is coming too.' He disappeared back to his cellar and Matt went to join Kitty at her table.

'Come on,' she murmured and stood before carrying her glass carefully across the scrubbed red quarry tile floor to where the unfortunate Mr Whitlock sat nursing his pint.

'Mr Whitlock, may we join you? The landlord was just telling us about your ordeal.' Kitty took a seat opposite the man.

She could see that the lenses on his glasses were extremely thick and wondered what Inspector Lewis had been thinking to arrest the poor man.

Mr Whitlock peered myopically at them as Matt took the chair beside Kitty. 'I only got let out of custody yesterday. I kept telling them I didn't know what they were on about. I don't own a gun. I never fought, my eyes was too bad.'

Kitty sipped her sherry and tried not to shudder at the syrupy sweetness. Outside there was a distant rumble of thunder as the storm grew nearer to the village. 'Where do you think it came from?' she asked.

'I reckon as somebody come in here when it was empty and snuck up the stairs there at the back. My room is the first one as you come to. They could have took the key from the back of the counter.' Mr Whitlock shook his head gloomily. 'Just my bloomin' luck. I only come here to try and get what I was owed from that Galsworthy chap. Now, Alf, that's the landlord, reckons as he's dead and all. Somebody dropped a blessed great rock on his head. Is that a fact?' He peered at Matt.

Matt confirmed that this was indeed the case.

'I don't reckon as how I'll see a penny of my money now.' Mr Whitlock sighed and took a pull of his beer.

'Did he owe you much money?' Kitty asked.

Mr Whitlock snorted. 'One hundred and fifty pounds. That's a lot to me.'

'Forgive me for asking, Mr Whitlock, but what did Mr Galsworthy owe the money for?' Matt asked.

'Wine and spirits. I've a small business and his credit is well overdue. I tried the housekeeper, but it was Mr Galsworthy what had his name on the orders, and she said as he had to sort it out. Give me short shrift she did when I tried to speak to him or his missus. I couldn't get a hold of him and when I learned as he was here for this society wedding, I reckoned as he would most likely pay up so as not to be embarrassed in front of the other nobs.' Belatedly, Mr Whitlock suddenly seemed to realise that Kitty and Matt might be some of those very nobs and attempted to backtrack. 'Begging your pardons, miss, sir, but you catch my drift.'

Kitty swallowed the last of her sherry with a shudder. 'I do indeed, Mr Whitlock. You have been most shamefully treated. By the way did you ever write anonymously to Mr Galsworthy just to try and encourage him into paying you?'

Mr Whitlock looked affronted by the suggestion. 'Not anonymously no, miss. I invoiced him and sent reminders. Not that I ever got any response other than vague offers to pay at some point in the future. I run a legitimate business and I've a wife and six children to keep. You can't live off promises.'

'Thank you, Mr Whitlock. I do hope you get your money.' She glanced at her wristwatch. 'Gracious, I hadn't realised the time, we really must go. It's almost lunchtime already.'

Matt finished his pint and shook hands with the unlucky Mr Whitlock. 'I hope you manage to get paid, and I'm sorry for all your troubles.'

There was another loud crack of thunder as they hurried towards the waiting car. The electricity from the storm in the air prickled at Kitty's skin and stirred her hair. All around her the ground smelt of earth and coming rain while the birdsong in the trees had ceased.

The chauffeur saw them approaching. He folded up his newspaper and straightened his cap as they scrambled into the back of the car as the first drops of rain began to fall.

'In the nick of time, miss, sir. 'Tis black as pitch over there,' the man observed as he started the engine.

Kitty peered ahead as the chauffeur turned on the windscreen wipers. Lightning ran like a white streak across the sky, swiftly followed by a deafening clap of thunder. Rain started to pelt down, droplets bouncing off the metal body of the car like bullets.

'We'd better get back into the dry of the castle,' Matt remarked. He glanced at Kitty and murmured, 'And compare notes.'

CHAPTER SEVENTEEN

The storm crackled and roared its way around them all the way back to Thurscomb. At times they were forced to slow as the wipers could not sweep the rain away swiftly enough from the windscreen of the car for the driver to safely see the road ahead.

Kitty was relieved to see the creamy yellow walls of the castle come into view above the rain-battered hedgerows.

'I'll pull as close as I can to the main door,' the chauffeur said as they drove over the wooden drawbridge into the courtyard.

True to his word he manoeuvred the car so they could scramble out and into the welcome dryness of the castle hallway.

'I think I've saved my hat,' Kitty remarked as she unpinned her best straw summer hat from her blonde curls. 'What a storm.' She brushed the water spots from her skirt.

'Shall we go and see if anyone is in the drawing room? It would be good to discover the whereabouts of Inspector Lewis. We might discover what he learned from talking to Moira and Ralston this morning.'

Kitty gave a ladylike snort as she fell into step beside him. 'I'm starting to wonder how Inspector Lewis ever became a policeman let alone an inspector after our meeting with Mr Whitlock. I'm starting to think he could not investigate his way out of a paper bag.'

Kitty's aunt and uncle were in the drawing room seated on either side of the vast inglenook fireplace. Lucy and Rupert looked every bit the cosy newly-weds together on the sofa. A rather mournful

Muffy lay on the floor at Lucy's feet looking as if her furry nose had been put out of joint.

'Ah, Kitty m'dear, we were just talking about you and Matthew. Good thing you made it back with this storm going on. That Lewis fellow said you had gone to the village looking for clues. Any joy down there?' her uncle asked as soon as they entered the room.

'We had an interesting talk with Mr Whitlock, the gentleman that Inspector Lewis arrested at the Plume of Feathers,' Kitty said as she sat down on one of the smaller tapestry-covered occasional seats.

'Oh?' Lucy straightened up from where she had been leaning against her new husband.

'The poor man was owed money by Sandy, but it was obvious as soon as you met him that he could not possibly have fired the gun that killed Evans.' Kitty explained about Mr Whitlock's poor vision.

Her uncle made a dismissive noise. 'I knew that policeman was a fool, it's a good job you two are on the case.'

'We found out some other information too, sir, but we aren't quite certain how it all ties into the murders. Do you know if Inspector Lewis is still here?' Matt asked.

'The last I saw of him he was harassing my staff in the kitchens. I rather fear he may be the reason why luncheon is delayed,' Rupert said with a sigh.

Kitty's stomach gave a faint grumble at the mention of lunch. She glanced at her watch again as the gong sounded from the corridor.

'At last, shall we go through?' Rupert offered his arm to Lucy. Kitty's aunt and uncle followed behind them, with Matt and Kitty at the rear. Muffy trotted at her mistress' heels, clearly anxious not to be separated from her.

Hattie hurried into the dining room just as they were being seated, with Sinclair and Calliope not far behind her.

'No Daisy or Aubrey today?' Lady Medford asked as she spread her linen napkin across her lap.

'Daisy is still indisposed, and Aubrey is staying with her. I don't know where Adalia is,' Rupert said.

'I believe Adalia has taken to her bed,' Hattie informed him. 'Ralston is still unwell and is resting upstairs, and Moira is remaining in her room. She sends her apologies.'

Calliope gave her husband a meaningful look at this piece of information.

Outside the castle the storm continued to grumble overhead. Conversation around the table was muted and Kitty suspected that Calliope and Sinclair's presence was somewhat inhibiting.

It was something of a relief when the meal was ended, and the last portions of apple pie and custard had been cleared.

'I think I'll go and find Inspector Lewis. See if there is a progress report.' Rupert looked at his father-in-law.

'Excellent idea, m'boy,' Lord Medford agreed.

'Could you ask him when we might be free to leave for London?' Calliope asked. 'Sinclair has several very important meetings planned and we really do need to leave soon.'

Kitty wondered if these meetings were the results of his telephone calls from the village post office. She had a feeling that they must be of a nature of which neither her uncle nor Rupert would approve. There could be no other reason she could think of why he would need to make the calls from the village rather than the castle.

Rupert nodded and left the dining room. Sinclair and Calliope wandered back to the library where they appeared to spend much of their time. Kitty and Matt accompanied her aunt and uncle, Lucy and Hattie back to the drawing room.

The sounds of the storm finally appeared to be dying down and Kitty went to look out of the window to see if the rain had slowed or ceased. Muffy had made the most of Rupert's absence to jump up on the sofa beside Lucy to rest her head on Lucy's knee.

After a moment Rupert's elderly butler appeared in the drawing room doorway.

'Excuse me, Captain Bryant, Miss Underhay, his lordship requests your presence in the study.'

Kitty exchanged a glance with Matt, and they excused themselves from the room.

'I wonder if Inspector Lewis has any news for us?' Kitty murmured as they hurried through the hall to the study.

'Perhaps he has managed to make an arrest,' Matt suggested.

Kitty raised her eyebrows. 'I think that is most unlikely, don't you?'

*

Matt was still smiling to himself as they knocked on the oak panelled door of Rupert's study. On entering they discovered the inspector seated once more behind Rupert's desk with Rupert sitting in the leather club chair to the side.

'Matt, Kitty, do come in and take a seat. I thought it would be useful for us to pool our discoveries. I've asked the inspector to share the results of his investigations so far today with you, and I know that you will reciprocate with whatever you have learned,' Rupert said.

Kitty took one of the spare chairs and Matt took the other vacant one next to her.

'Thank you, sir. I'm sure it can only prove helpful to combine our knowledge at this point,' Matt addressed the inspector, mindful that it would do little good to antagonise him.

The sour expression on the policeman's face suggested that he didn't agree with Matt but had been coerced into cooperating.

'Mr Barnes remains unwell today. I'm led to believe he has a heart condition.' Inspector Lewis began flicking through the pages of his notebook. 'However, he has claimed that he was in the dining room collecting more food from the table for himself and a Miss

Merriweather when Mr Galsworthy was killed. He saw no one and this cannot be corroborated.'

The inspector's statement tied in with what he and Kitty had worked out already. It was always possible that Ralston's heart condition had been made worse by a hurried trip to and from the attic, combined with the exertion of toppling a large rock onto his son-in-law's head. However, unless the man was exaggerating his health issues this seemed unlikely.

'And your interview with Mrs Galsworthy?' Matt asked. He was curious to know how the inspector had found Moira after he and Kitty had seen her attempting to access the attic only a few hours ago.

'Quite naturally, Mrs Galsworthy remains very distressed by her husband's death.' Inspector Lewis' expression became even sourer.

'Did Moira say where she was when Sandy was killed?' Kitty asked.

The inspector consulted his notes once more. 'She had slipped up to her room to collect a handkerchief.'

'I presume again, that she wasn't seen by anyone?' Kitty asked.

'No, Miss Underhay.' The inspector closed his small black notebook. 'I have questioned all the staff and it seems they were enjoying Lord Woodcomb and Lord Medford's hospitality and didn't come into the main house until Lady Woodcomb raised the alarm and requested assistance.'

'And presumably she saw no one herself on the stairs?' Kitty murmured.

'No.' Inspector Lewis clearly didn't see the need to waste words.

'Thank you, sir. That has been most helpful.' Matt shared what they had learned in the village from the chemist and the post office but didn't mention their interview with Mr Whitlock. He also had no intention of sharing that they had seen Moira attempting to gain access to the attic.

From Inspector Lewis' sneer it seemed that he attached little value to their findings in the village.

'I didn't think you would find that I had missed anything of any great importance.' The inspector replaced his notebook in his pocket.

'So, what are your conclusions so far, sir? Some of my guests are extremely anxious to return to London, and I must admit I shall be happy to see them leave,' Rupert said.

'It seems obvious to me that if someone inside the castle did not kill Mr Galsworthy, then I cannot exclude the possibility that someone came in from outside and hid up on the roof waiting for the opportunity. No doubt they expected it to be dismissed as an accident,' the inspector said.

Matt saw Kitty's mouth drop open in astonishment. 'Then how did they get away unseen afterwards?' she asked. 'And why go to such lengths? They could have entered, stabbed him and been long gone before anyone here would have realised anything had happened.'

The inspector bridled. 'Like I said, Miss Underhay, that is merely one possibility.'

Matt was certain he heard Kitty mutter, 'Nonsense,' under her breath.

'Forgive me, Inspector, but it seems far more likely, unpleasant though this possibility is, that one of our fellow guests killed Mr Galsworthy,' Matt said.

'And what of Mr Evans?' Kitty asked. 'The two deaths must surely be linked. You said before that you thought Mr Evans was killed in error. So, did the same person kill both men or was it two murderers working together? And for what end?'

'Yes, the lack of motive is very strange. I know there were those letters Mr Galsworthy is said to have received in London and Mr Whitlock was owed a large sum of money, but what else was there that would drive someone to murder?' Matt asked.

The inspector got to his feet, clearly nettled by their questions. 'My investigation is not yet complete. You may rest assured, Miss Underhay, Captain Bryant, that I shall continue to dig. In the meantime, Lord Woodcomb, I must inconvenience you and your guests a little longer by asking them to remain here for the time being. Good afternoon, sir.' He took his leave of them and they sat together in silence for a moment.

'Oh dear,' Kitty was the first to speak. 'I'm so sorry, Rupert, we did try to be tactful.'

Rupert grinned. 'Please don't worry, Kitty. I agree with Lucy's father, the man is a fool. I'd rather put my faith in you two. If anyone can solve these murders you can.'

'I think I'm going to take a cup of tea up to Moira and see if she is willing to talk to me,' Kitty said thoughtfully.

'I think I may call on Ralston.' Matt smiled at Kitty.

Rupert rose. 'You may do whatever you wish to solve this thing. Lucy and I are due to leave for our honeymoon in two days' time. I'd hate for it to be delayed, especially after everything that has happened.'

'We'll do our utmost to get to the bottom of all this, I promise,' Kitty assured him.

Once he had left to return to the drawing room, Kitty picked up a piece of paper and a pencil from the desk.

'I'll tackle Moira about what she was up to this morning and where she said she was when Sandy was killed. You see Ralston and check out what he's told the inspector. Then we really must have a word with Adalia. What was she doing at the Plume of Feathers and why was she so flustered in the chemists that day?'

Matt nodded. 'Yes, someone put that gun in Whitlock's room. It could have been any of the people who were in the village that day, including Ralston, but who shot Evans?'

Kitty's lips compressed into a thin line. 'Exactly, and was the person who hid the gun in Whitlock's room the same person that fired it? Is Whitlock innocent or did he know the killer and agree to hide the gun knowing he couldn't be convicted of having shot Evans?'

She placed the pencil down.

'A lot of interesting questions,' Matt said.

'I think then that it's time we went and asked more questions.' Kitty tucked the list inside her bag.

CHAPTER EIGHTEEN

Kitty enlisted Alice's aid to procure a tray of tea and biscuits before carrying it carefully to the door of Moira's room.

'Moira dear, I've bought you some tea. May I come in?' Kitty tapped softly on the door as she juggled the heavy tray, trying not to spill the milk.

There was silence from inside the room. She feared for a moment that Moira wasn't going to answer, and she had raised her hand to knock again when the door opened a crack.

'That's very kind of you, Miss Underhay. Come in.' Moira's voice was dull, and her soft American accent seemed slightly more pronounced. She still hadn't dressed for the day and wore the pale-green Chinese style negligee and wrap they had seen her in earlier when she had tried the attic door. Her mousey brown hair was unbrushed and the end of her nose was red from crying.

Kitty carried the tray into the bedroom and placed it down on the small table in front of the fireplace. The room was of a similar size to that of her own room except this one housed a rather elaborately carved oak four-poster bed with tapestry drapes. It seemed too that Moira was happy for her maid to sleep with the castle servants in the staff quarters as there was no side room.

The fire was almost out and the air in the room felt cold. Kitty added some wood and stirred up the embers until there was a more cheerful blaze in the hearth.

'Come and have some tea. I know you must not feel like eating anything right now, but you must take care of yourself.' Kitty seated herself on one of the old-fashioned wing-backed armchairs beside the fire and poured two cups of tea.

Moira sank listlessly onto the seat opposite Kitty's. 'I feel dreadful. I've lain awake nearly all night. The sleeping draught the doctor gave me didn't seem to help at all.'

'You poor thing. It must be awful.' Kitty handed Moira a cup of tea, settled herself in her chair and waited to see if Moira would be willing to confide in her.

Moira stirred her tea. 'I keep seeing him lying there, with that great stone and all the blood.' A tear leaked from her eyes and rolled down her cheek. 'Poor Sandy. I kept telling him about smoking.'

Kitty felt in her cardigan pocket and produced a clean handkerchief. 'Here, take this, yours is quite sodden. It was awful but you must console yourself that at least he would not have suffered. It would have been quite quick.' She was at something of a loss to know how to comfort her companion.

'I suppose that is true, but I keep asking myself why would someone do such a thing?' Moira paused and blew her nose before continuing. 'I have a confession, Miss Underhay. It was on my mind so much during the night that perhaps it was an accident. That maybe the police were wrong, that I thought… Well, I thought, perhaps if I went onto the roof, and saw it for myself it might help.' She sniffed and continued. 'I went this morning, first thing, but of course the door to the attic was locked. I suppose the police must have done it. Then I realised I was being foolish.' She gave Kitty a faint wan smile. 'I was never any good with heights. I don't know what I thought I would achieve.'

'It was a natural instinct I suppose to want to see for yourself, but perhaps it was better that you couldn't go up there.' Kitty guessed this answered what Moira had been doing when she and Matt had seen her. In some ways it was almost a relief. Seeing how distraught Moira appeared to be she might have been considering throwing herself from the roof to join her husband.

Moira took a sip of her tea. 'I keep thinking why would someone kill Sandy? And that whoever it was must have truly hated him. Even worse, it must be someone in this house. I don't see any other explanation.' She gave a visible shudder and turned her red-rimmed gaze on Kitty. 'You and your friend, Captain Bryant, have experience in these kinds of matters. What is your opinion?'

Kitty sighed and set down her cup knowing that she needed to tread carefully. 'Is there someone amongst the guests who you think might have harboured ill feelings towards your husband?' she asked.

Moira gave a small sad smile. 'Sinclair was once a great friend of Sandy's when they were young but ideologically their politics have diverged quite drastically. We had been seeing less and less of them as Sandy felt politically it could be damaging to his future. You know, with his cabinet position and all. Although we still ran into Calliope quite often in our social groups.' Her nose wrinkled in distaste at the mention of Calliope's name. 'Sinclair, I think, resented Sandy's political success and he, himself, is increasingly involved with the Fascists and the Blackshirt movement. As you witnessed for yourself, that has led to several arguments and heated moments since our arrival here at Thurscomb. But, that is a long way from wanting Sandy dead.'

'Did Sandy know anyone else, here at the castle?' She knew what Moira meant when she said that Sandy and Sinclair differed now politically. Rupert had expressed the same feelings to Matt. However she had to agree with Moira that those differences were a long way from wishing to kill someone.

'We knew Daisy and Aubrey, of course, from before they were married. And we both know Adalia slightly. She would be at some of the party fundraising soirées we attended in London.' Moira drained her cup and set it down on the tray.

'And there was no one else?' Kitty asked. 'I bumped into a Mr Whitlock this morning in the village. He was the man Inspector Lewis arrested over Mr Evans' murder. He said Sandy owed him quite a large sum of money.' Kitty tried to phrase her statement delicately. She was keen to know what Moira knew about Sandy's debts and his alleged affairs.

Moira certainly appeared to be quite grief-stricken but Kitty was aware that it could just be remorse.

A humourless smile appeared on Moira's face. 'I have no doubt that when we return to London there will be a good many people come crawling from the woodwork to claim from Sandy's estate. What was this man owed money for?'

'Wine and spirits, I think. Did Sandy owe a great deal of money?' Kitty asked.

Moira nodded and bit her lip. 'He wasn't what you might describe as the ideal husband. He liked to live the good life, wine, food, cards and, of course, there were other women.' She sniffed and dabbed at her eyes with her handkerchief. 'I expect you wonder how I stood it?' She looked at Kitty.

Kitty had been pondering exactly that question and wondering if Moira could suddenly have had enough and snapped, sending the rock tumbling onto Sandy's head. Mr Evans' shooting could have been the work of an accomplice or a hired hand. 'It must have been painful for you.'

Moira blinked. 'I loved my husband, Miss Underhay, and I blame myself. If we could have had a child together.' She broke off in a gulping sob and it took her a moment to collect herself while Kitty made soothing noises. 'We tried everything. I saw the best doctors, the worst doctors, even the quack doctors and nothing. My father would have loved a grandchild. Nothing worked. Not even—' She stopped suddenly, and Kitty saw a look of fear pass across her face.

The words of the girl in the chemist shop floated into Kitty's head. 'Not even the potion you collected from the pharmacist in the village?'

Moira gasped. 'How did you know? Yes, but…' She buried her head in her hands for a moment, her shoulders shaking.

'That day in the chapel?' Kitty was feeling her way, the different pieces of this part of the puzzle were beginning to tumble into place.

Tears were falling down Moira's pale face freely now. 'I'd had a huge argument with Sandy. Oh, Miss Underhay, you'll think I'm a terrible, wicked person.' She stopped and blew her nose once more. 'The tonic from the chemist was for Sandy. I had to put a dose in his food or drink twice a day. It was supposed to help us conceive.'

Kitty could see where this was going. 'He didn't know, did he?'

Moira shook her head. 'Worse than that. That night when he was so ill and he said someone had tried to poison him. It was me. I accidentally put too much in his drink and it made him sick. I was so scared. I couldn't tell him what I'd done so I got the doctor to come and check him.'

'How did he find out?' Kitty asked.

'He went in the bathroom cabinet looking for aspirin for his head and found the bottle. He guessed what had happened. We had a terrible fight.' Moira hiccoughed to a halt.

'You poor thing.' Kitty gave Moira's hand a compassionate squeeze.

'I keep thinking that he went to his death with there still being this niggling distrust between us.' The woman scrubbed her face fiercely with Kitty's now sodden handkerchief.

'I'm sure he understood.' Kitty attempted to reassure her. Moira's explanation certainly cleared up quite a few things. 'Why did he assume he had been poisoned? Was it because of the letters, do you think?' After all, he hadn't appeared to think Moira was the culprit when he became ill.

Moira shrugged. 'I don't know. I suppose so.' She frowned. 'He had been different lately, as if there was something on his mind. I had been frightened by it, thinking perhaps he was going to leave me.' A frown creased her forehead and her cheeks pinked. 'But, he was still affectionate with me so I began to think perhaps it was his work. There was a lot going on there, so much pressure. His role as a junior minister was a huge step up you see, and he was involved with several projects.'

Kitty wondered if any of these projects might involve clamping down on the role of the Blackshirts. There had been several very unpleasant incidents lately and rumours in the press were rife that more were to come. It would certainly explain the animosity between Sandy and Sinclair.

'How is your father this morning?' She wondered how Matt was doing with his part of the investigation.

'He came to visit me briefly after breakfast. He and Sandy never really saw eye to eye you know, Miss Underhay. Papa tolerated Sandy for my sake, but he often begged me to end the marriage.' She gave Kitty another sad smile. 'He always wanted the best for his little girl, and he could see that I wasn't always happy.'

'Your father said he has a heart condition. Certainly, when Evans was killed he was quite unwell,' Kitty mused.

Moira nodded. 'Papa has a bad heart, any undue exertion or stress makes him quite unwell. I think it's gotten worse in the last few months as he needs his pills more often these days. He misses Mr Evans too. The murder upset him terribly.'

'He said Evans had been his right-hand man.'

'Papa may be a frail old man but he's also a ruthless businessman. You don't get to be as rich as my father without being one tough old cookie. Evans was his go-to man. He would check people out, ask questions, deal with documents and telephone calls. Father relied on him a lot.' Moira dabbed at her nose.

'I take it he did some snooping for him?' Kitty asked.

The blush on Moira's cheeks deepened as she nodded.

Kitty wondered if Ralston was ruthless enough to kill his son-in-law. He'd failed to convince Moira to leave Sandy. But then there was Evans' murder. Had that been an attack gone wrong? Had Sandy been the target? Or had Evans discovered something about one of the house party? Then if Sandy had learned who might have killed Evans then he would have had to die too.

*

Matt stumbled across Ralston sitting quietly in the chapel gazing at the stained-glass window above the altar. It was only by chance that he had opened the door and looked inside to find the older man sitting there.

The flowers from yesterday's wedding had made the air in the chapel heavy with their scent and a few of the larger white lilies had already begun to droop. It was not a scent that Matt cared for. He always associated it with death and decay rather than anything joyful.

Ralston didn't turn his head at the sound of Matt gently closing the small oak door in its stone arched frame.

'May I join you, sir?' Matt asked as he took the vacant seat next to Ralston.

The man gave a small shrug of his shoulders, which Matt took as an affirmative. They sat side by side in silence for a moment.

'I assume you are investigating the murder of my son-in-law?' Ralston asked eventually.

'Yes, sir. Rupert has requested that Kitty and I make some enquiries to assist Inspector Lewis.' Matt saw no point in dissembling. Ralston was a shrewd man and would know which way the ground lay.

The older man appeared weary. His complexion held a faintly grey tinge and he looked exhausted.

'It's no secret that Sandy was not the man I would have chosen for my daughter, or that I have tried to persuade her to leave him many times without success. However, I would not have wished him dead, Captain Bryant.' His gaze flickered towards Matt for a second before returning to his study of the window.

Matt nodded. 'Do you know anyone who would have wanted Sandy killed?' he asked.

Ralston sighed. 'Sandy owed a great many people money. He also had a lot of liaisons, which were perhaps not wise. Husbands tend to be very unforgiving. He always skirted with scandal although since his promotion to junior minister I think that side of his character had abated somewhat.'

'What about anyone staying here at the castle? Is there anyone here who you would have thought may have wished to harm Sandy?' Matt knew there were those who had disliked Sandy, but disliking someone was one thing. Hating them enough to murder them was something else.

Ralston turned to look at Matt. 'Sinclair and his wife had arguments with Sandy, but it didn't seem to be anything major. Calliope dislikes Moira but I think that was down to their history. Jealousy, I think, on both sides. I guess if you're asking me for someone's motive for killing him then I just don't know.'

'I'm sorry I have to ask all of these questions, sir,' Matt said.

Ralston shrugged. 'You have a job to do, and Moira will want answers, as do I. It seems impossible that both my manservant and my son-in-law have both been killed in a matter of days. Here, of all places, in such a setting, at a wedding.' He shook his head.

'Inspector Lewis believes that Evans was killed in error. That whoever fired the shot was really aiming for Sandy. I presume you have the same belief? That you don't know of anyone who may have wished to kill Evans?' Matt knew they had covered this ground before. In the light of Sandy's death, however, he wanted to revisit it.

Ralston's shoulders sagged. 'Evans was my right-hand man. He was my eyes and ears. Also my legs since my heart has weakened over the last twelve months. It's possible I suppose that he may have learned something that he wasn't meant too but if he did, he never shared that knowledge with me.'

Matt frowned. He had entered the chapel half convinced that Ralston's millions may have been used to employ someone to murder Sandy. It had made sense that with Ralston's failing health he was unlikely to have physically been capable of pushing the stone from the roof. It was also impossible for him to have shot Evans.

'May I ask a somewhat delicate question, sir?'

Ralston's brows raised. 'Ask away. I expect you want to know the financial arrangements for Moira in the event of my death.'

Matt's face heated a little. 'Yes, sir.'

'My will is quite straightforward. There are, of course, bequests for some of my staff and for charities that I have supported for many years. Beyond that everything goes to Moira and any children she might have in the future.'

'There was no provision for Sandy?' Matt asked.

Ralston shook his head. 'My intention is to ensure my daughter retains control of her own fortune. That she has a comfortable life. If you were a parent, Captain Bryant, you would understand. Once you have a child that child is everything to you.'

Matt stiffened and swallowed. An image of little Betty's face flashed in front of his mind. 'I was a parent, sir. My wife and daughter were killed during the war. Betty was only a few months old.'

A look of understanding showed in the older man's eyes and his expression softened. 'I'm very sorry for your loss. Then you do understand. I wanted to protect Moira from the fortune hunters. Sandy was a cad in many ways, but my daughter loved him. I tried, when they first got together to buy him off, but he wouldn't be bought. Once they were married then I knew it would have to be

Moira's decision if it were to end. I could have tried again but if I had succeeded and she had found out, then I would have lost her.'

Matt understood what Ralston was saying. 'I see.'

Ralston patted his hand in a fatherly way. 'I believe you do.' He returned his gaze to the window above the altar. 'I'm not a religious man, Captain Bryant, but I've always found the peace and sanctity of a church very soothing.'

Matt looked at the window and realised the image in the glass was that of St Christopher bearing the Christ child on his shoulders.

'I shall leave you to your thoughts, sir, and thank you.' Matt took one last look at the window and slipped quietly from the chapel.

CHAPTER NINETEEN

Kitty shivered as she made her way back down the stairs. The aftermath of the storm had left the interior of the castle feeling damp and stuffy. The loss of sunshine combined with the thickness of the walls was oppressive and she longed to be back on the Devon coast. Outside in the clean, fresh air, with the scent of the sea.

Someone had turned on the electric lights in the stairwell and in the main hall. No doubt it was an attempt to dispel the gathering gloom of the afternoon. As Kitty reached the foot of the stairs the lights fizzled and flickered ominously before coming back on.

She wondered where Matt had got to and if he had managed to speak to Ralston. Her mind was busy turning over everything she had learned from Moira. How had the gun made its way to the Plume of Feathers? The large grandfather clock in the hall chimed the hour. Four o'clock. Teatime.

Kitty went to the front door and took a peep outside. The gravel and paving stones of the courtyard were wet from the storm. Puddles had formed in the dips reflecting the grey sky overhead, but for now the rain had ceased. She took a quick glance upwards, then making up her mind she headed out across the square to the gatehouse.

'Oh, Miss Underhay, I'm very sorry, miss, but Miss Daisy is indisposed.' The young housemaid who'd opened the door to Kitty appeared flustered.

'That's quite all right. It's Mrs Adalia Watts I've come to see, if she is receiving visitors.' Kitty had scarcely got the words out of her mouth when she heard Adalia's imperious reedy tones.

'Who is it, Jane?'

The girl flushed. 'Miss Underhay, Miss Adalia, come to call on you.'

'Well, don't keep her waiting on the step.'

Kitty gave the girl an apologetic smile and followed her into the hall.

'Miss Adalia is receiving in her sitting room, miss.'

Kitty's brows rose slightly at this statement but obediently followed the girl along the hall and into a long, narrow sitting room. It took her a moment to adjust as the room was quite dark and gloomy and filled with all kinds of furniture that looked as if it had come originally from the castle.

Eventually, she located Adalia, reclining on the couch with the back of her hand pressed to her forehead in an attitude of woe.

'I'm sorry to disturb you, especially right on teatime, but I didn't see you at lunch and wondered how you were feeling after yesterday,' Kitty said.

Her stomach gave a low growl at the thought of tea and she hoped her hostess might take the hint.

'Thank you, Miss Underhay. It's so good to know that not all young people are so regardless of the well-being of their elders. Jane, tea, please, and the seed cake that Miss Daisy keeps in the blue tin.' Adalia glared at the maid and the girl whisked away leaving Kitty to take a seat on one of the old-fashioned overstuffed chairs.

'How Aubrey manages with just that girl I really don't know. It's simply too bad when Rupert has so many servants that he can't spare an extra one for Aubrey,' Adalia said with a sniff as she levered herself into a more upright position on the couch.

'The maid said that poor Daisy is indisposed. I do hope she didn't overdo things yesterday. It was such a busy day and then with Sandy's murder…' Kitty deliberately allowed her voice to trail away as she waited for Adalia's response.

'Daisy is young and fit. I daresay she merely wants to avoid the unpleasantness of that Inspector Lewis poking around the estate asking questions.' Adalia clearly didn't believe that there was anything significant wrong with Daisy. Kitty wondered how she would react when she learned she was to become a grandmother.

The rattle of tea things at the door signalled the return of the maid pushing a small gilt trolley.

'Shall I stay and serve madam?' the girl asked Adalia.

'No, I'm sure Miss Underhay will oblige me.' She dismissed the girl who fled with a thankful look on her face.

Kitty duly set out the pink floral-patterned china cups and was relieved to see the maid had indeed found the seed cake.

'Have you seen much of the inspector?' Kitty asked as she handed a cup and saucer to Adalia.

'He was here this morning asking all kinds of impertinent questions about when I had visited the village and some other nonsense. Why Aubrey didn't just send him away I'll never know.' Adalia watched as Kitty carefully cut them a slice each from the cake.

'I suppose he has his job to do but it must have been very distressing for you,' Kitty soothed.

'Exactly, my dear Miss Underhay. If you knew how I've suffered with my health since Aubrey's father died then you would understand how terribly distressing this has all been for me.' Adalia took a generous bite of cake.

'Oh, I do sympathise. Life can be terribly difficult for a woman alone.' Kitty hoped she wasn't laying it on too thick but Adalia appeared to be revelling in having a sympathetic listener.

'Exactly. Aubrey is an excellent son, of course, or at least he was until, well, one cannot choose for one's children and the dear boy is easily led.' Adalia heaved a large sigh.

'I understand Aubrey and Daisy were married in London.' Kitty had soon finished her own piece of cake and wondered if Adalia would think her greedy if she cut another piece.

'To be deprived of the pleasure of seeing one's only child married.' Adalia shook her head. 'I must confess, Miss Underhay, I was quite distraught. Naturally Aubrey was only thinking of me, of course. He knew my nerves wouldn't stand the strain of a large society wedding. But to think that he could have been married here, well, it is very hard, Miss Underhay, very hard indeed.'

'Of course.' Kitty wanted to steer the conversation back around to Adalia's visit to the Plume of Feathers.

Adalia set down her empty plate to take a sip of her tea. 'I can't begin to tell you how nice it is, my dear, to have someone who understands my feelings.'

'I must admit it seems incredible that two people have been killed in such a short space of time and at what should have been such a joyous occasion.' Kitty shook her head and tried to gently change the topic of conversation.

'I quite agree. It's absolutely shocking. That servant of Mr Barnes. What was his name? Evans. I assumed that must have been an accident of some kind, but then for Mr Galsworthy to be killed in such a horrible way.' A ladylike shudder travelled along Adalia's thin frame.

'Captain Bryant and I ran across Mr Whitlock, the unfortunate man that Inspector Lewis arrested, while we were in the village this morning.' Kitty sipped her tea and looked innocent.

Adalia pressed her hand to her throat, a faint flush highlighted her cheeks. 'Oh dear, I had heard that the police had let him go.'

'Yes, it's quite extraordinary how he came to be suspected and to have the gun used to murder Mr Evans in his possession,' Kitty said. She watched Adalia's reaction from under her lashes.

The older woman fidgeted uncomfortably on the sofa. Kitty looked around the room at all the treasures that she was certain Adalia had acquired from the castle. The huge painted vases, wax flowers and ugly dark furniture. An idea was building in her mind as to how the gun might have come to be in Mr Whitlock's possession.

'The assistant at the chemist shop said she saw you coming out of the Plume of Feathers the day the police found the gun.' Kitty kept her tone light and gossipy.

'Yes, well, I'd lost my glove and thought someone may have found it and taken it into the inn.' Adalia's tone increased in pitch. She tore her gaze away from Kitty's and started to smooth the silky skirt of her dress.

'You had not long left the chemist's shop. Why didn't you simply retrace your steps?' Kitty's tone was firmer. She was certain now that she was on the right path.

The colour deepened in Adalia's cheeks. 'I don't know. I was distracted.'

'By the gun in your bag?' Kitty asked.

The red patches on Adalia's face vanished as quickly as they had formed leaving her cheeks chalk white. Her eyes widened and darkened. 'It's not what you think, Miss Underhay. I didn't shoot Evans. Why would I? I didn't know him and I have never fired a gun in my life.'

'But you did hide the gun in Mr Whitlock's room. Where did you get it from and why did you hide it there?'

Adalia clutched at the top of her dress gasping for air. 'My smelling salts, in my bag. Can't breathe.' She flapped her hand ineffectually in the direction of her handbag, which was on the side table.

Kitty picked up the large cream kid leather bag.

'Hurry, my heart, palpitations.' Adalia's breath was raspy.

Kitty looked inside the bag and pulled out the smelling salts and passed them over. She wasn't at all fooled by Adalia's acting. She had seen her grandmother deal with guests for years who had tried to gain reductions on their bills by falsely making such claims. The older woman fumbled with the cap and wafted the salts around near her face wrinkling her nose as the smell hit her.

While she continued with her histrionics Kitty sat patiently and waited. Eventually Adalia rested her head back against the couch, her eyes closed.

'The gun, Adalia?' Kitty said firmly.

The older woman's eyes snapped open. 'I found it inside that vase. It's one of a pair, the other one is in the spare bedroom. Such beautiful things.' She indicated the huge oriental vase Kitty had noticed earlier. A matching one for the vase they had puzzled over the other day. 'The gun was wrapped inside a towel and stuffed inside. I didn't see it until I got the vase back here and peered inside.' She sounded sulky.

'Where in the house did the vase come from?' Kitty asked. She guessed it had come from the castle, but she hoped perhaps the location might help to identify who might have placed it there. She vaguely remembered Lucy saying something about the telephone table.

Adalia pouted. 'Both vases were in the main hall near the portrait of the late Lord Woodcomb, near the telephone. It was going to be moved for the wedding reception, so I brought it back here. It would be awful if it had been damaged. Such a lovely piece of porcelain. Daisy and Lucy have no appreciation for such things.'

Kitty sighed. That meant anyone could have hidden the gun inside the pot at any time. 'Why didn't you tell Inspector Lewis what you'd found?'

The older woman squirmed uncomfortably on the sofa. 'How could I? Rupert may have misunderstood about why I'd moved the vase and it could have looked bad for Aubrey. The inspector may have believed I was stealing the vase or even that I had killed

Evans.' Adalia's eyes widened. 'I panicked when I realised what it was, and I didn't know what to do. My only thought was to get rid of it as quickly as possible.'

'Then why take it to the Plume of Feathers and hide it in Mr Whitlock's room?' Kitty asked.

'I was going to throw it in the river but there were so many police around and I was frightened someone would see me. I thought that if I took it with me when I went to the village then I might have the opportunity to hide it there somewhere. I saw the room keys behind the bar and that no one was round then, so I took the key to the nearest room and just got rid of it. I didn't know the room was Mr Whitlock's or whatever his name is. I certainly never thought he would be in any trouble.' Adalia's tone had become defensive.

Kitty couldn't believe her ears. Adalia had been prepared to allow an innocent stranger to be arrested and possibly charged with murder simply because she didn't want to confess to appropriating Rupert's property.

'Well, you must tell Inspector Lewis all of this now,' Kitty said firmly.

A low moan escaped the older woman's lips. 'Oh no, Miss Underhay, I really don't think…'

Kitty glared at her. 'If you don't tell the police then I will, and it would be better if it came from you.'

Adalia opened her mouth as if to protest but subsided when she saw the glint in Kitty's eyes. 'Very well. This Mr Whitlock has been released anyway so it didn't do any harm.'

Kitty looked around the room at all of the things Adalia had liberated from the castle. 'You may also wish to return all of these things too. I can't think that Daisy will want them here and they belong to Rupert.'

Adalia clamped her lips together and looked as if she were about to cry.

'I must go back to the castle. If I see the inspector, I'll ask him to call on you.' Kitty rose from her seat. 'Thank you for the tea, I'll see myself out.' She escaped quickly before Adalia could find her tongue.

The air in the courtyard still felt sticky and close as she walked back to the main entrance. As she opened the heavy front door and stepped inside the main hall she saw the inspector standing next to Rupert beside the fireplace.

Rupert smiled at her as she approached. 'Kitty darling, we were just talking about you. How goes the sleuthing?' Rupert beamed at her while the inspector looked uncomfortable.

'I'm so glad I've seen you. Actually, I was about to look for you, Inspector Lewis. Mrs Adalia Watts wishes to speak to you about the gun that was used to kill Mr Evans,' Kitty said.

Rupert's eyebrows lifted and Inspector Lewis spluttered into speech.

'Mrs Watts? What does she know about the gun?'

'If you go over to the gatehouse, she is expecting you and she will explain everything,' Kitty said.

'She had better not be wasting my time.' The inspector turned on his heel and marched away.

'What a rude man,' Kitty observed once the front door had closed behind him.

'And stupid,' Rupert added thoughtfully. 'Adalia, eh?'

Kitty smiled at him. 'It's a long story.'

'If Adalia is involved it would be,' Rupert remarked drily. 'I rather think my sister is finding that Aubrey's mother has considerably overstayed her welcome.'

Kitty wondered what Aubrey made of the matter and if he knew about his mother helping herself to items of furniture from the castle. She had the feeling that Aubrey had probably been too concerned about Daisy to take much notice of his mother and her activities.

'By the way, Matt was looking for you earlier. I think he's in the drawing room,' Rupert added.

'Thank you, I'll go and find him.' There wasn't much time before she needed to go and change for dinner. She had spent longer with Adalia than she had intended, and she wanted to share all she had learned with Matt.

She walked across the hall and entered the corridor leading towards the drawing room. She hadn't taken many steps when the sound of raised voices reached her from the library.

CHAPTER TWENTY

Kitty glanced around and saw there was no one else in sight. Rupert had gone from the hall, presumably to either his study or up the stairs to dress for dinner. She crept along the passage and paused nearer to the partly open library door and listened.

'That Inspector Lewis has been all over the castle again all day asking questions.'

Kitty recognised Calliope's voice and guessed she must be speaking to Sinclair.

'And what if he has? The sooner he finishes up here the sooner we can return to London.' Sinclair's voice was lower and more moderated in tone than that of his wife.

'That private detective is poking about too, and the blonde girl. They've both been going about the place. They've been to the village too,' Calliope said.

Kitty reflected that her grandmother had warned her on more than one occasion that eavesdroppers seldom heard good of themselves.

'Rupert has asked them to assist the inspector. You can hardly blame him, it's obvious to anyone that the man is a fool.' Kitty had to strain to hear Sinclair.

'A fool who is suspicious of where you were when Sandy was killed.' Calliope's voice was sharp.

'Darling, there is really no need to fret.' Sinclair attempted to soothe his wife.

'Well, I won't lie for you, Sinclair. We both know you weren't in here when Sandy was killed.'

Kitty stifled a gasp. So, she had been right to be suspicious of Sinclair and Calliope's statement that they had been in the library looking for Calliope's wrap.

'You do realise, darling, that if you don't support my alibi then there will be questions raised about yours too. It's in both our interests to back one another up, then the sooner we can get out of here and back to London,' Sinclair said silkily.

Whatever else they might have gone on to say was lost when Muffy came racing down the corridor towards her. A shoe hung from her mouth and her tail was high. Hattie emerged from the drawing room and came panting along behind her.

'Kitty, do stop her. She's stolen Hortense's slipper again.'

Kitty thought quickly. She didn't want Sinclair and Calliope to realise that they may have been overheard so she made a point of clattering her shoes on the stone flags at the side of the Turkish rug as she caught hold of Muffy's collar.

'Lucky I was just coming along,' Kitty called as Muffy sat down nicely in front of her to drop the shoe at her feet.

Hattie puffed up to her. 'Honestly, this dog is such a thief.'

Kitty laughed. 'I know, but she's devoted to Lucy and is frightfully brave.'

Sinclair and Calliope didn't emerge and there was silence from inside the library.

'At least she hasn't chewed it. I'd better return it to Hortense.' Hattie retrieved the shoe and wagged a plump finger at an unrepentant Muffy.

'I was on my way to look for Matt. Is he in the drawing room?' Kitty asked as she fell into step beside Hattie.

'Yes, my dear, he was just getting us a drink when I spotted this miscreant absconding with the spoils.' Hattie pushed open the door to the drawing room.

Matt was at the drinks trolley. He grinned at Kitty and Hattie as they entered.

'I see you caught her then? Good show.'

'Thanks to, Kitty. She came along at just the right moment. I think I had better move Hortense's shoe out of the wretched animal's reach. I'll take it up when I go upstairs.' Hattie gave Muffy a glare of exasperation mixed with affection.

Muffy curled up on the sofa next to Kitty and started to lick her paw with an air of smug satisfaction. Hattie placed the shoe safely out of the dog's reach and accepted the cocktail that Matt had mixed for her.

'Kitty?' Matt waved the silver cocktail shaker at Kitty.

'Yes, please,' She rather thought she had earned a drink. It had been quite a day and all sorts of information was sloshing around now inside her head.

Hattie took a seat on the chair opposite Kitty and sipped her drink. 'I saw Inspector Lewis with Rupert earlier. I think he's interrogated everyone inside the house within an inch of their lives. Although I must confess I really don't know how it could have been helpful to him at all. Poor Lucy and Rupert, what a start to married life.' Hattie shook her head. 'How was Moira by the way? I heard you took her some tea?' She looked at Kitty.

'Still very distressed, as you might expect,' Kitty said. 'The whole thing is completely mystifying. I keep coming back to Sandy. What could he have done that was so awful that someone wished to kill him?' Kitty accepted her drink from Matt as he took his place at the other end of the sofa.

'And poor Mr Evans too,' Hattie said mournfully.

The clock struck the hour and Hattie gave a squeak of despair. 'Oh my goodness, look at the time! I must go and bathe before dinner. The hot water here is so unreliable.' She swallowed the remainder of her cocktail, collected the shoe and hurried from the room.

Matt looked at Kitty. 'How did you get on this afternoon?'

Kitty shared everything she had learned with Matt, including the snippet of conversation she had just overheard between Calliope and Sinclair. In return he told her of his conversation with Ralston.

'So, where does that take us now? Inspector Lewis has gone to see Adalia. I presume he hasn't spoken to you about anything else that he may have learned today?' Kitty kept her voice low, all too aware that someone might be listening in from the hall outside the drawing room.

'I don't know what to make of it all. It seems to me that we still have several people with some kind of motive, opportunity and means to have killed Sandy.' Matt's tone was thoughtful as he took a sip of his pre-dinner whisky.

'And what of Evans? Where does his death fit in all of this? Was he killed by mistake or was he the intended victim and then Sandy found something out that placed him in danger?' This last idea had been playing on Kitty's mind all afternoon, ever since her talk with Moira.

'I can't help wondering if we are looking for two people working together or one killer working alone.' Matt scratched his chin. 'It'll be dinner time soon. Let's see what this evening brings.'

*

Matt remained in the drawing room for a while after Kitty had gone upstairs to change. He was about to leave when Sinclair ambled in and headed for the bar.

'Hello, thought I'd have a pre-dinner snifter, can I top you up?' Sinclair lifted the cut glass whisky decanter and indicated Matt's empty glass.

'Just a spot for me.' Matt held out his glass and Sinclair poured a small measure. He hadn't intended to have another drink, but it was a good opportunity to talk to Sinclair alone. Usually Calliope was at his side and conversation tended to be somewhat awkward in her company.

'What a week,' Sinclair said with feeling as he sat down in the vacant armchair.

Muffy watched him with disdain for a minute before jumping from the sofa and trotting away to presumably find Lucy.

'Quite. One doesn't expect an invitation to a wedding to end in a double murder,' Matt remarked.

'I don't suppose that inspector chappie has indicated to you who he thinks might have done the deed?' Sinclair asked. His tone was light, but Matt noticed a fine tremor in the hand holding the whisky glass.

'Inspector Lewis hasn't confided in me, I'm afraid.' Matt wondered what Sinclair hoped to learn from the conversation. It was clear he was out to do some probing. 'I expect he's just trying to verify everyone's alibis and to see where everyone was when Sandy was killed.' He waited to see what effect this might have on the other man given what Kitty had overheard earlier.

'I just thought that you and Miss Underhay were assisting him. At least that's the impression Rupert gave me. You know Sandy and I had our differences, especially politically these last few years, but murder...' Sinclair stared at the contents of his glass.

'It seems impossible, doesn't it?' Matt mused. 'You and Calliope were together in the library I think you said when he was killed?'

Sinclair looked up, slightly startled. 'Um, yes, hunting for some wrap thing of Calliope's, she'd left it lying around. You know what women are like with their stuff. I went with her to help her look.'

'Hmm, I thought the inspector said one of the staff had seen you elsewhere around that time.' It was a blatant lie, but Matt knew that Sinclair would be unaware of that and it had to be worth a punt.

'No, I don't think so. Well, unless it was around the time that I'd gone to check something with Rupert. I mean I suppose I did go in and out of the library. I thought he might be in his study. Calliope had found her shawl so maybe that was it. I don't know, after all we'd been celebrating, and the champagne had been flowing all day by then,' Sinclair rambled to a halt.

Matt shrugged. 'Perhaps, I wouldn't worry too much about it. After all, Calliope was with you all evening so she can vouch for you I expect, although it would only have taken a few minutes to get up to the roof, lever off that stone and be back down in time to rush outside with everyone when the alarm was raised.'

Sinclair's face reddened. 'Are you insinuating that I killed Sandy?'

'Me? Oh no, not at all. I'm just saying that you can see that the inspector may believe it possible. But as you said, Calliope can vouch for you and you for her. You can vouch for her, I suppose?' Matt swallowed the last of his whisky and set down his glass.

'What? Well, yes, of course.' Sinclair sounded quite flustered.

Matt rose from his seat ready to head off to dress for dinner, satisfied at having rattled Sinclair's composure.

*

'You'm very thoughtful this evening, miss. How did your investigating go today?' Alice asked as she assisted Kitty into a pale-blue shot silk evening gown.

Kitty told Alice everything she and Matt had discovered. 'I wish I could stop feeling that we're looking at these murders all wrong.'

'In what way?' Alice asked as Kitty took her place in front of the dressing table mirror so her friend could style her hair.

'Inspector Lewis insisted that Mr Evans was killed by mistake. That whoever shot him did so by accident and they were really aiming for Sandy. But what if they weren't? What if Evans were the real target all along?' Kitty's gaze met Alice's in the mirror reflection.

'Well, what could Mr Evans have or know that would get him murdered?' Alice asked as she started to brush Kitty's short blonde curls.

'Evans knew Sandy, Moira and Ralston intimately. He was in their company all the time as he was in Ralston's employ. Then he knew Calliope and Sinclair as they met with Sandy and Moira socially.' Kitty frowned. 'I don't know about Adalia, but he could have discovered something about her since his arrival at the castle.' Adalia had made it clear that she would do anything to promote Aubrey's interests. Was it too big a stretch to consider that she might kill someone who could harm them in some way?

Alice fixed a pretty, pale-blue silk hair ornament with a diamanté setting to the side of Kitty's head. She stepped back and surveyed her handiwork before making a tiny adjustment.

'Mr Barnes and Mr and Mrs Galsworthy were with Mr Evans when he was shot,' Alice pointed out. 'So unless as one of them was working with somebody else, then it couldn't be them. The constable told us downstairs as the shot had been fired from a distance.'

The crease on Kitty's forehead deepened as she applied her lipstick. 'I know. Then there is the business of those anonymous letters. I'd thought it might have been Mr Whitlock. That he may have been so frustrated at Sandy ignoring him that he'd tried to threaten him into paying up. That doesn't seem to have been the case, however, so are those letters connected to Sandy's death in some way?'

'It sounds like a regular pickle to me, miss. None of them have been very honest, have they? Seems to me that if you keep your eyes and ears open one of them will trip themselves up soon enough,' Alice said sagely. 'What does Captain Bryant think?'

Kitty replaced the lid on her lipstick. 'I think he is as confused as I am. I'd dearly love to know more about where Calliope and Sinclair actually were when Sandy was killed. One or neither of them was in the library, that much is now quite clear.'

'Well it sounds to me like as if it could be either of them or it could have been Mrs Galsworthy that killed her husband and Mr Evans was murdered by her accomplice.' Alice's face brightened. 'There was a film like that I saw last year. What was it called?'

Kitty grinned. 'You and your films.'

'You can learn a lot from the pictures, miss,' Alice replied primly.

'I don't doubt it.' Kitty gave her appearance a last check in the mirror. 'Wish me luck then, Alice, I'm going to do some more sleuthing over dinner.'

'Well, you be careful, Miss Kitty. You almost got yourself killed in January with that Esther Hammett.'

Kitty smiled at her friend. 'I promise I'll be careful. I'm hardly likely to get stabbed with a fish knife over dinner.'

Alice tutted and emitted a disapproving sniff as Kitty giggled and let herself out of the bedroom to head downstairs.

She was still smiling as she entered the drawing room. Her uncle and aunt were already seated. Her uncle dapper in his evening attire and her aunt in a pale-grey gown, her pearls in place around her neck. Calliope was at the bar.

'You look charming, Kitty dear.' Her aunt smiled her approval of her choice of gown.

Kitty suspected that Calliope's rather daring crimson backless dress did not meet with her aunt's ideas of suitable attire for young women. 'Thank you, Aunt Hortense, you look rather fabulous yourself.'

She was rewarded by the pleasure on her aunt's face at the compliment.

Calliope sauntered over to a nearby seat and placed her cocktail glass down on the small rosewood side table. She opened her silver cigarette case and placed a cigarette in her black ebony holder. There was no offer from Calliope to obtain a drink for anyone else or to hand around her cigarettes.

Lord Medford's bushy eyebrows bristled and unbidden he immediately went to pour a sherry for Kitty and one for her aunt. Calliope appeared unmoved by Lord Medford's unspoken disapproval of her lack of manners.

'Have you had a good day, Kitty m'dear?' her uncle asked.

She knew immediately what he was asking. 'I think so, Uncle.'

Lord Medford beamed avuncularly at her. 'I'm sure you and Matthew will be successful in your endeavours.'

Calliope blew a thin stream of smoke into the air causing Lady Medford to cough. 'I presume this is your sleuthing? I heard you had been to see Moira this afternoon. Did she confess?'

Lady Medford gasped.

'I took Moira some tea and checked to see how she was feeling. She has lost her husband in the most terrible way.' Kitty held Calliope's gaze until the other woman was forced to look away.

Kitty was relieved to see Matt enter the room accompanied by Ralston.

'Mr Barnes, I do hope you are feeling better?' He was using a silver-topped walking cane and he appeared a shadow of the man she had met on her arrival at Thurscomb.

'A little, my dear, a little.' He sank down on the sofa beside her, and Matt immediately went to the bar to pour him a drink.

'Whisky and soda?' Matt asked.

Ralston nodded. 'Thank you, very kind.'

Calliope turned her attention towards the older man. 'And have you received a grilling from Inspector Lewis or Captain Bryant and Miss Underhay?' Her lip curled slightly as she spoke.

'I have spoken to the inspector, yes. I have nothing to hide.' Ralston accepted his drink from Matt. 'And neither does my daughter.'

A low ominous growl of thunder reverberated around the exterior of the castle.

Lady Medford shuddered. 'I think the storm has come back around. Do turn the lamp on, m'dear, it's grown quite dark in here.'

Lord Medford put his hand on the switch, the lamp came on, the bulb flickered and died with a sharp fizzing sound.

'Rupert really does need to get these electrical problems sorted out,' Kitty murmured to Matt.

The rest of the house party entered accompanied by Daisy, Aubrey and a somewhat chastened looking Adalia now clad in a black evening gown.

'That wretched fuse has gone again. The lights should be back in a minute,' Rupert assured them.

'My dear, are you feeling better?' Lady Medford asked, peering through the gloom in Daisy's direction.

Kitty thought Daisy still appeared quite pale.

'A little, thank you. I think it's this weather. I always get terrible headaches whenever there is a storm.'

Sinclair joined Calliope, although Kitty noted that they did not appear to be on good terms. Calliope turned away from her husband and affected to not hear him when he said something to her.

The only person missing as they mingled for drinks was Moira. She had sent her maid to give her apologies to Lucy.

'Poor thing, she really needs to rest. I've asked for a tray to be made up for her,' Lucy told Kitty as they chatted whilst waiting for the dinner gong to sound.

'She was in quite a state when I took her tea this afternoon.' Kitty thought that Moira's grief had certainly seemed very real and the argument she'd had with Sandy before his death had added to her pain.

'That was kind of you. Rupert and I can't help feeling somehow responsible for all of this. If Sandy hadn't been Rupert's best man and if we had known about the depth of Sinclair's, well, political leanings, oh, Kitty…' Lucy broke off, wringing her hands.

'Oh darling, please don't fret. None of this is really to do with you or Rupert. It's horrid that it's happened here to spoil your lovely wedding. But in a few days you're going to be sipping cocktails with Rupert in the South of France and all of this will fade away like a bad dream.' Kitty jumped up to hug her cousin.

'I do hope so. I really hope that whoever did this will be caught soon.' Lucy's voice wobbled.

'I'm sure they will. We've learned so much today, it won't be long now,' Kitty assured her. 'I've had a few ideas.'

Lucy's face brightened at Kitty's reassurance. The gong sounded from the hall summoning them to dinner. Kitty went to accompany Matt and noticed that Sinclair and Calliope were standing much closer to her and Lucy than she had realised. A small shiver ran down her spine and she wondered who else had heard what she'd said to Lucy. Adalia, perhaps, or Ralston?

CHAPTER TWENTY-ONE

The lights were still out in the hall as they made their way to the dining room. The dining table looked curiously intimate now the extra leaves had been removed. Lit like a stage set with fat creamy wax candles on the enormous silver candelabras and a few lanterns on the side tables at the edge of the room. The flickering lights threw shadows in the dark corners near the vast china-laden dressers.

Rupert's butler said something in his ear as he took his place at the head of the table. He nodded and sat down.

'I'm afraid that I've just been informed that the electricity in the castle has failed, and the staff are unable to effect a repair this evening. We have plenty of lanterns and a good supply of candles. I would ask, however, that candles are used with caution. Thurscomb has already suffered one major fire in its recent history.' Rupert looked around the table at his guests and a murmur of consent rippled around the room.

Dinner was served surprisingly well considering the difficulties the kitchen must have been facing working by lanterns and candle-light. Rupert, supported by Lord Medford, appeared determined to keep conversation away from anything contentious such as politics or murder. Instead, there was a relatively cheery discourse on Rupert and Lucy's honeymoon trip and the merits of aubretia, led by Lady Medford, as a suitable plant for difficult areas of the garden.

By the time the cheese course had been served Kitty was a little more relaxed. The occasional rumble of thunder could still be heard rolling around the exterior of the castle as they walked back along the darkened corridor to the drawing room. The air within the castle had cooled as the evening had drawn on but it still felt curiously sticky and damp.

The staff had been into the drawing room and had placed lanterns at strategic points within the main parts of the room. While the main seating areas were well lit the corners remained in shadow.

Daisy, Aubrey and Adalia all excused themselves to return to the gatehouse. Daisy wished to rest and Adalia pleaded a headache. Ralston also decided to retire early as he wished to check on Moira before turning in for the night.

'I simply cannot believe how the weather has turned,' Lady Medford said with a sigh as she accepted her coffee from Hattie. 'Do we know if these storms are to continue?'

'I believe they should be gone by morning, at least that's what my estate manager tells me,' Rupert replied. 'Hopefully the electric people will be able to sort out the wiring and the fuses tomorrow. It was an area that my late uncle neglected. I believe he preferred the oil lamps. He always said they were kinder to his eyes, although I suspect he thought them kinder to his wallet.'

'Well, I for one hope Inspector Lewis will permit us to leave tomorrow. We have several important meetings to attend in London in the next few days. Really it is quite insupportable to keep us here for much longer.' Calliope sat neatly on an occasional chair and crossed her slender legs before lighting yet another of her cigarettes.

Kitty saw her uncle exchange a meaningful glance with Rupert.

'I'm not sure what the inspector will decide to do about allowing anyone to leave. I think he may still have more questions for everyone,' Rupert remarked apologetically.

'It's quite ridiculous,' Calliope huffed and glared at her husband. 'Sinclair, can't you do something? It is really intolerable.'

Sinclair, to his credit looked uncomfortable with Calliope's demand. 'I think we have no choice but to comply at present, my dear.'

The angry stream of smoke that met this response indicated that Calliope didn't like Sinclair's answer.

'Do you think the inspector will discover who killed Sandy?' Hattie asked as she settled herself down with her coffee.

Matt glanced at Kitty. 'I think he has made some progress today.'

Kitty knew that any progress that had been made was entirely down to her and Matt.

Calliope made a scoffing sound, earning her a severe look from Lady Medford.

'I rather think I should finish the thank you notes for our wedding gifts. If we are to leave on time for France then they need to be completed before we set off.' Lucy looked at her husband.

'Yes, we had better thank everyone for all the toast racks and egg coddlers we seem to have acquired.' Rupert grinned at her. 'Don't strain your eyes though, darling. I'll come and set up a lamp for the desk.'

'I'm going upstairs too. I must admit I feel quite exhausted,' Hattie proclaimed and Kitty's aunt and uncle concurred with her sentiments.

'It really has been the most exhausting few days.' Lady Medford took her husband's arm and bade them goodnight.

Kitty was unsurprised when Calliope and Sinclair each decided that they too had other things to do.

'Well, we don't seem to be terribly popular this evening.' Kitty smiled at Matt. A rumble of thunder growled outside the castle and the shadows inside the drawing room seemed to lengthen as most of the lanterns had been taken.

She was quite glad of Matt's company. The eerie rolling of the thunder echoing around the vast gloomy room was enough to scare even the most level-headed of women. He settled in next to her on the sofa and draped his arm around her shoulders.

'I hope you were not planning to take advantage of our being alone, Captain Bryant?' Kitty couldn't resist teasing even though she was privately quite enjoying this shared intimate moment. If nothing else, the murders had definitely brought them closer together again.

'Miss Underhay, you wound me deeply.' His dark-blue eyes twinkled as he spoke.

He snuck a quick kiss on her cheek and her pulse speeded. She could smell the now familiar bergamot notes of the soap he used and the distinctive masculine odour of his skin.

Kitty made no objection to this display of affection and snuggled into his embrace. 'I must confess it is quite pleasant to have some time away from everyone even if we are in the middle of a murder case again.' Kitty frowned. The case bothered her. There was something missing, something that didn't sit right about the whole business.

Matt sighed and adjusted his arm. 'Why do I suspect your mind is more on murder than romance?'

Kitty giggled. 'I'm sorry, it's just that this business about Evans being killed by mistake is really playing on my mind.'

'You think Evans' murder was deliberate and he was the real target?' Matt asked.

'I think we should consider it. Suppose that during his work Evans had learned something about one of the people here. We know he wanted money for his daughter.' Kitty's frown deepened.

'Blackmail?' Matt suggested. 'But who and why?'

Kitty wriggled into a more upright position. 'Let's go through the possibilities.'

'Well, the most obvious would be Ralston. He's his employer, he's very wealthy and there is more scope to discover something about him than anyone. However Ralston was with Evans when he was killed and the shot was fired from a distance. So unless you think he has an accomplice or paid someone to kill Evans, then he lacks opportunity. I also think that unless he is a much better actor than we give him credit for that physically he couldn't have killed Sandy. The climb to the roof and the rushing around afterwards would be too much,' Matt said.

'I agree, unless of course we consider the accomplice theory or paying someone, which I think seems unlikely.' Kitty could see Matt's point. He had voiced what she herself had been thinking but it felt good to be able to test her ideas out.

'Moira would have been another possibility, but she seems scandal free and while I could see that she would have a motivation for murdering Sandy, I can't see her arranging for the murder of Evans.' Matt looked at Kitty.

'True. Then the next person is Sinclair. We know he is a member of the Blackshirts and is connected with Oswald Mosley. Is there anything there that Evans could have found out and blackmailed him over? Calliope said she and Sinclair were both excellent shots.' Kitty disliked Sinclair's politics but he had seemed quite open about them.

'I don't think that Sinclair is particularly wealthy. Rupert said he had lost a lot of his business connections since he had changed his political beliefs. That might be one of the sources of friction in his marriage,' Matt suggested.

Kitty could see that. 'Calliope does like nice things. Her gowns are all couture and frightfully expensive. Does she come from money?' She couldn't help smiling a little as she heard herself. She sounded like Millicent Craven, her grandmother's busybody friend.

'I don't know. I'm not sure how well Rupert and Lucy know her. Sinclair was always Rupert's friend. Moira and Sandy married about three years ago, so Sinclair and Calliope met at around that time.'

Kitty could see Matt trying to work it all out. 'Calliope could have killed Evans and Sandy, but what could Evans have found out about her?'

'Rupert believes that she is the driving force behind Sinclair's changed beliefs,' Matt said thoughtfully.

'Sinclair always behaves like a man who can't quite believe his luck when they are together. They make an odd couple, don't they? She is so beautiful she could have chosen anyone and Sinclair, well, they don't match.' Sinclair with his receding hairline and mild sheep-like face was a strange choice for the beautiful, if acerbic, Calliope. Kitty wondered if Calliope had been seeing someone else. Could that be what Evans had discovered? But Calliope didn't appear to be the kind of woman who would care about something like that.

'Adalia?' Matt suggested. 'We know that Evans had come across her a few times socially with Aubrey in the course of his employment.'

'Adalia will do anything to protect her son. She wouldn't want anything she may have done wrong to reflect back on Aubrey in case it harmed him or his prospects in some way. She is determined to be respectable,' Kitty mused.

'She had the opportunity to kill both Evans and Sandy, and she admitted taking the gun to the Plume of Feathers.' Matt looked at Kitty.

'I know, it doesn't feel right as a theory though, does it? Perhaps the inspector was right and Evans' death was an accident after all.' Kitty felt unaccountably frustrated by that idea.

Lightning lit up the room and thunder cracked sounding as if it were right above the castle.

Kitty shivered. 'The air is cooling, I've got goosebumps on my arms.'

'Time we went upstairs, I think. We had better take a lantern each.' Matt rose and picked one of last of the coachman style lanterns from the mantel and passed it to Kitty before collecting one for himself.

They walked together along the corridor into the dark, deserted hall. The light from the lanterns flickered across the suits of armour and the vast empty inglenook fireplace.

'Walking through here in the dark almost makes you believe in Lucy's ghost, doesn't it?' Kitty's whisper seemed magnified by the stone of the walls.

'It's definitely quite creepy.' Matt took her hand as they reached the foot of the staircase.

Lightning flashes illuminated the stairs through the small slit windows until they reached the landing with its larger leaded casements. Somewhere to Kitty's left there was a curious rumbling sound followed by a dull thud.

'What was that? That came from inside the castle, not outside?' Kitty's grip tightened around Matt's hand. The pieces of the puzzle were beginning to click into place in her head.

'I think it came from the chapel area.' They moved quietly together towards the chapel entrance. The carved oak door stood open, and Kitty was sure she could hear a scuffling sound from somewhere inside. Something about the sound was furtive and muffled, as if someone didn't wish to be heard.

She gave Matt's fingers a warning squeeze before releasing her hold. He nodded and she knew he had heard the same sounds. He pushed the chapel door open wider and Kitty prayed it wouldn't squeak.

To her surprise, as they entered and raised their lanterns to look around, the chapel was empty. She ventured further inside and peered around to try and see where the sounds might have come from. Matt copied her actions, walking further along the aisle to look into the far corners beyond the altar.

Neither of them spoke, still alert to the possibility that someone could still be lurking somewhere in the shadows. Kitty was about to suggest they give up when she heard it again. A scrabbling noise and the muffled sound of a dog crying.

'That's Muffy,' Kitty whispered, her voice sounding too loud in the empty chapel.

The noises were coming from the back of the chapel near the door where they had entered. Kitty held the lantern nearer to try and locate the source of the sounds. A vast faded tapestry in green and golds covered the wall with a depiction of the story of St Christopher carrying the Christ child across the river.

'It sounded almost as if Muffy were somehow inside the wall.' Matt had joined her.

'Another secret passage or priest hole, perhaps? But how did Muffy get inside?' Kitty started to examine the edge of the tapestry and discovered it hid a section of carved wooden panelling.

Matt began to tap experimentally on sections of the panelling while Kitty held the tapestry to one side.

'Here, this bit sounds hollow, listen.' Matt rapped on it again and Kitty heard what he meant.

She pressed her ear to the wooden panelling. 'There must be a way in.' She could hear Muffy howling from somewhere inside the wall.

'Perhaps she followed someone inside without them noticing and then the door closed and she's trapped in there,' Matt suggested.

Kitty knew Lucy would be devastated if anything happened to her beloved dog. 'We have to get her out.'

She started to feel around the carving searching for any kind of hidden lever that might open a door in the panels.

'Wait, I think I might have it.' Her fingers had detected a small groove at the top of a ledge. She pressed down and the panel clicked open revealing a small narrow entrance way.

'Well done.' Matt held his lantern closer, and Kitty could see a flight of steep stone steps leading down inside the curtain wall of the castle.

Muffy's crying was louder now the door was open. She glanced at Matt and saw a sheen of perspiration on his brow. He hated confined spaces, a legacy of his time in the trenches. He was still haunted by memories of being trapped in the mud with the walls caving in and horses and men drowning, suffocated.

'Stay here, I'll go and see if I can find her. This opening is too small for you.' Impulsively Kitty darted forward before he had time to object.

The space was scarcely wide enough to allow her inside and she was forced to duck her head until she had gone down the first few steps. She heard Matt urging her to return but Muffy's squeaky howls of distress urged her forward. She hoped the little dog wasn't injured. It would be easy to fall on these steps especially in the darkness.

The passage appeared to follow the gentle curve of the castle wall and before long she was walking along a flat passageway barely the width of her shoulders. Even with the aid of her lantern it was hard to see what might be ahead of her.

Matt's voice had faded now, and she hoped he wouldn't attempt to follow her. It would be far better if he remained in the chapel and kept the door open. She had no desire to become trapped between the castle walls.

Muffy's cries became louder, and Kitty guessed she must be close to wherever the little dog might be. The flame inside the glass lantern flickered and Kitty hoped it was not about to go out. If it did her situation would be perilous indeed, imprisoned in the inky blackness.

She kept edging her way forward and eventually she felt the stir of air on her face. The blackness started to lighten, and she could smell the rain-drenched earth. The storm was louder too with ominous growls of thunder.

There was another scent, stale, smoky and burned. The destroyed wing of the castle. Was this the route the so-called ghost had taken? Finally, she emerged into what remained of a room. The centre of the floor had been burned away but the boards around the edges remained.

To her relief she spotted Muffy sitting whimpering in a corner on the opposite side of the room.

'Hold on, girl, I'm coming to get you.' She could see the little dog was shivering and bedraggled but Muffy made no move towards her.

Kitty held up her light and looked to see if she could edge her way safely around to retrieve the dog. It looked as if it were possible if she kept to the walls and watched her footing.

She decided as she set off that the next time she went down a secret tunnel she would ensure she was not wearing an evening gown. Especially when it was one of her best ones. Alice would be furious when she saw the state of this one.

The wind gusted through the empty window frames and she tasted the rain on her lips. Kitty was forced to move more slowly than she would have liked. The boards creaked under her weight and she gingerly tested each one as she went to ensure it was sound. She had no desire to plummet down into the cavernous blackness of the burned-out ballroom below.

As she drew closer, she could see Muffy was next to a closed door beside what had once been a small, ornate iron radiator. The dog grew more excited as she approached and tried scrabbling on the boards with her front paws as if trying to reach her.

'Wait, stay there. Good girl.' Kitty edged the last few feet and bent over the little dog to see what was wrong. How had Muffy managed to get out here? Had she followed someone?

Her worst fears were confirmed as she examined Muffy's collar. Someone had tied a thin cord around it and had secured the dog to the radiator preventing her from moving. Her fingers were cold and refused to obey her as she fumbled with the rope. Kitty's heart raced. Discovering Muffy like this could mean only one thing. Someone else was out here in the shell of the ruined wing.

CHAPTER TWENTY-TWO

Kitty fussed the top of the little dog's damp head and realised she had a dilemma on her hands. Muffy's big brown eyes looked up expectantly at her and her stumpy tail wagged happily at the sight of a familiar face. She stopped trying to undo the knot.

If she released Muffy she would have to hope the dog would be able to safely navigate her way back around the damaged floor and up through the tunnel in the dark to the chapel. If she tried to hold on to Muffy using the rope as a leash the dog could easily send them both onto the floor below.

How had the dog managed to get out here? Kitty's hair was becoming plastered to her head with the rain sheeting in through the open roof and damaged windows. So far there was no sign of anyone else having come that way.

Kitty swallowed hard. Was she brave enough to try the door beside Muffy to see if there was a safer route back into the castle? Her teeth chattered as she straightened and tried the door handle.

The light from her lantern danced and flickered as she opened the door. She was surprised to find another room, relatively undamaged by the fire. The floor at least appeared intact and a large portion of the ceiling. Tattered remnants of curtains fluttered wildly in the window frames and what appeared to be a large mahogany wardrobe stood in the far corner.

Her breath stilled in her throat. Another lantern stood on the floor next to the wardrobe. Kneeling before it, intent on recovering whatever had been stored inside, was a figure wearing a hooded black cloak. Whoever it was must be Lucy's ghost.

The pounding of the rain and the noise of the thunder meant that whoever was there hadn't heard Kitty open the door. She glanced around her looking for some kind of weapon. This person could be harmless, or it could be the same person who had already murdered both Evans and Sandy. Whatever they were up to, Kitty was certain it was something no one else was meant to see.

To her dismay there was absolutely nothing to hand that she could use. She toyed with slipping back out and reclosing the door reasoning that she and Muffy would have to take their chances in the fire-damaged room. Even as the thought crossed her mind however the figure turned their head and saw her.

Kitty froze in place as whoever it was tucked something inside their robes and advanced towards her carrying the light. With the darkness of the room and the shadow of the hood falling across their face it wasn't until they were closer that she realised who it was.

'Calliope! What are you doing out here?' Even as she spoke, she realised how foolish her question sounded.

The other woman had changed from her evening attire into some kind of trousers under the long robe. Her beautiful face was stony as she looked at Kitty.

'I could ask you the same question, Miss Underhay. Dear me, you look like a drowned rat. I take it you're poking your nose in everyone's affairs again?' Her tone was not exactly friendly and even wearing her evening shoes Kitty was at a distinct height disadvantage.

'I came to find Muffy. I heard her crying and thought she had somehow become trapped in a passageway. What are you doing here?' Kitty asked again.

Calliope's kohl-lined eyes glittered in the dim light. 'I came to collect something that belongs to me. That stupid mutt of Lucy's followed me into the passage. I tied her up to keep her out of the way. I decided that by the time they found her in the morning I would be long gone.'

'Just you? Or both you and Sinclair?' Kitty asked.

Calliope's mocking laughter was swallowed up in a clap of thunder. 'My dear Miss Underhay, why on earth would I wish to take Sinclair with me? He has fulfilled all his uses to me now.'

'Did he kill Evans or was that just you?' Kitty's pulse raced and she edged backwards slightly so her hand was on the handle of the door behind her.

Something metallic gleamed in Calliope's free hand. A chill ran along Kitty's spine when she recognised the long slim blade of a stiletto knife.

'Now you're disappointing me, Miss Underhay. I was so sure earlier this evening that you had started to work it all out. Why would poor dumb Sinclair do anything? He was simply my alibi and my passport to meet the people I needed to meet for the good of the cause.'

Kitty's hands shook at the look on Calliope's face. 'Was that why Evans died? It wasn't an accident, was it? You intended to murder him. Had he discovered something that he wasn't supposed to know?' If she could keep Calliope talking perhaps Matt would either come down the passage and find her or raise the alarm and get help.

Calliope's mouth stretched in a humourless scarlet smile. 'Evans was spying on Sandy as per dear Ralston's instructions. That was how he discovered that Sandy had been – how shall we put it – assisting me? Passing on a few pieces of useful information from the cabinet meetings. So helpful to know things ahead of time.'

'I presume Evans tried blackmailing you? He wanted money for his daughter.' Kitty tried to hear if any help might be coming over the continued noise of the storm.

Calliope admired the silvery blade of her knife in the lamplight. 'Better, Miss Underhay. Yes, he wanted money, so I had to get rid of him. He had tried blackmailing me and sending anonymous letters to Sandy hinting at what he knew. Sandy was quite rattled so I told him that I would deal with the problem. It would no doubt have only been a short matter of time before Ralston would have discovered what was going on.'

Muffy had clearly grown tired of waiting for Kitty to return and began to howl again.

'How did you persuade Sandy to help you? I presume he did not do so willingly or you would have had no reason to kill him?' Kitty hoped that with all the noise Calliope wouldn't hear the tremor in her voice.

Calliope's smile widened. 'I see I was right not to underestimate you, Miss Underhay. I had a little insurance on Sandy. Some indiscreet photographs and a whole pile of debts that Moira would never agree to pay if she found out about them. A politician has to be quite careful and with his promotion Sandy had started to develop a conscience. He told me it had to stop. After the wedding he would no longer be able to assist me. I had thought Evans' death might persuade him to continue but instead he was rapidly becoming a liability. It was all terribly inconvenient.'

Kitty ran her tongue over lips that had become dry as she'd listened to Calliope's matter-of-fact recital of her crimes. 'I suppose you couldn't believe your luck when Adalia found the gun after you had hidden it in the vase?'

'I had intended to dispose of it in the moat but thought it might be useful to divert suspicion elsewhere at some point should that fool Lewis prove to be smarter than I had anticipated. And then the nitwit arrested Mr Whitlock even though the man is clearly as blind as a bat and I hoped the issue might be resolved without my having to do anything.' Calliope rolled her eyes as Muffy's howls reached a crescendo. 'That wretched noisy dog! I should have dispatched her when she first followed me into the passageway, she'll rouse the house if she keeps that racket up.' She flexed her hand around the knife.

'You can't hurt Muffy!' Kitty moved to completely block the door, her heart racing in terror.

'Please do not get in my way, Miss Underhay. You appear to have forgotten that I also need to rid myself of you.' Calliope went to take a step forward.

'Matt is waiting for me in the chapel. He saw me come down the passage and he knows that Muffy is here too. He or Rupert could be here at any minute.' Kitty was aware she was gabbling but she was determined to save Lucy's beloved pet.

'There is more than one way out of this part of the castle. My dear husband was very useful showing me all of his childhood haunts and hiding places. Perhaps an accident for you and the dog might be the best solution.' Calliope lunged towards Kitty with the knife blade extended.

Kitty flung open the door that was at her back and stepped smartly to the side. Calliope was taken off balance by the unexpected move and dropped her lantern, extinguishing the flame. She whirled around in the doorway to face Kitty but discovered she had been pre-empted. Kitty had moved away from the door towards the wardrobe on the far side hoping there might be something there she could use as a weapon.

Kitty had abandoned her own lantern as she ran across the floorboards praying they were as sturdy as they appeared. That lamp too was now extinguished leaving the room in virtual darkness with only the flashes of lightning from the storm outside to offer brief moments of illumination.

Calliope recovered her wits and advanced on Kitty, knife extended. The wardrobe was of the old-fashioned solid kind and

Kitty had little hope of finding something useful but there was nothing else in the room.

The doors had been left open and she spotted the rail that had once supported the clothes hangers. More in desperation than expectation she grabbed it and tugged. To her surprise it was the kind that rested on two small brass cups rather than being fixed in place, so it came away in her hand.

Kitty grasped the wooden pole with both hands holding it up in front of her as she faced her assailant.

'Why not just get out of here, Calliope? Make your escape?' Kitty yelled above the noise of the storm.

'And leave a witness? Never.' The hood had fallen back on Calliope's cloak and Kitty caught a glimpse of the determination in her dark eyes as the lightning flashed.

The two women circled one another. Calliope occasionally lashing out with the wicked-looking blade and Kitty preparing to smack the rod in her hands down on her assailant's head if she had the opportunity.

Calliope lunged forward, the blade nicked Kitty's arm and blood started to run down onto her hand. The sight seemed to amuse Calliope and she smiled evilly at Kitty. Somewhere in the distance above the noise of the thunder Kitty thought she could hear something else.

'First blood to me,' Calliope called.

Kitty had hardly felt the wound. She was more annoyed that the woman had caught her.

Suddenly there was a scrabbling noise and Muffy's barks grew louder as the little dog rushed into the room. Excited to see people she rushed at Calliope, taking her by surprise. With her opponent momentarily off guard Kitty brought the pole down onto the other woman's head with as much force as she could muster. She was terrified that Calliope might turn her knife on Muffy.

Calliope dropped her knife and attempted to kick out at the dog. Kitty took her chance to hit her once more. This time the force was too much for the ancient piece of wood and it broke in her hands.

Kitty threw the pieces away and looked around for Calliope's knife. The other woman was on her hands and knees, shaking her head as Muffy danced around her trying to lick her face, clearly convinced this was all some kind of mad game.

The knife had skittered away across the boards back towards the door that Kitty and Muffy had used to enter the room. Calliope appeared to sight it at the same time as Kitty and lunged towards it.

The other woman's height advantage won her the race and Kitty found herself once more facing the wicked point of Calliope's weapon. Muffy had become distracted by the wood Kitty had thrown down and was now ignoring them as she sniffed her new prize.

'You little witch.' Calliope advanced on Kitty, murderous intent in her eyes.

Kitty took a step back away from Calliope through the open door and prayed the burned boards would take her weight and she wouldn't step back into thin air.

Calliope's crimson lips thinned into a grim smile and she lunged forward once more. Knowing she had little choice, Kitty flung herself sideways towards the radiator where Muffy had been tied just a few moments before. As Calliope moved forwards the toe of her shoe appeared to catch in the hem of her long black cloak and she stumbled. The momentum of her weight carried her forwards and onto the edge of the missing floorboards.

Kitty could only watch as the scorched boards cracked under her weight and the woman plummeted from sight. Kitty closed her eyes and winced as she heard the sickeningly soft thud of Calliope landing on the stone flags of the floor below.

Muffy came trotting to the doorway, a broken piece of the rod in her mouth, wagging her tail happily.

'Muffy, stay there.' Kitty held onto the radiator to pull herself upright against the wall. Her heart was racing, and her palms were clammy with both sweat and the blood that was still trickling from the cut on her arm.

'Kitty!'

She looked across the ruined room to see Matt emerging from the tunnel holding a lantern.

'Stay there. The floor is unsafe. Calliope has fallen,' she shouted a warning. She couldn't begin to imagine the courage it had taken for him to force himself to travel through that dark, narrow tunnel to come and find her.

'Help is on the way. Rupert is coming with the keys to unlock the other side.'

Kitty could have collapsed with relief. She caught hold of the rope fragment that was still attached to Muffy's collar, determined the dog wouldn't fall. She could hear more voices now and shouts mixed with the sound of motor vehicles rumbling into the courtyard.

*

Matt remained at the end of the tunnel until he saw lights appear behind Kitty and Rupert emerge to help her through the doorway back to the relative safety of the other room.

Relief that she was safe washed through him and assuaged some of the nausea that had consumed him as he had made his way through that tortuous passage to reach her. He had alerted Rupert as soon as she had gone from sight knowing that he would know where the passageway ended.

Alarmed by the idea that whoever had entered the tunnel was most likely the killer, Rupert had also telephoned the police station at Ripon and roused a belligerent Inspector Lewis from his slumbers.

Rupert had then taken his keys and crossed the courtyard to enter the ruined wing from the other end while Matt had returned to the passage entrance in the chapel. His concern for Kitty's safety had overridden his horror at having to enter the passage and he had forced himself to make his way in the darkness to try and find her.

The same fear he had felt only a few weeks earlier when he had discovered her body limp and unresponsive in her crashed motor car filled him once more. Rising alongside it was a cold tide of anger. It was all very well Kitty demanding her right to determine her own destiny and actions. She kept reminding him that she was a modern, independent woman, but not when it meant that those who cared about her, loved her, had to watch and worry.

If anything had happened to her, he would have never stopped blaming himself for failing to prevent her from entering the passageway. It had taken him years to get over the sense of having failed his wife and daughter when they had been killed during the war. Could he go through all of that again if anything happened to Kitty?

His hand automatically went to his coat pocket and he fingered the small burgundy leatherette covered jeweller's box that nestled there. The box his aunt had slipped into his hand after she had met Kitty and given her approval.

More lights appeared, shining up through the vast hole of the ruined floor and he heard men's voices calling instructions. Kitty said Calliope had fallen. He estimated the drop had to be between fifteen and twenty feet, possibly more, onto the unyielding stone floor below. The sprung hardwood dance floor of the ballroom that had once covered the flags having all been destroyed in the fire.

Matt waited until the last glimmer of the pale-blue satin of Kitty's evening gown had gone from his view. The storm was finally beginning to die away with the gap between the lightning and thunder growing longer and the sound more distant.

He paused for a moment to gather his courage knowing that he had little choice but to return to the chapel via the passage as it would be foolhardy to make his way around the walls. At least on his return he knew what he was walking towards and that Kitty was safe.

CHAPTER TWENTY-THREE

Kitty was glad of Rupert's strong arm around her waist as he led both her and Muffy to safety back through another burned out room and down a narrow stone staircase to the courtyard. Servants and policemen were scurrying about carrying lanterns and torches.

'Calliope?' Kitty asked.

Rupert shook his head, his expression grave. 'I fear there will not be much hope with a fall from that height onto the flagstones. The police are in there now.' He glanced towards the doorway leading into the former ballroom and Kitty could see a cluster of figures gathered around a dark form on the floor.

Shock set in at her own narrow escape and she started to tremble.

'You're bleeding. Come, let us get back inside and we can attend to your arm.' Rupert supported her as they made their way back into the castle hallway and on into the drawing room. More lanterns had been set up and a confused and frowsy young maid was busy at the fireplace.

Kitty was deposited gently on the end of the sofa and Lucy appeared dressed in her night attire bearing blankets, a worried expression on her face.

'Kitty darling, are you all right? Oh, your arm, you've been hurt.'

The fire having been lit, Lucy dispatched the maid to find the first-aid tin so she could examine and dress Kitty's wound. Muffy, delighted to see her mistress again bounced about happily wagging her tail.

Matt entered the drawing room just as Lucy was winding a bandage around Kitty's arm.

'What happened?' He looked at Kitty and she saw his face was still pale with the shock of the night's adventures.

'She tried to kill me with a knife. It's all right. I'm not really hurt, it's just a small nick.' Kitty could see from the set of his shoulders that he was angry, and she guessed that a portion of that anger had to be directed at herself.

'It's fine, Matt. I've dressed it and the wound is quite small. Let me get you both a brandy. You've had the most horrible time.' Lucy glanced at Matt and Kitty knew her cousin had seen his expression.

He took a seat at the other end of the sofa and she tried not to cry at the gap he had put between them.

Lucy handed them both a balloon-shaped glass with a generous measure of brandy inside.

'Take a sip, Kitty dear,' Lucy urged, her dark eyes anxious in her small, pale face.

Kitty forced herself to obey her cousin even though she still felt nauseous from her experience in the ruined wing. Her teeth chattered on the rim of the glass and the fiery liquid made her cough.

Rupert re-entered the room and she could tell by the grim look in his eyes that Calliope was indeed dead.

'I have asked for the house to be roused. Inspector Lewis will be joining us shortly.' Rupert placed his arm around Lucy's waist.

'Sinclair?' Kitty asked.

'Inspector Lewis is speaking to him before he joins us.' Rupert turned his head as the drawing room door opened and the rest of the house party clad in their dressing gowns began to file inside.

'What's happened?' Hattie, her hair tied up in curling rags plumped herself down next to Lucy.

Kitty's aunt and uncle followed accompanied by Ralston, his complexion an unhealthy grey at being woken. Moira, red eyed and bewildered slipped in after him. Aubrey also appeared accompanied by Adalia who seemed to have the remnants of cold cream around the edges of her face.

'Whatever is happening? The noise and lights woke us.' Adalia glared at Rupert as if she held him personally responsible for her disturbed night. Kitty presumed that Daisy had remained in bed.

'Inspector Lewis should be joining us shortly and then I think Kitty and Matt will explain what has happened.' Rupert's gaze travelled over them both.

Adalia suddenly appeared to realise that Kitty was not only still in her evening gown but was also soaking wet. She opened her mouth to speak, only to close it again as the inspector entered, accompanied by a shaken-looking Sinclair and a uniformed constable.

Sinclair was escorted to a chair with the police constable standing next to him. Kitty thought he appeared in more need of brandy than she or Matt given that presumably he had just learned that his wife was dead.

Inspector Lewis stood in front of the fireplace, his hands behind his back as he rocked self-importantly up onto his toes as he surveyed them all.

'I regret to inform you all that Mrs Calliope Davies is dead, killed by a fall in the damaged wing of the castle.'

There was a horrified gasp from the group and people turned in their seats to look at Sinclair, who was holding his head in his hands. His face was ashen, and Kitty feared he was about to collapse.

Lucy jumped from her seat and hastily poured another glass of brandy and pressed it into his hand.

'Catherine, my wife's name was really Catherine. She just preferred Calliope as she thought it fitted her better,' Sinclair murmured before taking a restorative sip.

'I am more interested in what she was doing in that part of the castle and why she had confidential government documents concealed about her person.' The inspector reached inside his trench coat and pulled out a manilla folder stamped with red lettering and a black government symbol. He waved the file in the air and glared at Sinclair.

Kitty could see her uncle's complexion had turned puce at the sight of the folder, knowing all too well what it implied.

'Calliope, that is Catherine, was responsible for both the murder of Mr Evans and for Sandy Galsworthy,' Kitty said.

Everyone except Sinclair, who appeared uninterested, turned their attention back towards Kitty.

The inspector glowered at her. 'Perhaps you would care to enlighten us, Miss Underhay.'

Kitty glanced at Matt who gave her a small nod of encouragement and plunged into her story. Lucy cried and hugged Muffy to her when Kitty told them of what had happened in the ruins.

'So Calliope was my ghost? She must have been meeting Sandy to receive that file and to hide it.' Lucy lifted a tear-streaked face from Muffy's damp fur. Lady Medford looked concerned as Lucy quickly explained her request to Kitty to find the truth behind the figure and lights she had seen in the ruined wing.

'I thought I had seen the nun's ghost,' Lucy said.

'I think they exchanged the file in the ruins and Calliope left it in there for safe keeping, intending to retrieve it when she was ready to leave,' Kitty said.

'She knew none of the staff would try and go there because of the ghost.' Rupert nodded.

'And it wouldn't be searched after Evans and Sandy's murders as it was deemed too dangerous for anyone to enter that part of the castle,' Matt said.

'Did you know about this?' Moira jumped up from her seat and turned on Sinclair. Her hands were balled into fists and her voice was icy.

Sinclair lifted his head and Kitty stifled a gasp. In the few minutes since Calliope's death had been confirmed Sinclair looked like a dead man.

'Catherine was an expert shot and I knew she always carried a gun in her luggage. I asked her about it once and she laughed and said she had been in some tricky situations in the past. It was for her protection.' He gave a slight shrug. 'She was so beautiful. Men approached her all the time, it seemed reasonable to me. I couldn't always be there to protect her.'

Kitty considered Sinclair would have been an unlikely protector for Calliope, but she supposed that wearing his wedding ring might have deterred some men from pursuing her. She saw the Adam's apple bob in his long skinny neck as he swallowed nervously.

'I saw the gun was missing after Evans was killed and I knew Calliope must have been outside the castle that afternoon. That was when I started to suspect that the information she had been receiving to help our cause may have come from Sandy. Calliope was my wife, what was I to do?'

'You could have come forward. Told Inspector Lewis that Calliope owned a gun. Then Sandy, oh, Sandy…' Moira broke down sobbing and Ralston placed his arm tenderly around his daughter's shoulders and led her back to her seat.

'Did you know about the blackmail? How Calliope was obtaining information from Sandy?' Rupert asked, looking at his former friend.

Sinclair's gaze locked with Rupert's. 'I knew she was getting information, but I didn't know how or from whom. Not until Evans was killed. I knew Sandy would never have given her the information willingly, but I didn't know if she had intended to kill Evans or Sandy.'

'She said you were both excellent shots,' Kitty said.

Sinclair nodded. 'That was what made me believe Evans had been her intended target after all. I asked her and she said he had tried to blackmail her. That he wanted money and, well, sexual favours from her.'

Kitty could see from Sinclair's expression that he had believed Calliope's story. 'You felt he had deserved to die?'

'She was so beautiful, the thought of that man wanting to sully her.' Sinclair paused for another gulp of brandy. 'When I first met Catherine, she was the one who introduced the ideas to me. She was dedicated to bringing about change to the political system in this country. She had seen what was happening in Austria and Germany and other places. It opened my eyes. She did what she did for the cause.' Sinclair's voice had taken on a different tone and his eyes held the same fanatical gleam Kitty had seen in Calliope's gaze.

Rupert turned away in disgust. 'I am ashamed at ever having counted you as my friend.'

Sinclair went to stand, and the constable placed a meaty hand on his shoulder gently pressing him back in place.

'You are mistaken, Rupert old boy, this is the future.' Sinclair's voice held a hint of appeal but Rupert ignored him.

Lord Medford scowled and Kitty was positive she heard her uncle emit a growling noise from the back of his throat.

'You gave your wife an alibi for Mr Galsworthy's murder.' Inspector Lewis blew out his cheeks clearly affronted that Sinclair had lied to him.

'She was my wife, Inspector.' Sinclair had subsided back onto his chair looking for all the world like a balloon with the air let out.

'Disgusting.' Adalia pursed her lips disapprovingly.

'Madam, you were hardly forthright in this matter yourself,' Inspector Lewis rebuked her.

Adalia's cheeks turned crimson, and Aubrey blinked at her owlishly through his glasses.

'Mother?'

'Never mind, Aubrey,' Adalia snapped.

The constable responded to Inspector Lewis' nod and escorted Sinclair from the room.

'We shall be questioning Mr Davies further. After all it may be that he has committed offences under the official secrets act as well as aiding and abetting murder.' The inspector puffed out his chest, reminding Kitty of a self-important pigeon.

The shock from earlier had worn off. Her arm had begun to sting and she was cold and damp under the woollen blankets her cousin had piled around her.

'Yes, well, thank you, Inspector. I presume you will return later to take Miss Underhay and Captain Bryant's statements?' Rupert was already escorting the policeman to the door.

Once he had gone from the room her aunt took charge.

'Kitty, you look all in, my dear. A bath and bed for you.'

Kitty was bone weary. She was not about to put up an argument. Matt rose and offered her his arm.

'I'll see you up the stairs.' She accepted his offer even though she could tell he was still cross with her. Everyone else began to move, talking amongst themselves as they did so. As she left the room, she noticed Hattie move to assist Ralston and Moira.

She leaned on Matt's arm to walk through the dark hall and up the stairs, the blankets Lucy had provided still draped around her shoulders. All she wanted now were some clean dry clothes and her bed.

They called goodnight to the others as Matt took her to the door of her room where he halted.

'I'll see you in the morning, Kitty, when you've had some sleep.' His tone was grave.

She lifted her chin so she could see his expression in the dim light provided by the lamps the servants had placed at various points along the corridor.

'Please don't be cross with me, Matt.' Her eyes filled with tears as she spoke. 'I…'

He bent his head and his lips brushed hers. 'Go to bed, Kitty.'

He opened the door and Alice appeared, sleepy-eyed, wrapped in her dressing gown.

'Miss Kitty, whatever has gone on?'

'I'll leave her in your capable hands, Alice.' Matt released her and nodded goodnight to her maid before striding away towards his own room.

CHAPTER TWENTY-FOUR

Kitty remembered little else of that night. Alice bathed her, stuffed her into her pyjamas and tucked her into bed with a hot water bottle and a scolding before she had time to blink.

When she woke she had no idea of the time except her room was lighter than usual and she was hungry.

'About time you was astirring, Miss Kitty. That wretched policeman has sent three messages up already asking if you was awake.' Alice's anxious eyes looked into hers.

'What time is it?' Kitty frowned and tried to look for her clock.

'Almost lunchtime, miss.' Alice bustled about the room getting her things ready. 'I heard all what happened last night with that Mrs Davies having that terrible fall.'

Kitty tried to push herself up in her bed wincing as she took her weight on her injured arm. 'Ouch.'

Alice tutted. 'I think I'd best have a look under that bandage, miss. You might need a spot of iodine on that cut.'

There was a knock at the door and Alice went to see who was there as Kitty struggled into her dressing gown.

'Kitty darling, are you all right? I've bought up some tea.' Lucy popped her head around the door.

Alice held the door open for Lucy to enter.

'I'm fine, really. I must confess I've only just woken up.'

Her cousin placed a tea tray across Kitty's knees and perched herself like a pretty, petite, brunette pixie on the end of the bed.

'The inspector is downstairs. He's interviewed Matt and is waiting to see you. He's annoying everyone. Papa keeps making noises about his shotgun.' Lucy grinned impishly. 'Thank you for saving Muffy.'

Kitty drank her tea, savouring the drink. 'I couldn't let Calliope hurt your dog.' She frowned. 'I can't think of her as Catherine. That was quite a revelation, wasn't it?'

'Well, according to Inspector Lewis, she had good reason to change her name. He's done some digging in the police files. Before she married Sinclair, she was Catherine Earnshaw and had quite a record of misdemeanours. It seems that she escaped abroad and reinvented herself as Calliope. She had any number of liaisons with several very wealthy and important men before she met and married Sinclair.' Lucy's eyes widened as she told Kitty all she had missed from the morning's news.

'Have you seen much of Matt this morning?' Kitty asked. She knew Lucy had said he had been interviewed by the inspector, but she wondered if he had spoken to her cousin at all.

A pretty pink colour mounted on Lucy's cheeks. 'He saw the inspector and then he was closeted with Rupert and Papa in the study for an hour. I haven't spoken to him myself yet.'

Alice stepped forward to relieve Kitty of the tea tray. 'Excuse me for interrupting, Miss Lucy, but you'd best get a wiggle on, Miss Kitty, or you'll be late for lunch and we'll never get rid of that inspector.'

Lucy jumped off the bed. 'Gracious, yes, thank you, Alice. I'll see you downstairs shortly, Kitty.'

Kitty dressed with aid from Alice and subjected her wounded arm to her friend's ministrations with the iodine.

''Tis better safe than sorry, you were lucky as she didn't do you a worse mischief,' Alice remarked as she re-corked the bottle and packed away her small first-aid kit.

'I know. I was so concerned that Muffy may have been trapped or hurt in the passageway that I didn't stop and think things through. I knew Matt would have gone into the tunnel and I knew what it would have cost him to do so.' Kitty looked at her friend for understanding.

Alice bit her lip. ''Tis maybe not my place to say, miss, but Captain Bryant was terribly upset when you was nearly killed in your motor car a few weeks ago and you had that big row last summer about you putting yourself in harm's way. It seems to me that you might have wounded his pride, miss.'

Kitty sighed. 'I'm rather afraid you may be right, Alice, and I think I have some fences to mend. I can't apologise for wishing to be treated as an equal partner in all of our adventures, but I should have been more thoughtful and evaluated the risks first.'

The maid smiled at her. 'I'm sure if you tell him that he'll understand, miss. 'Tis only that he cares about you.'

'I hope you're right. Things have felt a bit out of kilter ever since the crash and everything that happened at Elm House. Then with meeting his aunt here at the wedding, well, I don't know if she approved of me.' Kitty had not been at all certain about the outcome of her interview with Matt's aunt Euphemia.

She knew Matt's parents were not convinced of her suitability as a prospective future wife for Matt. Then again, they had heartily disapproved of his first marriage too.

Alice looked indignant at Kitty's statement. 'How could she not approve of you, miss? You'm of good character, financially stable, hardworking and pretty. What more does she want?'

Her friend's spirited testimony as to her good points brought the smile back to her face and she arrived in the main hall just as the gong was sounded for lunch. Hattie and Lady Medford were just leaving the drawing room when Kitty caught them up.

'How are you feeling, Kitty dear?' her aunt asked as she scrutinised Kitty's complexion. 'Fully recovered from the shenanigans of last night?'

'Yes, thank you. I'm relieved the whole affair is over.' Kitty was surprised to find Lucy in the dining room alone with no sign of Rupert, Matt or Lord Medford.

'Are the gentlemen not joining us?' Hattie asked as she took her seat at the table.

Kitty saw Lucy exchange a glance with Lady Medford.

'No, they have gone into Ripon with Inspector Lewis. Moira is packing and has requested a tray and the same goes for Ralston,' Lucy explained.

Something was clearly afoot. Kitty placed her linen napkin across her lap and waited until the watercress soup had been served.

'Do we know what business has called everyone to Ripon?' she asked.

'Something to do with the case, I believe. Those documents that were recovered from Calliope.' Lucy glanced at her mother as if seeking reassurance for her statement.

'I understand that Adalia is packing too.' Hattie's eyes sparkled with mischief.

'Yes, it seems that some urgent affair calls her home,' Lady Medford remarked drily.

'How is Daisy today?' Kitty was concerned for her friend. The past few days had been very stressful, especially for someone in a delicate condition.

'Aubrey said she was recovering well and feeling much better this morning.' Lucy placed her spoon down in the empty dish.

'I'm sure her recovery will be much helped once Adalia is safely aboard the train.' Hattie beamed at them all.

The rest of the meal passed in pleasant conversation about Lucy and Rupert's travel plans and suggestions of local beauty spots for Matt and Kitty to explore during the remainder of their stay.

After lunch was concluded everyone went about their business. Lady Medford accompanied Lucy to oversee the packing of her trousseau. Hattie decided to see Moira and Ralston before stopping in at the gatehouse to visit Daisy.

Kitty was filled with restless energy. She wished she knew why the men had all decamped to Ripon. She still had to give her statement to the inspector and now she was finally downstairs the wretched man had departed for town.

The storm's aftermath had left behind a bright clear day with blue sky and the earth smelling fresh and green in the sunshine. When the others enquired about her plans for the afternoon Kitty declared her intention to go for a walk to the folly. She wanted fresh air and felt the need to escape the confines of the castle.

She set off shortly afterwards accompanied by Muffy who trotted happily ahead of her, tail in the air and head down sniffing at the grass. There were a few puddles on the path, but most were drying quite quickly in the warmth of the sun. The birds chirped from the trees lining the side of the path and butterflies fluttered along before her. An occasional dragonfly skittered across the river and Kitty found her spirits starting to settle.

She reached the folly and spent a contented half an hour with Muffy rambling about the ruins before stopping to sit on a low stone wall for a rest. In the peace and quiet of the pretty countryside it was hard to believe that two brutal murders and a death had occurred in such a place.

Kitty closed her eyes and tipped her head back enjoying the feel of the sun on her face. How long she stayed like that she wasn't certain. It was only the sound of Muffy barking in delighted recognition of someone approaching that roused her back to the present.

She shaded her eyes with her hand and peered along the path. Her heart lifted as she saw Muffy's plump, ridiculous body race towards Matt's tall, tweed-clad frame. The dog gambolled about at his feet and he bent to fuss her before sending her trotting back along the trail to where Kitty was sitting.

Matt raised his hand in greeting and made his way towards her. Kitty's pulse kicked up a notch.

'What ho, your aunt said I would find you here.' He took a seat on the wall beside her stretching his long legs out in front of him.

'I needed to get away from the castle for a while.' Kitty turned her head to look at him.

She was a little surprised when he drew his silver cigarette case from his pocket and lit up. Matt rarely smoked now, usually only when he was troubled by something or when he was under some kind of stress.

'Lucy said you had all gone into Ripon with Inspector Lewis. Is he waiting for me to give a statement?' Kitty asked.

Matt shook his head. 'It has been decided that there is no need.'

'Oh?' Kitty was shocked. 'What has gone on?'

Matt flicked some ash to the side of where he was seated. 'Lord Medford and Rupert have been speaking to someone at the Home Office. The story of Sandy's death has not yet broken in the press.'

Kitty frowned. 'What of Sinclair? Is he to be charged with anything? What is happening?' It was clear that whilst she had been dressing for lunch something had occurred to make the inspector change his mind about taking her statement. Her uncle had also become involved in the case too.

Matt finished his cigarette and screwed out the butt on the ground with the toe of his shoe. 'Sinclair is dead.'

Kitty stared at him, speechless for a moment.

'He was found in his cell hanging from a noose he had fashioned from his shirt. He left a note saying he no longer wished to live without Calliope.'

Nausea swept through Kitty and she pressed a trembling hand to her mouth. 'That's dreadful.'

'The powers that be have determined to let it be known that Sandy met with an unfortunate accident and that Calliope and Sinclair took their own lives after being responsible for accidentally causing the death of Mr Evans. The government wish to avoid any kind of scandal that may be attached to the discovery of Calliope's possession of confidential material. They have determined to rewrite history.'

Kitty was silent after hearing Matt's matter-of-fact summary.

'Sandy gets to keep his political reputation intact and thus that of Ramsay MacDonald's government. No shame will attach to Moira and there is a chance that they may be able to discover who Calliope's political contacts were.'

Muffy returned to snuffle around Kitty's feet as she blew out a breath. 'Of course with my uncle's presence here and as Rupert is now his son-in-law, I suppose it is for the best.' The idea of a cover-up did not sit easily with her, however, and she knew that Matt felt the same way.

'That's it then now. Rupert and Lucy can go on their honeymoon. Ralston and Moira are leaving for London.' He glanced at Kitty.

'Even Adalia is finally making her farewells.' She flashed a small smile at him.

The air around them seemed to suddenly become very still. Muffy now clearly bored wandered off to investigate a clump of dandelions in the nearby hedgerow.

'I suppose that just leaves the matter of us to be resolved.' Matt's blue eyes darkened, and Kitty thought her heart was about to fly out of her chest.

Was this to be it? Finally, had she pushed him too far?

Kitty couldn't bring herself to speak. Instead, she waited, determined that she was not about to allow Matt to throw away what they had together without a fight.

Matt looked down at his shoes. 'When I met you and Alice at the station in Torquay to see you both off, I was talking afterwards with Robert Potter.'

Kitty's brows drew together in a frown. This was not the start to the conversation that she had anticipated.

'Oh?' She was surprised her voice was audible her throat felt so constricted with anxiety.

Matt shuffled his feet on the path and a fine layer of dust from the newly dried mud coated the toes of his brown-leather brogues.

'Then you will recall when I arrived here I received the note from my aunt Euphemia.'

Kitty's spirits that had started to bubble with a fragment of hope immediately took a dive. She wondered how these two pieces of information were connected.

'Yes.'

Her one-word responses didn't seem to bother Matt and he plunged on regardless.

'After she had spoken with you, she came to find me before she left the reception.'

'I remember.' Kitty recalled that scene of Matt bending so the elderly woman could say something to him and his hand going to his pocket.

His mouth tilted up slightly at the corners. 'She observed that you were, in her words, an independent young miss and that if I wished to keep you then I must be prepared for all that it would mean.'

Kitty's eyes widened in surprise.

'She assured me that while we would probably not always agree, if we made a life together then it would not be boring.' Matt's expression had grown solemn once more.

'Oh.' Kitty was at a loss for words. This conversation was not the one she had been expecting after the events of the night.

'She also gave me something.' Matt's gaze locked with hers and he slipped down from his place on the wall to go down on bended knee before her in the dust. A small jeweller's box was open in his hand and Kitty saw a ring, sparkling in the sunlight.

'This belonged to my grandmother. Aunt Euphemia always intended that I should offer it to the woman I intended to marry. She was too late when I married Edith, my first wife. I love you, Kitty old thing, even though you will keep trying to get yourself killed. If you will do me the honour of marrying me, then I promise you a life that will not be boring.'

Kitty could see sincerity mingled with trepidation in his gaze and she knew for certain that he did indeed see her as his equal, however much he might struggle with that need to look after her.

'Oh, Matt, I love you too. My answer is yes, I'll marry you.'

He leapt to his feet to sweep her up in his arms. An action that brought Muffy trotting over to caper around them. After a short but satisfactory interlude Matt took the small diamond and emerald ring from its box and slid it firmly into place on her finger.

'I do love you, Kitty Underhay, even though you are the most exasperating woman I have ever met.'

'The feeling is mutual, Matthew Bryant, even though you are the most pig-headed man I have ever met.' She grinned at him and admired the ring's perfect fit on her finger. 'You didn't tell me what Robert Potter said?'

Matt grinned, the dimple in his cheek flashed. 'He said that one wedding tended to lead to the expectation of another.'

'I see.'

Kitty tucked her hand in the crook of Matt's arm as they prepared to return to the castle to share their news. Matt whistled to Muffy and they started for home.

'I thought your aunt didn't like me,' Kitty confessed.

Matt laughed. 'No, quite the reverse. She has little patience with my mother's opinions and none at all for my father's so was curious to meet you.'

Kitty admired her ring. 'I'll telephone Grams and Aunt Livvy. Although I suspect our news won't be too much of a surprise.'

Matt smiled. 'I expect your grandmother will enjoy breaking the news to Mrs Craven. I expect you will also wish to send a telegram to your father? I did speak to your uncle to ask his blessing as I know that you regard his opinion highly and with your father being in America…'

Kitty laughed. 'What did my uncle say?'

'He said that it wouldn't matter what he, your father, or your grandmother thought. If you wished to accept me then you would say yes regardless of their opinions. However, for the record, he said he approved.'

They had crossed the courtyard and were about to enter the castle when a skinny lad on a bicycle came tearing into the courtyard over the drawbridge to skid to a stop beside them.

'I've a telegram for a Miss Underhay.'

Bile rose in the back of Kitty's throat. 'That's me.' Her hand shook as she accepted the missive from the lad. She dreaded opening it fearing something had happened back at the Dolphin.

The boy waited as she ripped it open.

Hammett in custody. Advise return Dartmouth as soon as possible. Greville.

'Matt, they have him at last. Hammett is in custody. It's from Inspector Greville. He wants us to return home as soon as we can.'

Matt paid the boy and scribbled a response to be sent on the lad's return to the post office.

'This is it, Matt. Finally they have him. Perhaps I might yet get my answers to how my mother came to die in that cellar.' Tears blurred her vision as he held her in his arms.

'Let us hope that we can get him to talk.' Matt kissed her forehead.

It seemed her engagement was a lucky omen. Now they needed to make haste back to Devon to find out what they could from her mother's murderer. Perhaps, at last, she would discover the truth and bring her killer to justice.

A LETTER FROM HELENA

Thank you for choosing to read *Murder at the Wedding*. If you enjoyed it and want to keep up to date with all my latest releases, just sign up at the following link. Your email address will never be shared and of course you can unsubscribe at any time.

www.bookouture.com/helena-dixon

If you read the first book in the series, *Murder at the Dolphin Hotel*, you can find out how Kitty and Matt first met and began their sleuthing adventures. I always enjoy meeting characters again as a series reader, which is why I love writing this series so much. I hope you enjoy their exploits as much as I love creating them. Readers have been asking for more stories featuring Kitty's cousin, Lucy, so I hope this book will please everyone. After all, who doesn't love a happy ending even when murder gets in the way?

I hope you loved reading *Murder at the Wedding* and if you did, I would be very grateful if you could write a review. I'd love to hear what you think, and it makes such a difference helping new readers to discover one of my books for the first time.

I love hearing from all my readers – you can get in touch on my Facebook page, through Twitter, Goodreads or my website.

Thanks,
Helena Dixon

 nelldixonauthor

 @NellDixon

 www.nelldixon.com

ACKNOWLEDGEMENTS

My thanks to my lovely readers and friends, especially those based around Ripon and Harrogate who helped me so much with the research for this book. My thanks to everyone at Markenfield Hall who helped me to research a suitable fortified house for Rupert and Lucy.

Thank you to the coffee crew, Phillipa Ashley and Elizabeth Hanbury, who give me huge support, advice and encouragement. Thanks to my lovely family and research crew who help me to source the material to make the books as accurate as possible, something that hasn't been easy over this last year.

You may have also seen that this book has a special dedication. Anyone who knows me knows I am a lifelong Bay City Rollers fan, and it has been a delight to reconnect with my youth and to get to know my musical heroes as people over the last few years. While finishing this book, we lost Les McKeown. Listening to the Rollers during lockdown, and chatting on social media, really helped me to switch off the present to write *Murder at the Wedding*. Les, Alan and Ian are much missed by everyone who connected with them, and I wanted to say a special thank you to all the guys and their lovely families and my fellow fans for the fun, friendship, and most of all the music. K.O.R.

My thanks also go, as always, to my lovely agent, Kate Nash, my incredible editor, Emily Gowers, and everyone at Bookouture who help bring Kitty and Matt to life.